Instead, she experienced a shock of recognition when she stared at the man standing before her.

Taking a step back, she examined him cautiously. With long black hair pulled back by a stark white tie, stunning blue eyes, and a fabulous face that managed to look both sensitive and sensuous, he could easily pass for a dangerous pirate.

Perhaps she was daydreaming or hallucinating. She hadn't gotten much sleep last night—or any night in the past month—and she *had* been reading a romance with a lusty pirate hero on the cover. Probably she still had pirates on the brain.

Although the man at her door was in desperate need of a shave, he intrigued her. Her "pirate" was a tall, imposing presence in tight-fitting but ragged khakis, with muscles bulging out of a snug, sweat-stained white T-shirt.

Good Lord! was the first coherent thought that pierced her brain. She might have said it out loud had she been capable of speech. Her grandmother had said someone would come for her, but certainly she didn't mean so soon and definitely not this brash pirate person. And what was he doing at her door, unannounced and unwelcome, on a Sunday afternoon, disturbing her peace and leaving her speechless? One look at this man and she was about to toss all thoughts of proper behavior out the window.

Praise for Marilyn Baron...

Winner of the Georgia Romance Writers
Unpublished Maggie Award for Excellence in 2012
in the Paranormal/Fantasy Romance category
Winner of First Place in the Suspense Romance
category of the 2010 Ignite the Flame Contest
sponsored by the Central Ohio Fiction Writers chapter
of Romance Writers of America
Finalist in the Georgia Romance Writers
Unpublished Maggie Award for Excellence in 2005
in the Single Title category

~*~

"Baron offers a bit of everything...There's humor, infidelity, murder, mayhem, and a neatly drawn conclusion."

~RT Book Reviews (4.5 Stars)

~~

"Expertly handled relationship...a page-turning journey...a riveting read."

~Anna K.

~~

"Wonderfully witty writing...sharp characterisation and...brilliant dialogue...humorous asides and...the quite fantastic twist at the end...left me with a real lump in my throat...highly recommended. Worth more than 5 stars if that were possible."

~Andrew Kirby

~~

"Ms. Baron's portrayal of her heroine's thoughts, feelings and actions was spot-on. Five stars! Highly recommended!"

~Pam Asberry

Under
the Moon Gate

by

Marilyn Baron

Under the Moon Gate

Cover Art by *Kim Mendoza*

The Wild Rose Press, Inc.
PO Box 708
Adams Basin, NY 14410-0708
Visit us at www.thewildrosepress.com

Publishing History
First Vintage Rose Edition, 2013
Print ISBN 978-1-61217-787-8
Digital ISBN 978-1-61217-788-5

Published in the United States of America

Dedication

In loving memory of my younger brother,
Paul Meyers,
who lost his valiant battle with cancer
on Valentine's Day 2012.
His fighting spirit and genuine goodness
will forever be an inspiration to me.
Paul, you are my hero.

Author's Note

After the Japanese attack on Pearl Harbor, Bermuda was surrounded by German U-boats. Although the move cut off vital supplies, the islands were never invaded. Why did the Germans stop short of capturing that tiny speck in the ocean, when the value of controlling such a strategic possession could have altered the course of the war? Under the Moon Gate, *a romantic thriller set in contemporary and World War II Bermuda, is a fictional account of why Bermuda was spared.*

PART ONE

The Princess and the Pirate

Tucker's Town, Bermuda, 2013

Chapter 1

Patience Whitestone struggled out of a familiar nightmare, agitated and bathed in a cold sweat. The curtains rustled slightly in the faint night breeze, and she shivered, although it rarely dipped below sixty degrees Fahrenheit in sub-tropical Bermuda. Smoothing moisture from her brow and her breast onto her cotton gown, she clutched the fabric as she stood almost frozen beside the bed.

She didn't remember leaving the window open. But since her grandmother's funeral a week ago, she'd been in a fog and hadn't remembered much of anything. Hesitating, she bit her bottom lip and cautiously ventured over to take a look outside.

Heart hammering, she stole a glance into the garden and sensed the movement even before she saw it. By the light of the full moon, an imposing shadow darted under the moon gate. The man glanced over his shoulder and, for a moment, her grandfather looked up at her. She could barely distinguish the man's features, but he had her grandfather's rugged build, and he moved like her grandfather, with the grace and power of a panther. That was impossible, of course, unless this presence was her grandfather's ghost.

She had been right there under the moon gate when William Whitestone's lifeblood had slowly seeped out of his body.

She slammed the window shut and sprinted down the hall toward her grandfather's study. But when she got to the door, she couldn't bring herself to enter. Before his death, this room had been her favorite place, their private place.

Her grandmother had little interest in her husband's business affairs, so as a rule she'd left them alone in his sanctuary.

As a little girl, Patience would push open the door and scamper over to her grandfather's chair. He'd scoop her into his arms and lift her onto his lap. He could be on a private business call, busy with his nose buried in files, or in an important meeting, but he always had time for her.

He would select a massive picture book from the shelf and let her leaf through it or set her up with crayons and paper so she could color while he worked. Her grandfather had been a notoriously ruthless businessman, but with Patience his gruffness disappeared. His arms had always been welcoming.

She hadn't had the courage to cross the threshold of her grandfather's study since his murder. Sallie, the housekeeper, assured her nothing had changed inside, that she had taken care of having the bloodstained carpet cleaned. But Patience knew if she walked into that room, the pounding in her head would start again, as it had after she'd followed her grandfather's blood trail to the garden. She couldn't bear to relive those final moments.

Now her feet were set in concrete, and she couldn't summon the strength to move forward.

Her grandfather's Walther PP 7.65mm with its eight-shot clip would still be in its place, in the desk drawer, right where she'd found it that day, surprised it hadn't been fired. Why, if her grandfather was such an expert marksman, so strong and fearless, such a dangerous adversary, hadn't he tried to defend himself? Obviously, the intruder had surprised him. But her grandfather had excellent reflexes, even at his age. He should have been able to rebound from any attack. It was almost as if he had let himself be bested.

The urge to enter the study, to pick up the weapon and feel the familiar weight of her grandfather's firearm in her hands, was strong.

Finally, her pounding heartbeat pulsed back to its regular rhythm. Just knowing the gun was there, in his desk, like having part of her grandfather there, made her feel safer. But she questioned whether she'd ever have the courage to use the weapon, even though her grandfather had raised her to be capable enough to handle any situation.

By the time she returned to her bedroom, she was convinced it had all been a nightmare. There had been no man below the bedroom window. How could there have been? Marigold House was a fortress. Her grandfather built it to be impenetrable. William Whitestone was dead, but the wall of protection he'd erected around her life was still intact.

Tears slipped down her cheeks. She tried to stop the flow of water with the back of her hand. She'd never fall asleep again tonight. She'd just have to find something to stop the incessant throbbing in her head and soothe the constant ache in her heart. She might as well stay up and wait for the next telephone call. Whoever was trying to scare her was doing a first-rate job.

Patience flipped on the light, strode into the bathroom, and discarded her drenched nightgown in the white wicker clothes hamper. At her closet, she slipped into an old pair of shorts and well-worn fuzzy bed slippers, pulled on a pale blue Rediscover Bermuda T-shirt, and entered the parlor to resume work on her latest watercolor, a beautiful seaside scene.

Naturally, whenever she saw beauty, her thoughts turned to her grandmother.

Her grandparents had lived for each other, had eyes only for each other, had existed in a world apart. Their world. But after their only child and her husband had been killed in an automobile accident and Patience cut from her mother's belly, they'd surrounded her with love. She was their "little miracle." They'd even adopted her, given her the Whitestone name. She'd always envied her grandparents' special connection, but never resented it. They were the only parents she had ever known. She loved them as a daughter.

At least Patience had been able to say a long goodbye to her grandmother. Diana Whitestone had been lucid until the day she lay dying in the hospital cot Patience had set up in her grandparents' bedroom. At the end, a round-the-clock nurse had made sure her grandmother wasn't in too much pain. Diana did suffer, but mostly from the loss of her husband the month before. After her beloved William's death, she said nothing was the same for her.

Despite the doctor's opinion, Patience knew her grandmother had really died of a broken heart. She simply couldn't go on without her husband. His unexplained murder had hastened Diana's rapid deterioration. Patience hoped she was finally at peace.

Patience and her grandmother had talked long and late into their last nights together, talked about how much they missed William and dreamed together about the future.

"Someone will come along," Diana promised, as though it were a certainty, not merely a prediction, "and you will never be alone again."

"But Grandmother, I don't need anyone," Patience had insisted gently, not wanting to upset Diana in her weakened condition.

"I know that, sweetheart. I just want you to always be protected, cherished, and loved, like I was."

"I'm never going to find the kind of fairytale love you and Grandfather shared. All it took was one look at you dancing in your yellow dress in the ballroom at the Castle Harbour Hotel and it was love at first sight."

Diana had smiled, sighed, blinked back the tears, and assumed that faraway look she wore whenever she remembered her husband.

"Of course your true love will find you, and you'll have your own storybook ending," Diana assured, struggling for each breath.

Well, Patience had certainly been waiting long enough. At twenty-seven, her prospects looked pretty bleak. To say her grandfather had been overprotective was putting it mildly. Her dating experience had been severely limited. No man was ever good enough for Patience Whitestone, according to Grandfather. She was his "Princess," safely locked away in the castle for all eternity. She had never even been allowed off the island. Now that her grandfather was gone, she had some decisions to make about the rest of her life.

"Grandmother, stop talking now, and try to get

some rest," Patience had whispered in their final hours together. She closed her hand around her grandmother's, hoping to ease her distress.

"I'll have all the time in the world to rest—well, maybe not in this world, but…" Her grandmother had suddenly shifted to a more serious, almost conspiratorial and softer tone, forcing Patience to edge closer to hear her words.

"Patience, you need to get away from here, get off the island," Diana whispered urgently. "I want you to experience things you never did when your grandfather was alive. He was so…protective…of both of us. I'm sure he had his reasons, and I was content with the way things were, content to be with him, but it was never fair to you."

A loud, insistent knocking at the front door interrupted Patience's memories, until the sound became a pounding that echoed inside her head. Annoyed at the intrusion, Patience put the finishing touches on her painting and wiped her hands on her T-shirt. She stretched her hands behind her and rubbed her lower back. Had she really been painting all day and lost track of another chunk of time?

Why didn't Sallie answer the door? She must be outside in the garden. Hadn't Patience let her friends know she wanted to be left alone? She needn't have bothered to make that request. She *was* alone, all alone. Probably it was another food delivery from one of the neighbors. As if she could eat anything now.

"For heaven's sake, I'm coming," Patience called out. She yanked open the thick Bermuda cedar door, ready to brush off the unwanted visitor. Instead, she experienced a shock of recognition when she stared at the man standing before her.

Taking a step back, she examined him cautiously. With long black hair pulled back by a stark white tie, stunning blue eyes, and a fabulous face that managed to look both sensitive and sensuous, he could easily pass for a dangerous pirate.

Perhaps she was daydreaming or hallucinating. She hadn't gotten much sleep last night—or any night in the past month—and she *had* been reading a romance with a lusty pirate hero on the cover. Probably she still had pirates on the brain.

Although the man at her door was in desperate need of a shave, he intrigued her. Her "pirate" was a tall, imposing presence in tight-fitting but ragged khakis, with muscles bulging out of a snug, sweat-stained white T-shirt.

Good Lord! was the first coherent thought that pierced her brain. She might have said it out loud had she been capable of speech. Her grandmother had said someone would come for her, but certainly she didn't mean so soon and definitely not this brash pirate person. And what was he doing at her door, unannounced and unwelcome, on a Sunday afternoon, disturbing her peace and leaving her speechless? One look at this man and she was about to toss all thoughts of proper behavior out the window.

"H-how did you manage to get through the gate?" Patience finally stuttered.

"Ah, she speaks."

"Of course I speak," Patience hissed, still stunned. "What are you doing here?"

"You mean how did I manage to access a place that's locked down tighter than the Tower of London?"

"I'm going to call the police now," Patience threatened.

"If you're talking about the two bozos at your front gate who are supposed to be patrolling your house, don't bother. They're snoring like drunkards. I didn't have the heart to wake them. I'd complain if I were you."

The pirate stuck an oversized deck shoe in the doorway as Patience tried to slam it shut.

"You're not going to get rid of me before you've heard what I came to say. It's about your grandfather."

The breath caught in her throat. "What could you possibly know about my grandfather?"

"I can't tell you if you won't let me in," he said.

Patience knew she should be cautious, but if the man truly had information about her grandfather, well, then, she wanted to hear it—now.

"If you have something to say, say it and leave," Patience insisted, preparing to do battle.

"It's obvious you've been misnamed, Patience. You don't seem to have any."

More indignant than ever, Patience snorted. Word of her notoriously sweet and tolerant disposition hadn't yet reached this man, apparently.

"Aren't you going to invite me in?" he continued. "It's teatime." The man flashed a smile and a hint of dangerous dimples.

"I think I've been more than *patient*, and I don't even know your name," Patience insisted, wondering how he knew hers.

"I didn't give it. And I scaled the fortress to get to the princess."

"I'm hardly a princess." Patience scowled.

"You're the closest thing Bermuda has to royalty, one of the most respected names on the island. Blood in Bermuda doesn't get any bluer than yours, does it, Patience? Your grandmother's family has been connected to all the big names on the island. You can't go anywhere in Bermuda without tripping over a legend—the Smithfields, and the Overbrooks, and the *Whitestones*."

"Why don't you come back later? This isn't a good time."

"I've come a long way to talk to you."

"I don't know you."

"But I know *you*," he said, eyeing her narrowly. "You're Patience *Katarina* Whitestone."

"Patience *Katherine* Whitestone," she corrected. No one had called her Katarina since her grandfather died. She'd loved the way the hard sound of her middle name had tripped off his tongue, like a lullaby, when she was half asleep and he thought she couldn't hear it. "If you don't leave this instant, I'll have to notify the authorities."

"I don't think you'll want to call the authorities after you hear what I've come to say."

The man was speaking in riddles again. And Patience couldn't take much more of his insolence—or the unsettling effect his strange behavior had on her.

"Are you threatening me?" Patience bristled, surfacing from her fog and summoning a burst of energy. "Because I'm not alone here. Sallie will be back in a minute, and I have a gun." Lifting her chin with a defiant jerk, she tried for a look of bravado she didn't really feel. For all she knew, the man could be a criminal—a murderer—or her stalker.

"I'm no threat to you," he assured her, as if he had the ability to read her mind.

"Tell me who you are, and I'll be the judge of that."

"My name is Nathaniel Morgan. You have something I want. And I have something you want. I think I may know who killed your grandfather."

Patience faltered. The color drained from her face, replaced by a look of panic.

"What do you know about my grandfather's death?" she demanded weakly as she faced him squarely, barely able to catch a breath, her knees about to buckle.

"More than you would want to know, I imagine, *liebchen*." He spoke the last word like a caress, lowering his voice, with enough of a hint of sensuality and familiarity, to stir something within her.

Liebchen—darling, love, sweetheart.

"Goodbye, *liebchen*," were the last words her grandfather spoke to her. But how could this man have known that, unless he'd been there? And that would mean... She could still *see* her grandfather's blood on her hands. Still *feel* the thickness that had oozed from his wounds and soaked her bright coral sundress. She needed to be on guard, but suddenly she was exhausted, overcome by a languorous feeling and a sensation of dizziness. Her mind clouded. Her pulse pounded as lightheadedness overtook her.

Chapter 2

What the devil? The woman's long lashes fluttered like a flag at half-mast. Her eyes glazed over. She was losing her sea legs. Nathaniel reached across the threshold as Patience Whitestone collapsed into his waiting arms.

Damn. He had a history of scaring women off, but he hadn't meant to frighten her into a dead faint. As usual, he had bungled it, and now she'd passed out.

"Patience, can you hear me?" Nathaniel called frantically as he closed the door and carried her to an overstuffed couch in the next room. He grabbed a magazine from the coffee table and tried fanning her, shaking her lightly, sprinkling her skin with water from a pitcher on the marble stand behind the couch, even stroking her face gently. He was at his wit's end. And that Sallie person she'd mentioned was nowhere to be found.

Helpless, Nathaniel looked down at Patience. Somehow he felt a connection with this woman. He had dreamed of her, or someone like her, on the deck of his boat, alone in the middle of the ocean, on a dark night drenched in moonlight, under a heaven sprinkled with stars, drifting in and out of sleep, of consciousness, as his vessel rocked toward Bermuda. But nothing could have prepared him for this visceral reaction to the flesh-and-blood woman who'd gone limp in his arms.

The truth of it had first hit him like a powerful wave when she opened the door to him earlier, nearly knocking the wind from his sails. And he'd detected a spark of recognition in her face, too. He was sure of it. She'd looked as stunned as he felt.

Before she died, his grandmother foretold he would find his destiny in Bermuda. He didn't believe any of that hogwash about destiny or fate. But she had made him promise to go to the island and hand deliver a letter and a small fortune in diamonds to William Whitestone. He was honoring that promise now; however, he intended to take something much more valuable back with him.

But William Whitestone was dead, and so was his wife. Was Nathaniel obligated to reveal the contents of the letter to Whitestone's granddaughter? And what was *his* grandmother's connection to the German spy William Whitestone and his dangerous wartime associate Nighthawk?

He had a purpose in Bermuda beyond humoring his dying grandmother. He had come for the gold his uncle had told him about, and he was determined to locate and leave with every last ounce of it. The trip was long overdue, and no woman, breathtakingly beautiful or not, was going to interfere with his business here.

Nathaniel expected Patience wouldn't be cooperative. He couldn't just come right out and tell her the reason for his visit. He would have to skillfully navigate the choppy waters.

Naturally, she'd be angry. Anger only seemed to make her more magnificent, if that were possible, and more vulnerable. He couldn't afford to have her fall apart. He wanted her alert when he questioned her. She was going to hear him out, whether she wanted to or not. But first he needed some information from her. And he could hardly get answers from an unconscious woman.

There was really no easy way to tell her about her grandfather. And no surer way to confirm whether she knew the truth about him than to question her face to face.

Looking into that face, Nathaniel acted on another impulse, one he couldn't have controlled even if he cared to. He reached to slide a lock of her golden hair between his fingers. Somehow he'd known her hair would feel like fine silk. If he were the poetic type he'd tell her, *if* she ever regained consciousness.

Nathaniel looked around the room and out the window at the expansive grounds. Prime Bermuda real estate in one of Bermuda's most exclusive residential areas—prestigious Tucker's Town. This quaint village of splendid properties was home to movie stars, prime ministers, a veritable Who's Who of the rich and famous in Bermuda and around the world. People with legendary last names like Astor and Rockefeller.

The sprawling stucco house, painted a pale yellow, was built in the island's traditional architectural style and comfortably but luxuriously furnished. Morning glory vines ran wild along the roadside. Marigold House was fronted by a pair of elegant gateposts and accessed by a sweep of tapered stone steps leading to the front door in the traditional welcoming-arms pattern. Unlike the tepid welcome Patience had given him. Why didn't the woman wake up?

Frustrated, he pulled her toward him and kissed her. That always seemed to work in the movies and in fairytales. The soft brush of her lips against his felt like the tiniest whisper of hummingbird wings. She stirred, and her arms wound around his neck involuntarily until the two of them were intertwined. She responded by kissing him back tenderly, barely conscious, apparently still in a daze.

No, actually, he was the one in a daze, an almost dreamlike spell. He clasped her tighter, gathered her closer and pressed her warm body to his. He wanted more, but romance was not part of his mission. In fact, it would be unacceptable in this instance. Not that he believed in romance. Love and romance was for fools, and he was very definitely not a fool, not anymore.

She sighed and moved in his arms.

"Patience," Nathaniel whispered. "Good. You're back."

Chapter 3

Patience awoke in the pirate's arms. He resembled a reenactor of *The Bermuda Journey,* just back from performing on St. George's. No doubt he was one of the parish's more feisty residents who belonged in the stocks or the pillory for committing a variety of public offenses, not the least of which might be scandalous behavior and taking unwarranted liberties with women. Yes, the man was definitely a St. Georgian, a consort of the devil, or at the very least, a sorcerer. Certainly he was an enchanter or a charmer. He was also hard and lean and rugged, and he looked better than any man or devil had a right to.

"Patience, say something."

Patience tried to speak, but her mouth was dry.

"Water," she finally whispered. "May I have some water?"

Nathaniel took a glass from the coffee table, filled it with water from the pitcher, and handed it to Patience.

While she drank, she recovered her composure, but common sense prevailed and fear crept back into her consciousness. Could he be the man who was threatening her? The one who'd broken into Marigold House, who'd called her every day since her grandfather's death, sometimes late in the night? The stalker who breathed heavily into the phone and spoke in a harsh, guttural language? The stranger who lurked in her nightmares? The police claimed they would patrol the house. Obviously they hadn't taken her concerns seriously or this man wouldn't have slipped through their net.

But the man before her seemed too young to belong to the gruff voice on the telephone. And she had to admit he didn't cause the same terrified reaction she felt when the stalker called. Her pirate sent chills down her spine, but they were chills of a different sort.

Patience placed the water glass on the coffee table and looked out the picture window. The sun, already settling lower in the sky, was still spreading riotous sparkles across the sea. Images that had horrified her in the middle of the night—shadows in the moonlight, strange sightings, and shallow breathing—seemed less intimidating in daylight. The immediate threat had receded.

But Patience faced a threat of another kind. She was entranced by this dark and dangerous stranger with the handsome face, this man she couldn't seem to dismiss. The pirate was downright dazzling, and he knew it. His nearness was making her lightheaded. Or maybe it was the fact that she hadn't eaten anything substantial in days.

Patience struggled out of his grasp. Her lips were warm. Had he kissed her? Or was that a dream? She looked down at her hands. Because she didn't seem to have the strength to resist, they were still firmly folded in his.

"Keep your hands to yourself," she said. Then she remembered his last words before everything went black.

"My grandfather. You said something about my grandfather." She fought to remain alert as she pulled away from him.

Patience followed the pirate's gaze as he scanned the room and settled on the large portrait hanging on the wall directly across from the fireplace.

"Is that a picture of you?" he asked, veering off the subject, nodding toward a portrait of a woman in a vintage 1940s yellow gown.

For some reason the man was stalling, drawing her attention away from the matter at hand. Okay, she'd play along. Humor him until she could get him out of her house. Because she wasn't entirely convinced he wasn't somehow connected to the man who was threatening her. His presence here now was too much of a coincidence to be circumstantial. And she didn't believe in coincidences. She was in a weakened condition and distracted by grief, but she wasn't stupid.

Maybe he intended to rob her. The papers had reported that the Whitestones were the wealthiest family in Bermuda. She would keep him talking until Sallie came back into the house. Where was she, anyway?

"No, that's not me," she said. "That's my grandmother. People make that mistake all the time. That picture was painted at the Castle Harbour Hotel, where my grandparents first met. That's the dress she was wearing when they danced together for the very first time.

"My grandfather had the portrait done because he wanted to freeze that moment in time, capture the way he remembered her, out in the garden, under the moon gate. All my grandmother's friends say I look exactly like she looked when she was my age. The Castle Harbour's gone. It's a private resort club now." *Just like my grandmother. Everything good goes.*

Now she was babbling like an idiot.

"She is very beautiful," Nathaniel said, and placed his hand over hers.

Patience flushed at his touch. If he thought the woman in the portrait was beautiful, then that meant he thought she was beautiful, too.

"Yes, she *was* beautiful," Patience agreed. "I guess you didn't hear that I buried my grandmother last week." Why did she feel compelled to talk to this stranger about her personal loss? She tried to gauge his reaction, but his face was inscrutable, and her gaze couldn't penetrate those vivid blue eyes.

"I don't appreciate your intrusion on my grief," Patience blustered.

****

"I'm really sorry to hear about your grandmother," Nathaniel said sincerely. She hung her head, so he gave her the necessary time and space to compose herself.

When he'd set sail from Virginia, it was with every intention of meeting with Diana Hargrave Whitestone. On his arrival in Bermuda, he'd been disappointed to read about her illness and death in *The Royal Gazette*. The event had merited extensive coverage. She was, after all, from one of Bermuda's most prominent families—a Smithfield on her mother's side. Before he learned of her death, Nathaniel had pinned all his hopes on questioning William Whitestone's widow in person. Now his only link to the past was a grieving, doped-up granddaughter.

He had seen Patience's fragility at the funeral.

Would her vulnerability make a difference? He couldn't let it. He had come too far to turn back now.

He was painfully aware of her grief. At her grandmother's gravesite behind St. Peter's Church, where a large crowd had gathered for the funeral, Patience had seemed isolated, even as she was surrounded by a tight-knit group of friends who closed ranks to protect her. She looked utterly lost, bereft, but she put on a brave front. She hadn't shed one tear. She held up her head regally, like a princess. And he had begun to think of her as one.

Nathaniel had gone to Bermuda's first church early on the morning of Diana Whitestone's funeral, waiting to see Patience. The beauty of the church's whitewashed façade drew him, the rich historical feel and the peacefulness of the place, saturated with the aroma of cedar, impressed him. And, even at a distance, he was blown away by the stunning beauty of the granddaughter.

At the conclusion of the service, Patience knelt in front of her grandfather's grave and gingerly placed a clutch of colorful flowers there. Then she'd raised her head, drifted through the crowd of mourners, and silently walked down the chalk-white steps to the limousine waiting in front of the church.

He hadn't talked with her then because the timing was all wrong. He watched the house for a whole week, waiting for her to show herself. Since she didn't so much as peek her head out the front door, he felt he had no choice but to go in after her. He was tired of waiting.

Now the only one who could give him the truth was Patience—if, indeed, she knew it. And he surmised that she did. How could she live in the same house with her grandfather all these years and not know something as basic as his true identity?

He wondered how William Whitestone had answered his granddaughter when she asked, "What did you do in the war, Grandfather?" Wondered whether he had been honest with Patience and whether she would be honest with him when he confronted her. He could see she was still grieving for her grandmother, but her first instinct would be to protect her grandfather's memory at all costs.

Suppressing another urge to run his fingers through that glorious mop of blonde curls that crowned her head like a halo, Nathaniel stood there for a minute, drinking her in. He tried his best not to stare at her long legs in those short shorts or feast his eyes on the clingy T-shirt that barely disguised her curves. Even the fluffy bunny slippers looked sexy on her. He couldn't resist reaching out to press his finger to her cheek.

Patience shivered and blushed at his touch.

"Just trying to remove a smudge from your face," he answered. "Is that a capital offense in Bermuda?"

Her hand flew up to her cheek. "Oh, it must be the watercolors." She sighed.

Nathaniel began studying another portrait on the far side of the room.

"That was my great-grandfather, Vice Admiral Sir Stirling Hargrave, my grandmother's father. He was stationed here during World War II."

"Yes," Nathaniel said, grateful for the opening. "And that is the reason I came to talk to you today." When he turned around they were almost touching.

Patience fidgeted with her hands. Nathaniel took them into his and stilled them. The heat from her body seemed to flow into his.

"You're not going to like what I have to tell you," Nathaniel said.

"Just say it," Patience demanded. "What are you really doing here?"

"I'm just trying to have a rational conversation," Nathaniel said. Somehow, he was going to have to make Patience feel comfortable with him in the space of an afternoon. He had come this far. He may as well put it all out there. She'd probably never let him back into the house again. This might be his last opportunity to talk with her alone. He would have to start somewhere.

"*Sprechen Sie Deutsch?*"

Chapter 4

The man definitely had a screw loose, Patience thought. She needed to call the police and let them know a crazy foreigner was loose in Tucker's Town.

"No, I don't speak German," Patience said.

"*Unternehmen Teufels Insel,*" Nathaniel said next.

"I don't understand. That sounds German, too."

"It is. Roughly translated it means *Operation Devil's Island.*"

"Is that supposed to mean something to me?"

"Does it?" he asked pointedly, eyes narrowing.

"Not a thing. Except that Devil's Island or the Isles of Devils is the name sixteenth-century Spaniards gave to Bermuda when they first foundered off the coast in the 1500s, at Spanish Point—which isn't too far from here, as a matter of fact."

"*Unternehmen* means to undertake or to attempt," explained Nathaniel. "Many of Hitler's plans began with that name. For example, *Unternehmen Seelöwe,* Operation Sea Lion, referred to the full-scale German seaborne invasion of Britain." He looked at her inquisitively as if expecting a reaction.

"Hitler?" Patience was genuinely puzzled. "What does that monster have to do with anything?"

"If you know your history, you know that after the Japanese attack on Pearl Harbor, Bermuda was surrounded by German U-boats. The move cut off vital supplies, but the islands were never invaded. I'm guessing it was some secret plan that Hitler and his henchmen at German High Command devised to isolate and occupy Bermuda when the time was right. Bermuda is only a tiny speck in the ocean—only twenty-one square miles—but they say location is everything. After all, the British Navy has always viewed Bermuda as the central focus in their operations in the Atlantic and Caribbean," Nathaniel explained. "This was especially true during World War II because of Bermuda's strategic location between the United States and England. Can you imagine the value of controlling such a possession?"

"I've studied the history of this island extensively, and I've never heard of a Nazi plan like that."

"You wouldn't have. The mission was probably scrubbed before the order was issued, but I assure you it did exist. Do you doubt the Germans got this close? In 2012, a shipwreck hunter discovered the remains of a World War II merchant ship that was torpedoed by a German U-boat off Cape Cod. Certainly they would have been here, too."

"Even if what you say is true, what could that possibly have to do with my grandfather? Or his killer? My grandfather wasn't German. He was Swiss."

"It seems being Swiss is a cure for all ills these days," Nathaniel said. "Are you certain of his nationality?"

"Of course."

"Well, perhaps the person you knew as your grandfather wasn't really who he claimed to be."

"Not who he claimed to be?" Patience repeated, confused. "What are you talking about? I think I knew my own grandfather."

"Only what he wanted you to know."

Patience bit her lip, hard.

"And how do you know so much about my family?"

"How did your grandfather die?"

Patience lowered her head. "He met with…foul play."

"Foul play? You mean he was brutally murdered, don't you?"

"Yes," she whispered, twisting the hem of her shorts in agitation. "Why are you being so cruel? And why are we talking about this?"

"Suppose he had assumed another identity before he married your grandmother?" Nathaniel proposed. "Suppose he was a sleeper agent, sent over to Bermuda by the Germans before the war to mingle among the population, waiting to be activated and used to further the Führer's agenda?"

"You're delusional," Patience accused. "How did you find me? Are you one of those ghouls who prey on other people's misfortune? Did you read about my grandmother in the newspaper and hope to somehow profit from her death?"

"On the contrary, Patience. You stand to profit enormously from my discovery if you'd only listen to me."

Patience was more than furious. "I assume you have proof of my grandfather's connection to this so-called plan? Or did you just make this giant leap in your twisted little mind?"

"How else could I have found you if I didn't have proof? Your grandfather's real name was Wilhelm von

Hesselweiss. His code name was *Insel Adler*—Island Eagle—and his rank was *Kapitänleutnant* in the *Kriegsmarine*, serving under Rear Admiral Wilhelm Franz Canaris, the same man who headed up the *Abwehr*, Germany's spy agency. I've also uncovered some details of your grandfather's service record and training. For instance, he did a stint with the *B-Dienst*— that's German naval communications intelligence, if you don't know, also reporting up through Canaris."

"Why would I know something like that?" Patience scowled. "And how do *you*? What are you, some kind of pervert? How dare you spew your venomous lies about a decent man like my grandfather? The war's over, in case you haven't heard, and no one wants to hear about it anymore." She shot up from the couch, pointing to the door. "I want you to leave now!"

Nathaniel bristled at the insult but remained calm as he took her hands and gently pulled her back down. "Now, would you please let me continue? Don't you want to know the truth?"

Patience gritted her teeth but listened.

"I have retrieved some documents with his undercover address, which is still *your* address, his papers, maps of the island, and schematics of the U.S. military bases in Bermuda. He had all the bases covered, so to speak, from A to Z," noted Nathaniel, "from the U.S. Army base on St. David's Island, Fort Bell, to the U.S. Navy telecommunications center on Zuill's Park Road."

"Tell me again how you came across these documents?"

"My uncle used to do a lot of shipwreck salvage. He left a trunk with my grandmother before he died

25

unexpectedly, and she willed it to me when she died. After her funeral, when I finally got a look at the contents of the chest, I was fascinated by what I discovered. I've studied the papers thoroughly, and there's no doubt about their authenticity. I think you'll be surprised by the significance of what else my uncle hauled up from the bottom of the Atlantic."

When Patience remained silent, Nathaniel continued.

"Receipts for large shipments of gold, which are still unaccounted for, with only clues to the location of the treasure, to which you have a partial claim. And lastly, there was this."

Nathaniel lifted a thick battered brown leather volume from his jacket pocket.

"What is that?" she said, eyeing the package suspiciously, refusing to take it.

"Your grandfather's personal journal. I imagine it has the answers we need."

A journal with her grandfather's words? Something of his left behind? That was priceless. But this man was wrong about her grandfather. She was certain of that.

"Answers *we* need? I'm not interested in any dirt you think you might have unearthed that would tarnish my grandfather's reputation and that of my family."

"Yes, think of the scandal," Nathaniel mused.

"And if this journal truly belonged to my grandfather, why is it in your possession and not in his vault here at home? And why would he have left a trail at all?"

"Isn't that obvious?" Nathaniel said. "The Germans were notorious record keepers. They documented everything, because of course they never doubted they would be victorious. After the war, he probably wanted to sink the evidence so deep it would hopefully never be found, especially by his family. Or maybe someone else betrayed him and placed it where it would eventually be found."

"And where exactly was that?"

"At the bottom of the Atlantic."

"What kind of sea chest was it?" Patience pressed, intrigued. "Was it a pirate's chest? Sunken treasure from a shipwrecked Spanish galleon?"

Not exactly, he thought suspiciously, but she was close. Too close. With her reference to treasure, was it possible she knew? Nathaniel didn't believe her choice of words was a coincidence.

"The kind that's emblazoned on the side with a Nazi swastika," said Nathaniel.

Patience got up, rounded on Nathaniel, and stared him down.

"You have quite an imagination. This sounds like something straight out of a Jules Verne novel. You asked me to listen. Now I'm through listening. I'm not interested in anything you have to say. So please leave."

"There's more," Nathaniel said. "Did your grandfather ever mention a man called Nighthawk?"

Patience looked puzzled. "Nighthawk? No."

"Well, it was probably a code name."

"Why are you doing this to me? If your so-called proof is in here, what do you need with me?"

"Because a man's journal is his own. As a historian and a gentleman, I respect the privacy of the dead. This belongs to you. I just want to discuss it with you after you've read it."

"You read my grandfather's private diary?"

"Like I said, it was the property of my grandmother. I inherited it. But I need your help in interpreting it."

"And in return?"

"I promise not to say a word to anyone about what I've found. If you promise to let me look on your property for the gold referred to in those papers."

"Oh, gold? Well, if it really exists, that's why you're here. So why hasn't anyone found it after all these years?"

"That's a mystery I intend to solve."

"If there's any truth to your theory, you can keep your bloody fortune. I want no part of it."

"Ah, now there's the catch," he said. "I don't actually have the gold. But I think you hold the key to its whereabouts. Is anything worth more than your family's reputation?"

"I didn't think *gentlemen* engaged in blackmail, Mr. Morgan," Patience fired back.

"I never claimed to be a saint. But *this* was meant for you." Nathaniel handed Patience the diary.

The book felt heavy in her hands. "If what you say is true, then whatever you find is contaminated. I don't want the money. You're welcome to it. I do want the truth. I can't believe my grandfather would be involved in anything so despicable. I want to read my grandfather's journal, if it really is his. Maybe there's more I can learn about him. I'll talk with you about it, but not for your sake. I want some answers, for my own peace of mind."

****

Nathaniel wasn't making any promises. He was

calling all the shots now. And he had some questions of his own about his grandmother's role in this whole affair and her relationship with Nighthawk and William Whitestone. For instance, why did she keep William Whitestone's sea trunk and make sure it went to Nathaniel?

"Has anything unusual happened since your grandfather's death?" Nathaniel asked. "Have you been contacted by anyone?"

Patience turned on him, fury blazing in her eyes.

"Did you make those calls?" she shouted, poking her index finger sharply into his chest, causing Nathaniel to retreat to the other side of the couch.

"You did, didn't you? How else would you have known about them? I told no one. My house was broken into, but nothing of value was taken. I thought it was someone who read about my grandmother in the newspapers and assumed I'd be easy prey."

"That's why you called the police?"

"Yes, but about the break-in only."

He grabbed her arm roughly.

"The voice on the phone, how did he sound, what did he say?" Nathaniel demanded, as his grip tightened.

"Nothing that made any sense. He spoke in German, like you. Please let go of my arm. You're hurting me."

Nathaniel scowled and ignored her.

"And?" Nathaniel questioned, sensing there was more that she wasn't telling him.

"Someone had been blackmailing my grandfather," Patience whispered.

"How do you know?" Nathaniel prodded, refusing to release her.

"After his death, I was reviewing my grandfather's accounts and noticed large sums of money had been transferred out on a monthly basis to an unknown source. I found that strange. My grandfather was not the type of man to submit to blackmail."

"Perhaps he made an exception to protect his family."

No wonder she was so skittish. It all made sense now, Nathaniel thought. The same person who was blackmailing her grandfather, who had very probably killed him, and had broken into her house, that person had also been snooping around his, Nathaniel's, boat.

"For a while, the calls stopped. I was hoping..." she sighed. "But then there was the note."

"What did the note say?" Nathaniel insisted.

"It said I would be next, that I would die just like my grandfather. It said my time was up and not to call the police or I wouldn't live to see tomorrow."

Nathaniel grimaced. The man was circling and closing in for the kill, like a vulture or a predatory hawk in the night.

He could see how his revelations were affecting Patience, and he regretted it. Seeing how the winds were blowing, Nathaniel decided to try a safer tack.

"I'm sorry, Patience, if I was too rough on you," Nathaniel apologized, releasing her arm.

"Just get out of my house and let me read my grandfather's words in peace," she pleaded, tears threatening to spill over.

Just then Sallie entered with a laden tray and a cheerful, "Tea, anyone?"

Later, steering his rental scooter down the driveway, Nathaniel reviewed the situation. He had involved Patience in this affair, and now he couldn't in good conscience leave her unprotected. Whoever was threatening her was the same person who was now after him and the contents of the sea chest. He had a pretty good idea who the stalker was. Or at least that his codename was Nighthawk—Island Eagle's dangerous associate. But he hadn't had any luck locating the man. Was Nighthawk still in Bermuda after all these years?

****

Patience watched Nathaniel saunter out to the circular driveway, where he took off recklessly on his scooter. Hopefully, the police would catch him on the way out, throw him in jail, and make sure he never came near her again.

Locking the door after him, she wandered back to the sofa, where her legs buckled beneath her. Thank goodness the arrogant man was gone. She was having trouble catching her breath around him. His accusations were disconcerting, and every time he got near her, she lost control of her thoughts.

The journal had been preserved in plastic, so the inside pages were in fairly good condition. As the sun began to move to the back of the house, lowering the level of light in the room, Patience switched on a table lamp and became absorbed in the past.

Yes, it was her grandfather's familiar handwriting she was seeing on the pages, but the story she was reading was about a stranger, and the man who had written it was one she didn't know at all.

Chapter 5

Patience was still reading her grandfather's journal when she heard the knock at the door. This was the second time today. Why couldn't everyone leave her alone? She dried her eyes and hid the journal in the cedar chest under the stairwell before opening the door. The first pages had been damning, but she refused to believe a stranger's accusations of the grandfather she had known and loved all her life. There had to be some other explanation. And she would find it or force Nathaniel to help her find it.

She could hardly keep her eyes open. Her head felt muzzy. It couldn't be the black tea Sallie had prepared for them after she'd finally shown up and insisted on being hospitable to the "gentleman caller" just when Patience had been on the verge of throwing him out. Black tea was supposed to be invigorating. And she felt anything but invigorated. At this rate she was going to sleep her life away, she thought, opening the door.

"Cecilia," she said as she stared into the face of her best friend. "Come in."

"I thought you might be up for some company. It's been a whole week, and I haven't heard a peep from you. I've sent food to the house. Did Sallie tell you? I didn't want you wasting away. I know you didn't leave the house for the entire month your grandmother was sick, except for the funeral. You've cut yourself off from everyone. You could stand the company. I was starting to get worried. We all were."

Cecilia continued to chatter as she followed Patience into the drawing room. "I just came from the Rediscover Bermuda committee meeting. I presented your ideas for the annual celebration. They loved everything you proposed, especially the idea about the expanded Dine Around program. That will benefit all the restaurants on the island. They're going to adopt all your recommendations.

"Oh, and they loved your ideas about the special celebrations planned throughout the year, to coincide with Bermuda's holidays and sporting events, especially the personal tour of the current homes of some of the original families. I reminded them that the celebration will touch every parish, every part of the island, every aspect of our culture, our history, and our future, just like you told me to.

"They were thrilled with the brochure copy, and the watercolor you painted will look great on the postcards we're having printed for the travel agencies. Everyone misses you. They want to know when you're coming back. There's a lot of work yet to be done on the campaign. We've arranged for all the advertising agencies to make presentations next week. You absolutely have to be there."

"I'll try. Can I get you something to eat? Maybe some of those cookies you sent over?"

"They fed us at the meeting," said Cecilia as she joined Patience on the couch.

"I want a local agency, Cecilia."

"One you can control?" Cecilia smiled. "Or one that won't mind working with a theme you've already selected, even if it is terrific?"

"You know that's not why. I think it's important that a Bermuda agency be given the contract for the celebration. It will be more meaningful."

"I agree with you. I'm just playing devil's advocate here, but you have to be prepared that some people on the committee will question your opinion because you've never been off the island. You've been insulated. You don't really know what's out there. The New York and London agencies are slick. They know the market we're targeting. Their argument is bolstered by the fact that Bermuda has only 69,000 citizens but about 600,000 tourists a year come here, more than half of them by cruise. And eighty-five percent of all those visitors are from the United States."

"Just because I've never left Bermuda, it doesn't mean I don't know what's available. Bermuda is such a jewel. In my opinion it's the best-kept secret in the world. The island is such a surprise to first-time visitors that almost half of Bermuda tourists are repeaters. People who live here understand that better than anyone. I feel strongly about that. It's just the right thing to do. I'll try to be there for the presentations, but I'm still mourning my grandmother."

"I know, but you've shut off everyone just when you need people around you."

"I'm not in the mood for company," Patience protested. "I don't really feel like talking right now. I want to be left alone."

"Well, sorry, I can't do that. You shouldn't be alone. I've told you that. I'm not going anywhere. You don't have to talk. I'll just sit here with you. If this is going to be a clash of wills, I'll win."

"Speaking of letting you in, how did you get around the police? They're supposed to have guards posted at the gate."

"Patience, you know I can get around *any* man, *any* time. Each of those young officers asked if he could walk me to your door, and I told them to knock themselves out. And that's exactly what they did. They actually came to blows over which of them would get to escort me."

"Who got the honors?" Patience said, laughing.

"Neither. When they had picked themselves up off the ground and dusted themselves off, they discovered I had already walked away."

"Great." Patience sighed. "I might as well dismiss them, for all the good they're doing. They're supposed to be keeping people out."

"Surely, not your best friend," Cecilia said. "Anyway, they know me, so of course they let me in."

There was no help for her. Cecilia was like a bulldog driving a bulldozer. Patience knew her friend would not give in or accept any excuses until she got her way. She was overpowering. She was also the greatest friend in the world.

Cecilia looked at the coffee table.

"Tea service for two? Patience, are you holding out on me? If I didn't know you better, I'd say you were hiding a man in here. Where is he?" Cecilia bounded up from the couch and checked all the rooms on the first level.

"No man on the first floor."

"Cecilia, really!"

"Should I try upstairs?"

Patience blushed. Cecilia could sniff out a man

from a mile away. She probably smelled Nathaniel's lingering sea scent in the drawing room.

"Sallie and I were having some tea earlier," Patience said, not wanting to get into an explanation about the mystery man at her door.

"Who is he? I'm sure I know him. This island is so incestuous. Everyone already knows everyone else." Cecilia sniffed the air. "What we need on this island is some new blood to get the juices stirring."

"Cecilia, you're outrageous. I just buried my grandmother, for heaven's sake. You've already had every man on the island. Three times. And been married to most of them. There's no one left. And I never entertain men in my house, you know that."

"You never entertain men outside of your house, either. Just trying to raise your spirits. Don't mind me. You've been crying." Cecilia sat down beside Patience and took her friend's hand. "I'm so sorry. I've stuck my foot in my mouth. I'm awful. You should just kick me out."

"It's okay. You can stay…for a while." She couldn't stay mad at her friend for long.

"You're having trouble coping, aren't you?" Cecilia said sympathetically. "Well, we need a diversion. Why don't we go into town tonight and go clubbing? I know this great new bar. Or we could do something really touristy like the Swizzle Inn. I'm in the mood for some crab bisque and coconut shrimp and some of Johnnie's bread pudding with brandy sauce. And, of course, some Rum Swizzles. I could drink a pitcher myself. Swizzle Inn-Swagger Out?"

Patience laughed half-heartedly.

"Cecilia. I couldn't possibly. I don't want to leave

the house. I don't have any energy. And how would it look?"

"Since when have I cared about how something looked? And anyway, we won't know a soul. Nobody local goes there."

"Well, I care," Patience protested. "Listen, I think I need to catch forty winks, so maybe you could come back la—"

The conversation was interrupted by another knock on the door.

Patience sighed. What did they say in America? Her house was getting to be like Grand Central Station.

"Now who could that be?" Cecilia wondered. "I thought you hung out the *No Visitors Allowed* sign."

"A lot of good that did," Patience laughed. Maybe it was the police telling her they had dragged that dangerous pirate off to jail.

Cecilia was at the door before Patience could answer it.

"Wow!" she heard her friend say. "Excuse me while I swoon."

"There seems to be a lot of that going around today," Nathaniel remarked. "Must be something in the air."

Cecilia turned to her friend for an explanation.

"It's an inside joke," Patience said.

"You *do* know this man. You must, if you already have inside jokes. You *have* been holding out on me, you naughty girl. Aren't you going to introduce me to this delicious specimen?"

Patience joined them at the door and noticed with irritation that Nathaniel had shaved and changed clothes. He cleaned up nicely. He actually looked presentable. But he still smelled of the sea. She also noticed he was balancing a duffel bag over his shoulder.

"What are you doing back here?" she growled.

"I'm like a bad penny," Nathaniel said. "I keep turning up, and I'm going to keep coming back until I get what I came for."

Furious, Patience glanced at Cecilia, who seemed anxious for her to complete the introductions.

"Cecilia, I'd like to introduce you to Nathaniel Morgan, pirate and adventurer extraordinaire. Nathaniel, this is my best friend, the troublemaker, the outrageous but always entertaining Cecilia Overbrook."

He smiled and held out his hand. "Of *the* Overbrooks?"

She nodded. "I'm only an Overbrook by marriage, or rather an ex-Overbrook."

"She's working her way through every family on the island, and won't stop until she's married into them all," Patience said, amused.

"Patience, you know I'd have to deck you for that remark if you weren't in mourning."

Cecilia turned her attention to Nathaniel. "Looks like you're planning to stay awhile."

****

Now this woman was more his type, Nathaniel thought. Vivacious, busty, and gutsy. *If* he were in the market for a woman, which he was not. She was a knockout. But seeing the women side by side, he had to admit Patience had a quality that set her apart and left her stunning friend looking almost coarse in comparison. Where Cecilia was a blazing firecracker, Patience was more like a wondrous firefly or a silent symphony of fireworks.

"Are you really a pirate?" Cecilia asked, entranced.

"I look for lost treasures, so I guess I am a pirate of sorts."

"Where have you been all my life?" Cecilia purred, grabbing Nathaniel's hand. "Come right in. Patience, I think this man needs a drink. And after that, we'll find out just what else he needs."

Patience rolled her eyes heavenward.

"I'm sorry about my friend here," Patience apologized. "She seems to be on the prowl today."

"I'm always on the prowl, darling, you know that. And I'm suddenly famished." She looked as if she might ingest Nathaniel on the spot and swallow him whole.

"There's plenty of food in the fridge," Patience gestured. "Help yourself." Patience watched Cecilia smile at Nathaniel before she sashayed into the kitchen.

"Don't apologize for your friend. I think she's great," Nathaniel said.

"Yes, you would."

"Now just what is that supposed to mean?"

"Nothing. All men fall in love with Cecilia. That's why they never notice me. What are you doing back here? And how did you get by the guards this time?"

"I told them I was your cousin from Virginia."

"My cousin? And they bought that?"

"Of course. I also told them we wouldn't be needing them anymore," he said, lowering his voice so only Patience could hear. "We don't need them poking around in our business, and the letter you received specifically threatened your life if you called the police. Now that I'm on the island, I'm going to protect you."

"And who's going to protect me from you?"

"Patience, we have to talk," he said, "privately."

"I'm going to have Sallie call the police," Patience promised.

"She's not here. I saw her out in the garden and gave her the rest of the day off."

"You did what?" Patience was furious. "You can't order my staff around. I need her here. She's been spending the night because—well, I don't want to be alone right now."

"You're not alone. I'm here. And we've got a lot to discuss."

"I think we said all we have to say to each other earlier this afternoon. And what are you doing with that bag? Have you decided to leave Bermuda, please God?"

"I'm not going anywhere," Nathaniel said.

"If you need a place to stay..." Cecilia offered, wandering back into the drawing room to stand next to Nathaniel.

He dumped the bag on the floor inside the door before taking Patience's elbow in a proprietary hold.

"No, Patience has already kindly offered to put me up for a while."

"Patience? Put up a man at her house?" Cecilia asked bluntly. "Who *are* you, really?"

"I'm Patience's cousin from Virginia."

"Patience never mentioned any American cousins," Cecilia said suspiciously.

"Didn't she tell you about me? No, I guess not. I think she's ashamed of me. I'm the black sheep of the family. Sorry I missed the funeral, but I have decided to take you up on your generous offer, cuz."

Nathaniel gave Patience a very uncousinly kiss,

then explained to Cecilia, "We're kissing cousins."

"Get your hands off me," Patience said, growing more irate by the minute. "And I most certainly did not offer to put you up for a while or any other length of time. What I *am* going to do is boot you out of here on your backside."

"Patience is so kind, isn't she?" Nathaniel smiled at Cecilia, laying on the charm as thick as the marmalade on the scones Sallie had served with tea that afternoon.

"She'd give you the shirt off her back," Cecilia agreed. "And I'd be happy to give you the shirt off mine, Cousin Nathaniel."

"Interesting offer," Nathaniel said, winking at Cecilia. "I've read that Bermuda was a hostile, haunted place of evil spirits, inhabited only by wild birds and sea creatures, and that the 'dreaded islands of Bermuda...the Devil's Islands, should be feared and avoided by all sea travelers alive above any other place in the world.' And now I can see why. The natives are certainly less than hospitable. Although some are more hospitable than others." His eyes bore into Patience's as she glared back at him.

****

"How dare you?" said Patience, rounding on him angrily. She took personal offense at the remark about her hospitality. It was her job to promote Bermuda, to welcome people here, to laud the benefits of the island. His words were an insult to everything she stood for, everything she and her grandmother had worked so hard for during the past four years on the Rediscover Bermuda committee.

Patience had assumed her grandmother's position as head of the committee, begun for the 2009 celebration of the 400th anniversary of the discovery of Bermuda. It had been Patience's idea to keep the flame of the Rediscover Bermuda campaign alive by unveiling an offshoot of the campaign annually.

But she was secretly impressed. Nathaniel did know his Bermuda history.

"That's so typical," said Patience, masking her admiration as she continued her tirade, her lower lip in a petulant pout. "Shipwrecks, hurricanes, and the Bermuda Triangle. That's all most people remember when they think of Bermuda."

"You have to admit there have been a lot of strange occurrences connected with the island," Nathaniel pointed out. "Pirates running aground, sailors stranded on treacherous hidden barrier reefs, ships foundering in terrifying storms, and planes simply disappearing from the radar screen."

"All exaggerations," she countered, "and misconceptions. How is it you know so much about Bermuda?"

"I'm getting my PhD in Bermuda history. My dissertation is on Bermuda during World War II."

"Well, if you think you're going to barrel your way into my house like a barbarian, Nathaniel, you've—"

"*Cousin* Nathaniel," he corrected. "And it seems I already have. Now it wouldn't be right to turn a blood relative away, would it?"

"I can call a hotel. We've got the Pink Beach Club and Cottages right around the corner. They've very nice accommodations. Secluded, with tennis, two lovely beaches, two rather fine restaurants, and entertainment. In fact, they have a new executive chef. It's very exclusive. I highly recommend it. I know the managing director."

"Of course you do. You rich, elitist types tend to stick together, don't you? Private yacht clubs. Exclusive golf courses. Members only, of course."

"You're despicable, and you're also a hypocrite," Patience accused. "You mistake civility for snobbery. You apparently have enough money to waste coming over here and harassing me. Don't you have a job to go back to? Or someone to go back to? Or some place you have to be?"

"No," Nathaniel admitted. "I'm a student, completely unattached, and it's summer break. All I need to complete a PhD is my dissertation, and that's what I'm working on now."

Completely unattached. Interesting. But she wasn't going to let him know that made any difference to her. "Oh, so you just sail around the world without getting your hands dirty earning a proper living."

His brows lifted. Maybe that dig had hit a little too close to home?

"If you like to golf, Pink Beach Club guests have privileges at the Mid Ocean Club," Patience said, in a second attempt to lure Nathaniel into leaving her property. "It's one of the finest courses on the island— one of the top fifty golf courses in the world. Did you know Bermuda is home to more golf courses per square mile than anywhere else in the world?"

"I hate golf," Nathaniel announced, visibly agitated.

Patience and Cecilia each gave him wary sidelong glances.

"Okay," Patience said. "Calm down. We won't tal about golf, then."

"What are you two staring at?" His thunderous expression gradually dissipated.

"Nothing," Patience answered. "It's just that I've never seen anyone display such animosity toward a sport. Do you hate all sports?"

"No. Just golf."

"I see," said Patience. But she didn't.

"Were you hit over the head with a golf club when you were a child?" Cecilia ventured with a tentative smile.

Nathaniel wasn't laughing.

Cecilia leaned over to whisper in Patience's ear. "Talk about overreacting. He acts as if golf clubs are weapons of mass destruction. And while we're on the subject of tools, I wonder if he's a putter. Or do you suppose he prefers the long drive? I'd like to get a look at his nine-iron, and—"

"Cecilia!" Patience interrupted. "You're being rude and crude! You two deserve each other."

"I'll take that as a compliment." Cecilia laughed.

"While you two women are busy having a laugh at my expense, I'll just go down the hall and find my room, stash my gear and get settled."

"But," said Patience, chasing after him, "I didn't say you could—"

"Since I've already moored my boat at your dock," Nathaniel interrupted, "I may as well stay. I won't be ny trouble. You won't even know I'm here."

Patience ran over to the window. The light was ady beginning to fade. "Your boat? It's more like an n liner. How did you manage to maneuver that trosity into the bay?"

I'm a sailor, remember? And your house is sited

on a deep-water mooring."

"I never agreed to this. You can just turn around and leave, and take the Queen Mary with you."

"Now, Cousin, you're just distraught," Nathaniel soothed. "Sit down." He tried to guide her to the couch.

"Don't patronize me, don't order me around in my own home, or treat me like a child, and don't ever touch me again."

"You make a lot of demands."

"Patience," Cecilia said, puzzled. "What's gotten into you? For heaven's sake, he's your cousin. Be gracious."

"Precisely," Nathaniel agreed.

"Distant cousin," Patience corrected. "Get out, Nathaniel. I'm giving you ten seconds to get out, or I'll call—"

"The authorities?" Nathaniel laughed, his eyes flashing a warning signal. "You know you won't. We don't want to air our dirty laundry in front of your friend, now, do we? Cecilia, could you please leave us alone now? Patience and I have a lot of catching up to do."

Cecilia's eyes met hers and held a million questions.

"Don't worry, I'm harmless," Nathaniel assured her.

"Patience, you'll call me later, promise?" Cecilia implored. "You'll be all right, won't you?"

"Yes, because my *cousin* is not going to be staying." Patience let her friend out the front door and turned to Nathaniel.

"My cousin?" Patience was horrified. "That's pathetic, even for you."

"I'm moving in here. It's not safe for you. I can't protect you unless we're together."

"Protect me from what?"

"The evil that's stalking us."

"Are you hallucinating?"

"And we can't have people talking. We need to maintain a low profile. My boat was sticking out like a sore thumb at the yacht club. And we have your reputation to think about."

"A low profile? With that cruise ship berthed in front of Marigold House? I hardly think you're worried about my reputation. But even if you were, it's too late. I dearly love her, but talking to Cecilia is tantamount to taking out a front-page ad in *The Royal Gazette*. The news will be all over the island by this evening. 'Patience Katherine Whitestone is living in sin with her American cousin.'"

"Who else besides Sallie and Cecilia have access to this house?"

"Well, there's Andrew. He tends the garden."

"That fossil? I saw the man in the garden talking to Sallie. He doesn't have enough energy to put one foot in front of the other. I don't know how he even negotiates the steps down to the garden. The man is barely mobile."

"He's been with us forever."

"That's not hard to believe. My guess is your grandmother did all the work and he puttered around after her."

Patience blushed. "Well, she couldn't put him out of a job. He needs the money."

"And do you also collect all the stray cats and dogs around the island?"

Patience twisted the hem of her T-shirt and looked away.

"Don't answer that." Nathaniel rolled his eyes. "What's the story with Sallie? She's always skulking around the kitchen, making preparations, answering the door, and bringing in packages from well-wishers."

"Sallie doesn't skulk. She belongs here. She's trying to be unobtrusive, respectful of my feelings."

Her grandmother had hired Sallie many years ago and requested that Patience retain the housekeeper after her death, because she needed the work. But Patience knew the real reason. Diana hadn't wanted to leave her daughter alone after she was gone.

When her grandmother was sick, Sallie had cooked, cleaned, and handled the household. Patience and Sallie had always been close, but they had truly bonded during her grandmother's illness. She couldn't have made it through the last weeks without her. In fact, it had been Sallie who had gently pried Patience from her grandmother's lifeless body with soothing tones and tender words. "She's gone, luv. I've got you now."

"Well, that all stops today. There is to be no one in this house but you and me from now on, understood? Maybe Cecilia, or she'd get suspicious."

"Nathaniel, you're being unreasonable," Patience objected. In a corner of her mind she wondered why he was insisting that they be alone. What were his real motives?

"I'm being cautious. And I want the names and phone numbers of everyone who works at Marigold House, now."

She eyed him carefully. He was certainly in a strange mood. She didn't think she had any fight left in her to oppose him. She'd give in now, but as soon as he left, she would hire them both right back. She opened the nightstand and held out a small black address book.

Nathaniel walked out and was back within ten minutes.

"It's done."

"What did you do? Did you give them the ax? Make them walk the plank?"

"No, I'm not heartless. I gave them a well-deserved three-week vacation. Paid."

She smiled. "I'll write out the check in the morning."

"It's already been taken care of."

"How?"

"I have my own money, and I used it."

"It's pathetic, really," Patience said. "I'm a grown woman. Almost twenty-seven, and my grandmother had to hire someone to take care of me."

"This place is huge. You need help, there's no doubt about it, although I'm sure you could handle it."

Patience turned her head away, then whispered, "There might be a slight problem."

"What's that?" He cocked his head in her direction.

"Well, since you let Sallie go, I can't, that is, I don't know how, I mean I never learned to... Oh, bloody hell. We'll starve, Nathaniel."

"What do you mean?"

"I can't cook!"

He threw his head back and laughed until it hurt.

"Well, I can. And I'll teach you. Everyone should know how to cook."

"Can you clean, too?"

"I can swab a deck, so I guess I can sweep a floor."

48

"We have a vacuum cleaner."

"I'm not going to let an electric broom get the better of me. We'll manage until this mess is sorted out. We can always eat out."

"I'm not going out yet. I'm still in mourning."

Before he could comment, Nathaniel smelled smoke.

"Did you or Cecilia leave a burner on in the kitchen?" he inquired.

"No," Patience said. Nathaniel sniffed the air again and ran to the open window at the side of the house.

"There's a fire on the *Fair Winds*," he yelled, and dashed out the side door with Patience close on his heels.

"I'll call the fire department."

"No!" Nathaniel argued. "We don't need the authorities poking around here. We'll handle this ourselves."

"But you could lose your boat," she pleaded.

"There's more at stake here," he yelled back at her, taking the steps two at a time. "Bring some buckets."

Patience rushed back to the laundry room, grabbed a plastic mop bucket, and dashed into the kitchen to retrieve the deepest pot she could find. She followed Nathaniel down the steps and out to where the *Fair Winds* was moored. Nathaniel was already working furiously trying to extinguish the flames.

"Nathaniel," she called, and when he turned, she tossed him the bucket. He jumped off the boat, reached over, and dipped the bucket into the sea, fairly flying back to the source of the flames. Patience ran to the water, filled up the heavy stainless steel pot, and stood beside him, hefting its contents onto the fire. They worked in tandem for close to an hour without speaking. Fortunately, the fire had just started and hadn't done much damage. After interminable trips to dip their pails into the bay, the fire was finally under control.

Nathaniel was fuming. It was obvious this boat meant the world to him.

"The bastard," Nathaniel said, chest heaving. "He's been on the boat again. And this time he's left a dangerous calling card. That's it, Patience. He's gone too far. I'm going to have to kill him."

"You admitted, yourself, you don't even know for sure who *he* is," Patience reasoned. "All you have to go on is some codename in a journal. Calm down, Nathaniel, before you explode."

"He's probably watching us right now," Nathaniel seethed. "Get back to the house!"

"Stop ordering me around like I was a witless child," Patience said.

"Then stop acting like one!"

"You're insane," she spit, eyes flashing. "Why are you mad at *me*?"

"Because you're here! Now go, before I carry you into the house myself."

"Just try it," she challenged.

Patience didn't know if she wanted to laugh or cry at how ludicrous the situation was. All she was doing was trying to help. But she knew his anger disguised raw fear. He was on the edge.

Well, so was she. The unknown man hadn't threatened to kill Nathaniel, had he? How did he even know Nathaniel? She was his primary target, after all. If the man set Nathaniel's boat on fire, then it stood to reason Nathaniel couldn't be the stalker.

But he was still digging into her past. Was she wrong to be frightened of him? She knew somewhere in the back of her mind that he was out to hurt her, her family. But she was more frightened than ever of the stalker and thought maybe it wouldn't be a bad idea to keep Nathaniel around, even if he *was* irritating.

Deciding not to press her luck by further inflaming his temper, Patience stomped back up the steps to the side entrance, sulking as she slipped into the house.

****

He found her on the couch, the journal open on her lap.

"Damn," Nathaniel said, when he noticed her red, swollen eyes. "You've been crying."

"No, I haven't."

"Yes, you have. You've been reading his journal."

She didn't answer, but she bit her bottom lip and twisted her hands together, wrinkling the newly pressed skirt she had changed into after their bout with the fire.

Nathaniel covered her hands with his and took her into his arms. After the commotion of the fire, she was too tired to resist him, and it felt good to be held. She rested her head on his shoulder, just for a minute, until she could regain her strength.

"You didn't like what you read," Nathaniel said.

"I don't believe what I read."

"Or you don't *want* to believe it. Is it your grandfather's handwriting?"

Patience nodded.

"Are you finished?"

"No, I just started. I'm just so tired."

"Of course. Let me take you to bed."

She looked up at him in confusion, and her eyes filled. Did he mean what she thought he meant? No. But his lips were so close. So close she could feel his hot breath against her face. And she felt so warm in his arms. So safe. So protected. She didn't have the strength to struggle. She had no fight left. She simply couldn't move. She felt as if she were enveloped in a fog. And he was calling out to her.

****

"Patience," he murmured softly. He placed a gentle kiss on her lips. It wasn't right to take advantage when she was so vulnerable. He couldn't disguise the fact that he wanted her, which made no sense, because he had just met her.

But he felt like he belonged here, with her. He was drawn to her with a yearning that was physical. And even though he hardly knew her, he wanted to protect her. He tried to lead her down the hall, but she wouldn't or couldn't move.

She was practically asleep on her feet. He lifted her up and carried her into her bedroom, where he looked around. It belonged to a fairytale princess, floral chintz fabric on the windows for an English Country look and a soothing color scheme of lavenders, the palest blues, and yellows. Fresh, fragrant island flowers were everywhere. He had a flashback of a woman who might have been his mother, although he barely remembered her. Her room had smelled like this, like spring.

Nathaniel pulled back the crisp blue-striped duvet cover and placed Patience on the cool white satin sheets beneath it. Her clothes were constricting her. To make her more comfortable, he took off her bunny slippers and placed them on the floor. Then he removed her

52

skirt, slipped her T-shirt over her head, and folded both neatly on the settee at the foot of the bed. He thought about removing her bra but resisted the temptation. Tucking her snugly under the cover, he placed a kiss on her forehead, and she stirred. He thought he detected a touch of fever.

"Patience. You'll sleep now."

"You can't stay here," she pleaded, nodding off.

"Sssh," he said. "We'll talk about that when you wake up. I'll be close by."

Her lids fluttered shut and she grasped for his hand.

"Don't leave me alone."

"I won't," he answered.

Nathaniel sat down on the side of the bed and held her hand until she fell asleep. She was a wreck. She had probably not slept and had hardly eaten for the entire week.

Then she'd worked so hard helping him douse the flames on the *Fair Winds*. She needed complete bed rest. They would talk about other things when she woke. Soon he heard her rapid breathing as she slipped into slumber.

Once, in the middle of the night, she cried out. Nathaniel shot out of his bed in the guest room down the hall and rushed into her room.

She was sobbing, so he slipped under the covers with her, gathered her in his arms, and soothed her, smoothing her hair and rubbing her back, fighting the growing urge to kiss her.

"I'm here, Patience. I'm here."

Soon she was resting calmly. He stayed in the bed briefly—to be near her in case she needed him, he told himself.

He apologized to her, although he knew she couldn't hear him, as he repeated a line from her grandfather's diary: "I fear I have unleashed the evil, and we cannot turn back from this path."

Chapter 6

Nathaniel woke early and went into the kitchen to fix breakfast. He was greeted by stainless steel appliances and hanging pots and pans, much like a ship's galley. The polished Blue Pearl granite countertops and modern European sail-white cabinets trimmed in satin nickel hardware reinforced the nautical theme, enhanced by dazzling views of a restless ocean beyond the large windows.

The kitchen was well equipped and the refrigerator and pantry well stocked, as he expected. Probably Sallie or Cecilia had brought over the food earlier in the week. He doubted Patience had had a decent meal since the funeral. When breakfast was prepared, he left it to keep warm while he went to her room. She was still peacefully asleep, and he enjoyed watching her for a moment. In her hand was a well-worn paperback book with a pirate and a half-clad woman on the cover. He smiled. *Not so prim and proper after all, are you, Patience?*

She must have been restless and gotten up sometime in the night to get the book. Luckily, he had slipped out of her room and returned to his bed before she awakened and found him there. He traced his finger on her lips and pushed back a sunlit curl on her forehead, and she stirred and woke, still a bit disoriented.

"What are you doing here?"

"I'm staying with you, remember, Cousin?" he teased. She sat up instantly, ignoring her state of undress.

"Where did you sleep last night?" He caught her examining the pillow next to her, where a definite indentation was noticeable. "You didn't!"

"You were having a bad dream. I simply came in to comfort you and, well, I decided to stay until—"

"You decided to stay? You impudent rogue!"

Nathaniel threw back his head and laughed, a deep belly laugh.

"Now I'm a rogue. I seem to be descending in your estimation. First a pirate, then an adventurer, now a rogue. Cousin, you're priceless."

"I am *not* your cousin, and get out of my bedroom!"

"I'm sure we must have been related somewhere back in time."

"Impossible. Your line died out a long time ago…in the Stone Age. I suggest you leave, this instant. Kindly hand me my robe on your way out." He looked around and tossed her the sheer white silk robe draped over the settee. Only then did she notice what she wore.

"I don't remember undressing," Patience said, eyeing Nathaniel suspiciously. "You didn't…"

"I barely looked at you. You looked uncomfortable in that tight skirt, and you needed a good night's sleep."

"You drugged me, didn't you?"

"Don't freak out. I didn't *drug* you. When I spoke to Sallie, she confided that you hadn't been sleeping well. She was concerned about you, and she showed me where to find the sleeping pills your doctor prescribed in case you couldn't—"

"You *did* drug me, you bastard!"

She stood on the bed, hands on her hips, and faced Nathaniel like an avenging angel.

"In future, I'll let you know if I'm uncomfortable! Stop undressing me, and kindly keep your hands to yourself."

"I'm working on that problem." Nathaniel smiled.

Patience turned her back to him, trying to put on the robe with some attempt at modesty.

"You look just like the type who would take advantage. We didn't...you know...did we?" she asked turning her head in his direction.

"You would have known if we had," he assured her, laughing at her naiveté. "I made breakfast."

"I suppose you want to be knighted for that."

"I simply thought, since you probably haven't eaten in I don't know how long, that I'd..." He shrugged.

Patience bit her bottom lip and remembered her manners.

"I'm sorry. That was very sweet of you." She climbed down from the bed and followed Nathaniel into the kitchen. "I am hungry. What's on the menu?"

"Everything. Bacon, eggs, fresh fruit... I didn't know what you liked."

"Mmm. I'll take some of everything." She started to get a plate.

"Uh-uh, I'll wait on you this morning." Nathaniel got out plates, silverware, and napkins and sat her down with them at the kitchen table. "I even managed to make tea."

"Laced with drugs?"

"Dammit, Patience, there are no drugs in your tea. It's plain blackcurrant tea."

He moved the heavy silver tray he had prepared from the counter to the table, setting the teapot and the food where she could easily reach them, and watched as she poured tea from the teapot into the Wedgwood bone china cups. When her hands began to shake, he realized she really needed to eat something.

"Let me help," he said as he stilled her hands and took the teapot. When he touched her, all the nerve endings in his body went haywire.

He placed a lemon slice on the saucer, then spread preserves on a scone he'd found in a pastry box on the kitchen counter, and passed it to her on a delicate china plate. She refused with a wave of her hand.

"You don't have to serve me," she said.

"You were kind enough to let me stay last night, so—" He had the urge to rub his thumb tenderly under each of her eyes to remove the dark shadows, as an artist might do with the stroke of a brush.

"But that was..." She gazed uncertainly into the distance.

"When's the last time you ate?" he prodded gently. His breath caught as he responded to the intimacy in her voice. He wanted to touch her again but held back, not ready to weaken her defenses further as she looked at him and a tear slipped down her cheek, then another, until they came in a steady flow. Despite her night's sleep, he knew she was too exhausted to stop them, too despondent to care she was crying in front of a total stranger. She had been stoic at the funeral, hadn't shed any tears. Maybe she was overdue.

"I don't want to eat," she said.

When her tears became unmanageable, Nathaniel offered his linen napkin solicitously so she could wipe her eyes.

"Please, don't cry," he pleaded. He didn't know what to do about the tears. An only child raised without a mother, he had grown up cared for by his grandmother. Gran was a rock, the most in-control woman he'd ever known. And the most beautiful. More beautiful than any movie star. All his friends had said he had the hottest grandmother around. But it was her strength he really admired. She'd always been there for him. He suspected she had dark secrets, a past life she never talked about. But she didn't ever fall apart, and she never let him fall apart. In fact, he had never seen her cry. Soft and gentle? No one could accuse Gran of being either.

After Gran's death, he had wandered the globe aimlessly, all summer, without reason to put into any port more than a few days at a time, until now. With nothing to show for all that wasted time. He'd barely made a dent in his dissertation.

Nathaniel missed Gran. He tried to reach for memories of the past, a mother's tender kiss or comforting words spoken to heal hurts. He couldn't dredge up any. Perhaps he had once longed for them. Now they only existed in his imagination. He remembered his grandmother singing him French lullabies; that was all.

Yet, strangely, something deep inside of him responded to Patience, and he wasn't entirely unsympathetic to her frailty.

"Here, you need to eat something now. Have this scone. I insist."

She still didn't trust him, but, in all fairness, he *was* being polite. He had manners, when he chose to use them. She shook her head, but he lifted the scone to her mouth anyway and coaxed her to take a bite. It smelled heavenly, and though she must have been ravenous, she nibbled on the pastry slowly. When she was finished, he wiped the sugar-coated crumbs and preserves from her mouth efficiently with the napkin. He wanted to skim his fingers across her lips, to let her taste him; he refrained.

"I think you should go down to your boat now," she said. He wanted to kiss her and realized from the warm gleam in her eyes she might kiss him back, and who knew where that would lead?

"And I think you should eat something else before I go," Nathaniel said.

Patience relented.

Patience had beautiful hands to match that beautiful heart-shaped face of hers, so delicate and expressive as she finished her breakfast in silence. Her green eyes reminded him of the color of water in a calm sea.

****

"The food is delicious," she said. "Where did you learn to cook like this?"

"At sea, I guess. You learn to cook or you starve. Actually, my Grandmother Simone taught me."

"Did you mean what you said about teaching me to cook? I want to learn."

"Sure. Next time I make a meal, you'll be my assistant."

"Wonderful. Meanwhile, I'll be studying some of my grandmother's cookbooks."

Patience got up and stared out the window at the *Fair Winds*.

"It's still there. I thought the fire was just a bad dream. Why did you dock your boat here?"

"So I could keep an eye on both her and you. I'll take you out for a sail this morning."

"Is she seaworthy?"

"She's in great shape, thanks to you. You were a big help last night. I want to take her out for a while, and I want you to come, too."

"I don't think so."

"Are you afraid to be alone with me?"

"Apparently I was alone with you last night."

"There. You see? And nothing happened, did it?"

"I should hope not. And nothing is going to happen. I expect you to behave like a gentleman for the short time you're here."

"I won't attack you, if that's what you're worried about. Now where's the journal?"

"I've put it away in a safe place," she said, slipping out of the room to the cedar chest under the stairwell. "Where you can't find it." She opened the chest—and gasped. "The journal, it's gone! What have you done with it?"

He reached inside his coat. "Is this what you're looking for?"

She glared when she caught the glint in his eye. "Hand it over," Patience growled, reaching for it.

Nathaniel shifted it behind his back, and she reached her arm around his waist. He moved it to the other hand, and she reached around his other side until she had both arms around him.

"Darling, I didn't know you cared," he said,

closing his arms around her and pulling her roughly against him.

"Take your hands off me and give me back my journal."

"What will you give me for it? How about a kiss?"

"How about a kick?" she countered, kicking him in the shin.

"Ouch! You fight dirty." But he wouldn't let her go, instead bringing his mouth down and pressing it against hers, unlocking her lips with his tongue. Invading her. She fought to catch her breath. She tried to fight him but then found herself responding to his touch.

He was so tender, so gentle, and yet so demanding. She went soft, her vision blurred, and somehow her arms wound around his shoulders and she was nestled close to him, lifting her mouth to his for more. The kiss seemed to go on forever. She wanted it to. Her breasts felt full against his chest, and she felt his heart beating.

He grabbed her and lifted her up against him. "Patience," he whispered. "Closer, come closer. You taste so good. I knew it would be like this. I can't get enough of you."

She fought her way out of his embrace and grabbed the journal. "Well, I've already had enough of you," she answered as she spun out of his arms.

He grabbed her hand. "You want more. I felt it." His breath was coming in heavy spurts now.

"You're dreaming, sailor boy. I just wanted the journal, and now I've got it. Have you read it?"

"Only the first section."

Patience frowned. "Then I guess you think you have your answer. You've already made your mind up about my grandfather."

"I don't know what to think," Nathaniel said. "When will you read the rest?"

"As soon as you leave me alone. Which can't be soon enough."

"I'll get the boat ready. After you've read some more, come down and we'll set sail. Will you come?"

"Anything to get rid of you, to get a moment's peace," she said, then added playfully, "and Cousin…"

"Yes?"

"Thanks for breakfast."

He smiled and turned to leave. "We're going diving," he called back over his shoulder. "I have wetsuits and towels on board. Don't make me wait too long."

Patience sat on the couch in the parlor and tried to reclaim her equilibrium. The kiss and all the feelings that went with it were real. But she would never let Nathaniel know it. Her heart was still racing. She felt something she couldn't deny, something big. No one had ever kissed her like that. Made her feel like that. But she had to remember he was out to ruin her and her family's reputation. And he was manipulating her. Taking advantage. Playing her. Softening her up, damn him. And she didn't like being handled.

He was only spending time with her for the access he thought it would offer him to that precious stash of gold. Gold she wasn't even sure existed. Certainly she had no knowledge of its whereabouts. And if it did exist, she wouldn't make his job easier. Flustered at first, she soon settled down as she resumed reading about her grandfather's treachery.

There, well documented year by year through the

war, were her grandfather's activities, in her grandfather's hand. Her grandfather, codenamed *Insel Adler. The Island Eagle*. With its keen ability to observe. A bird of prey. Alert. Watchful. Always sharp. And, in this case, full of deceit.

Chapter 7

Patience rubbed her eyes and tried to hold back the tears. She looked out over the ocean in despair, trying to summon the image of the grandfather she remembered, to reconcile these words with the man she had known and loved all her life.

As she read the damning passages with growing horror, she was also gripped by the love and concern revealed for her grandmother. Of all the emotions described in the journal, these words rang the truest, further proof that William Whitestone had treasured his wife above all else in the world.

Patience descended the stone steps slowly, head bowed, and stepped onto the dock at the side of the house. Her eyes were dry, and she was determined not to sink into despair because of what she had read. One by one, the pieces of the puzzle were fitting together. The journal was painting a frightening picture of her grandfather as an insincere traitor.

But the real proof was missing, and she knew Nathaniel planned to confront her with his version of the truth on this sailing trip. A truth she wasn't ready to face.

Patience shielded her eyes from the sun as she caught her first real close-up look at Nathaniel's vessel. She hadn't paid much attention to the ship during the fire and had only caught glances of the craft from her window.

"Your sailing ship is marvelous. It's a replica of the *Sea Venture*. I don't know why I didn't notice that before."

"She's made of Bermudian cedar," Nathaniel replied. "Rare, I know, almost impossible to get these days, since the blight, but for the right price…"

"Why did you call her the *Fair Winds*?"

"Just a tradition in our family. Our house in Virginia is also called the Fair Winds."

"She's a beauty. We sure could use a vessel like this in our flotilla to kick off our celebration after the yacht race. It's going to be a parade of boats to launch all the festivities. Perhaps you'll agree to sail your boat in the flotilla in January."

"That seems like a lifetime from now," Nathaniel answered. "I don't plan to be around next year. Don't know where I'll be, but probably far away from here."

"Off to the next great adventure?" Patience wondered why the thought of him leaving bothered her so much.

"Do you sail?"

"Not much anymore, since my grandfather died," she admitted. He looked over at the boat docked in front of her house.

"Is she yours?"

"She was my grandfather's. But yes, she's mine now."

"She's magnificent," said Nathaniel, but he was looking directly at her. "I'd like to see how she handles, if you would care to take me out later," he said, and Patience suspected he might not be talking about the boat now.

His blue eyes pierced hers.

"Let's go, then," he said after a minute. "You can never really know a place until you've seen it from the water."

Patience watched him maneuver the boat expertly away from the dock, out of the bay, and into the open ocean. He was wearing khaki shorts and a white polo shirt, and she could see fresh scrapes and blood on his knees.

"Ouch. You're hurt. How did that happen?"

"I had a close encounter of the worst kind with a brick wall," he said, embarrassed.

"The walls are made of limestone, not brick," Patience corrected, "and that's about the worst case of road rash I've seen in a long time."

"Why do they put those damn walls in the middle of the roadway? I can ride a bike. But you people drive on the wrong side of the road."

"No, actually, it's the left-hand side," she joked. "The hospital is swelling with snowbirds who can't follow the rules of the road. And pale tourists who baste themselves and bake and broil in the Bermuda sun. The sun can often be deceptive. When we drop anchor, I'll tend to it, if you have supplies. Otherwise the salt spray will kill you."

"Will you kiss it and make it better?" He looked directly at her mouth.

Patience blushed.

"No, I'll use peroxide or something equally painful, that stings terribly."

"No, thanks, sister. I'll live with it."

"I thought I was your cousin," she teased, surprising herself. It wasn't in her nature to tease with a man. She was awkward around most men. And perhaps that was why she had never formed a long-term relationship with one. Flirting came easily to Cecilia. But never to Patience. She was what people called an odd duck.

She tired of the constant parade of proper suitors, bankers, politicians, businessmen, all "the right kind of people," from the right families, that her grandmother had trotted out before her, like she was Prince Charming, waiting to see if the slipper fit. Well, they were all her grandmother's kind of people. And instinctively she knew they were all wrong for her.

Her grandmother and Cecilia would have been surprised, shocked, if they knew what was in her heart. She yearned to be spirited away by a dark and dangerous swashbuckler, longed to be swept entirely off her feet, wanted to feel her heart race uncontrollably and be thrown off balance by the wrong kind of man. On the surface, a man like that would appear alien to her nature, but that would not be true. In fact, the man of her dreams was beginning to look a lot like Nathaniel. She stared at him as they got under way.

"So, you're American," Patience began.

"As American as they come. I'm from Virginia."

"Ah," she said reverently, and her eyes held a faraway look. "Virginia."

"Have you been there?" he asked, intrigued.

"No," she said, not wanting to admit that she'd never even been off the island. "But my family had many ties to the state. The two places are intertwined." Patience linked her hands to illustrate as she spoke.

****

Intertwined. What a strange word. From a strange

68

woman. *Patience*. Even her name was old-fashioned. But somehow it seemed to suit her and her surroundings. She was so prim and proper, and preachy, a real know-it-all, but so animated when she talked about her island. That was certainly her hot button, and maybe it was also the key to his quest. She spoke of the place as if it were Camelot. It was strangely arousing. He imagined what it would feel like to break through that reserve to the simmering woman he was sure he'd find inside. To peel that veneer back layer by layer. It would take a lot of patience on his part.

Patience would be surprised to know how much he had already learned about her. For instance, he knew she was named after the *Patience,* one of the two rebuilt ships that set sail from Bermuda to Virginia the year after the wreck of the *Sea Venture.* One of his ancestors had been aboard that vessel, which had foundered in a hurricane off St. George's Island in 1609 while on its way to resupply the starving colony of Jamestown, an occurrence that led to the accidental settlement of Bermuda. He knew her relatives were also among the first settlers of Bermuda. *Intertwined.* Yes. That was how he had always felt about the two places. How would it feel to be "intertwined" with the bewitching girl sitting in front of him?

"Where did you go to college?" she asked in an obvious attempt to find out more about the "houseguest" she hardly knew.

"University of Virginia."

"Ah, I thought I detected a bit of prep school polish under that gruff exterior.

He hesitated and then smiled.

"Were you really a history major?"

Nathaniel lowered his voice. "Yes. Does that turn you on?"

She shot him a glaring look. "Let's just say I have a soft spot in my heart for the subject."

"Any other soft spots I should know about?" He looked at her through shuttered eyes.

"None I care to share with you."

Nathaniel laughed, then decided to change course. "You know, aside from sailing from Virginia to Bermuda and back, this is my first real trip to the island."

"Bermuda is not really one island," said Patience. "It's a chain of more than one hundred twenty islands and islets that were created by a prehistoric volcanic eruption."

"Is there anything about Bermuda you don't know and aren't compelled to spout?" Nathaniel, privately captivated, tried to sound annoyed.

"I'm sorry. It's just that I sometimes get carried away when I talk about my home. It's what I do. Don't you find anything in Bermuda to your liking?"

Yes, I find you very much to my liking. "How could anyone sail and not love this place?" he answered, never tearing his eyes from her. "It's like a dream. I've never seen a place like it anywhere in the world," he admitted, his eyes gazing into hers. "The water, the beaches… They're breathtaking."

"Well, we've made enough small talk, so why don't you tell me where you're taking me?"

"First, I have to tell you the story of how your grandfather's chest was discovered," Nathaniel began. "My uncle was just a teenager when he sailed with Edmund Downing, who discovered the remains of the

Sea Venture in 1958 in the waters off Fort St. Catherine on St. George's."

"Your uncle knew Edmund Downing?" He had her complete attention now.

"My uncle was the real adventurer in the family. I guess I take after him. He never settled in any one place. His home was the sea. He instilled the love of sailing in me. I went with him on some of his expeditions when I was very young. He told me that when he and Downing discovered the wreck of the 1609 ship, they discovered something else at the bottom of the ocean. Downing wasn't interested in this particular find. On the surface, it appeared to be nothing valuable—just a bunch of papers in a large old sea chest. So he gave the chest to my uncle. I want to take you out to where my uncle first found it."

"Do you have the proper maps? There are still treacherous reefs surrounding the islands. During the last 450 years, more than 300 ships have wrecked on these reefs, including pirate ships."

"This isn't a pirate ship, and I'm a good sailor, Patience. Of course I know how to avoid the navigational hazards of the reefs. I managed to make it to Bermuda in the first place, didn't I? Anyway, I don't see any stone walls I could run into out here, do you?"

"They're hidden beneath the surface of the water," she said, laughing.

Nathaniel slowed the motor and dropped anchor. "Here it is. So close to the reef. That's why no one's been able to find it in all these years. I figure the chest was originally dropped off here by a German U-boat. Maybe in the same place your grandfather was dropped off to swim to shore."

"Pure speculation."

****

Patience bit her bottom lip as she contemplated the water. This was their special place. Hers and her grandfather's. It was both frightening and familiar to her. It was the place her grandfather had taken her when he first taught her to swim, then to sail and to scuba dive. There was no way Nathaniel could have known that.

Initially, Patience had been terrified of being out on the water, couldn't keep anything down when she was out on the boat. She still wrestled with that fear. But her grandfather had pushed her to conquer her fears until he thought she had made a complete turnabout. He teased her and said she was like a fish in water—had called her his little mermaid. She and her grandfather had gone diving together in these reefs, looking for shipwrecks. There were hundreds of wrecks, dating back centuries.

Conquer your fears. How many times had he told her that? Not just out on the water but on land, where he taught her to shoot, to defend herself, until she became an expert marksman, at home in any situation on land or in the sea.

Whenever she recalled her grandfather, she remembered them walking together, or swimming together, her small, tentative hand in his large, capable one. But her grandfather was no longer here to keep her safe, and when she thought of going into the water without him, the color seeped out of her face.

"You've been here before," Nathaniel said, posing it as a statement, not a question.

Patience turned toward him but refused to answer.

She had questions of her own. "How did your uncle manage to get the chest to the surface?"

"The chest had Nazi markings, so the crew was afraid it might contain an unexploded bomb. Divers went down and attached and inflated a flotation device to help get it to the surface. They took a cursory look inside, and when Downing saw the papers he dismissed the contents as having some historical significance but no monetary value. My uncle was a bit of a history buff, so when he expressed an interest in the chest, Downing turned it over to him. Years later, when I finally got a look inside, I saw the journal and your grandfather's papers. They led me to you."

"You're jumping to conclusions that my grandfather had anything to do with those papers," she protested.

"No, I have all the proof I need right here on this boat. Do you want to look inside the chest?"

"I'm hungry," Patience said, ignoring his question. "Do you have anything to eat?"

"Sure."

She was anything but hungry after that big breakfast, but relief washed over her when Nathaniel left the subject of her grandfather's past and stepped down into the galley. He brought back a hamper with a picnic lunch of cold chicken, a green bean salad, white wine, cheese, bread, and grapes.

"I want you to eat," Nathaniel prodded. "Captain's rules."

Patience frowned, but she dug into the hamper to take her mind off her fears.

"You're looking a lot better since you've gotten some sleep and some food in your stomach," he told her. "But you still look a little green around the gills. You need to put some meat on those bones, mate. If you don't eat your vegetables, you're going to get pellagra. That's what my uncle always used to tell me."

"Spoken like a true sailor. You think I look bony?"

"You could stand to fill out a little more," Nathaniel said, "in some places. Here." He traced a finger along her cheekbones. "And here." His finger ran lightly down her arm and across her stomach.

"In other departments, you're built just fine." His gaze focused on her breasts.

Patience blushed. Nathaniel turned away before he could act on his instincts.

They rested on deck. Nathaniel tried to lighten the mood. "You're a funny little thing, Patience. I've already seen how you constantly bury your nose in some history book or historical romance. You're obsessed with what *was*. You're steeped in the past while you ought to have your eye on the future. You should be searching for what will be."

"Those are strange sentiments coming from a historian," she chided. "But we're different, there's no doubt. The past is like a link in a chain. It often holds secrets to the future. It cannot be ignored. Sometimes the bond is strong, forged of steel. Sometimes it is faint and spidery, like a golden thread of the finest lace, or elusive, like a whisper. But still the tether that ties us to the past holds. It echoes through time, but no matter how tenuous the bond, the link stays strong. And I believe we are all bound together."

Nathaniel stood, seeming spellbound, as he watched her speak and gesture. Then he shook himself. "How about that dive?" he offered, looking away from her. "I've got my dive gear and some spare equipment for you. We can look around at the wreck site below. That is, unless you're scared to go down."

If the alternative was to open the trunk, then she didn't think she was quite ready. Maybe she'd never be ready. But she wouldn't back down from a challenge.

"I'd enjoy a dive." She resented his tone but fidgeted with her hands and looked away from the water. Conquer your fears, she thought, taking deep, cleansing breaths.

Patience donned the wet suit for protection against the coral and the coldness. The flippers fit snugly, and she tightened the goggles. Swinging on her oxygen tank, she grabbed the vest, checked the air in her tank, and adjusted her regulator for the deep dive before she picked up the knife Nathaniel had provided in case she got tangled in seaweed or needed to cut herself free from a rope. Nathaniel's equipment included a computer that could analyze how much bottom time they'd have. In this depth, they'd be down no longer than fifteen minutes. With all this gear aboard, Nathaniel was obviously an experienced diver.

Sensing her hesitancy, Nathaniel grabbed Patience's hand and pulled her along with him as he jumped into the water.

Once submerged, Patience began to appreciate the silence and the beauty, the changing play of light on the water. They came face to face with the creatures of the deep patrolling the wrecks, skimming along the reefs— a moray eel, an orange starfish, a sergeant-major, a bright blue tang, a blue angelfish.

She felt natural with Nathaniel, and she liked the sensation of holding hands in the deep. Her hand felt right in his. She wanted to do more than hold hands, but she knew her strange desires put her in dangerous waters.

When the dive was finished, Patience climbed up the ladder, with Nathaniel right behind her.

"Good thing we didn't run into any sharks," Nathaniel laughed as they shed their equipment.

"It's more likely we'd get nudged by some lumbering sea turtle."

He reached for her hand again. "Are you ready to take a look now?" he prompted.

"It's kind of like opening Pandora's box, don't you think?" Patience shifted her weight back and forth on the deck. "You already know what's in there. Why don't you just tell me?"

"Because I think you need to see for yourself."

Patience followed Nathaniel down the steps to his cabin, where she saw the locker—the elephant in the room. Then it was real, after all. But that didn't necessarily mean it was her grandfather's. She would prove that it wasn't, or get Nathaniel to help her prove it. After having read most of the journal entries, she had little hope left, but who knew what she might find in the box?

"Go on, Patience, open it. Unless you're afraid of what you'll discover."

Again she rose to the challenge and lifted the lid. *Conquer your fears.*

"It's just a rusty old locker, you see. It has nothing to do with my grandfather." Patience looked away from the Nazi swastika marked on the trunk.

"Look closer," he advised, rifling through the contents of the trunk, searching. "Here. This is a picture of the owner of the trunk. Is this man your grandfather?"

She forced herself to look at the passport. Yes, it was her grandfather, but this name was unfamiliar. It was a German name.

"Wilhelm von Hesselweiss," Nathaniel read. "Born in Dresden, Germany. This was your grandfather."

"This is some kind of mistake," Patience objected. "Documents can be forged."

"There's no mistake. Wilhelm von Hesselweiss translates to William Whitestone. Keep looking."

Patience sifted through letters, reports, and annotated maps, all in her grandfather's handwriting.

Her head began to throb as Nathaniel droned on, rattling off details—including the mounting body of evidence about stolen plans of long-closed Bermuda bases.

"In addition to the bases I've already mentioned, we have here plans for the U.S. Naval Annex on Tucker's Island, Morgan's Island in Southampton Parish, and the U.S. Navy submarine base on Ordnance Island in the Town of St. George, established right after the Pearl Harbor attack because German subs were taking quite a bite out of Allied shipping and nipping at America's east coast. And, of course, there are the schematics for the Tudor Hill U.S. Navy listening post/research base in Southampton Parish, a top-secret anti-submarine warfare and radar surveillance station, and the telecommunications center for the U.S. Navy on Paynter's Hill in Tucker's Town. Is that specific enough for you?"

Patience was more interested in the faded black-and-white snapshots. There was one of her grandfather, so young, with his arm around a beautiful young dark-haired woman in a garden—a wife, lover, sister? Not a sister. These two people were obviously in love. It was written all over their faces and transmitted in their body language, the way they were wrapped around each other. There was an inscription on the back. "All my love, Emilie. Dresden. 1934." Dresden? But her grandfather had never mentioned traveling to Dresden, had he? He was from Zurich.

Who was Emilie to her grandfather? Had her grandmother known about this other woman?

She came across another picture, this one of a woman and a man in uniform. The man's collar was decorated with an Iron Cross, and he held an infant in his arms. Looking at the man, she thought there might have been a family resemblance. Was the baby her grandfather? Did he have another family back in Germany that he'd planned to return to after the war? If so, why hadn't he gone back there? There were no relatives on her grandfather's side of the family by the time she was born. She had always wondered about that. Her grandfather had taken trips over the years, alone. To visit these relatives? To go back to Germany?

Then she lifted a German war medal from its presentation case—the prestigious Knight's Cross of the Iron Cross. Her grandfather's for distinguishing himself in battle in the Kriegsmarine? Patience slipped the picture of Emilie and her grandfather safely into the pocket of her bathing suit cover-up.

This was ridiculous. She was beginning to buy into Nathaniel's warped notions. True, there were plans for all those U.S. bases. Stolen from the office of her great-grandfather, the vice admiral? How else could Wilhelm have gotten possession of them? A drawing of their home, Marigold House. Receipts for British pounds, for diamonds, and for enough Swiss gold to buy a small country.

"There's no treasure—no gold or diamonds or pound notes," she stated flatly. "And if there were, then why haven't you found them? You've certainly been snooping all over my house."

"My hunch is he use the notes and buried the rest somewhere on the property at Marigold House. Marigold House? That's quite a coincidence. Your grandfather had a perverted sense of humor, don't you think? House of gold, bought with gold, buried over gold. My hunch is he either buried it or used it to finance his illegal activities during the war."

"My grandfather would never have done anything like that. You didn't know him like I did. There's no gold buried at my house. I know that house inside and out. I would know if such an amount of gold were hidden there."

****

What could Nathaniel say to a woman who wasn't ready to face facts?

"Oh, there's gold, all right," Nathaniel assured her. "And I'm not leaving until I find it. There's nothing you can do or say to stop me. I've worked too long and come too far to give up. We start digging outside tomorrow. Did your grandfather make any additions to the house after the war?"

"Most of the large Bermuda houses have been added to over the years," Patience stalled. "It's a very common practice. And I'm not going to let you dig up my house or my yard."

"You don't have any choice but to cooperate with me. If we don't get there first, whoever is stalking us will. And he will not be as understanding as I have been."

She had mentioned frightening calls in the middle of the night, and threatening letters. When she went silent, Nathaniel knew she was remembering those. She had to feel safer since he had come to Marigold House. Unsettled, maybe, but safer. Still, in some ways, he was perhaps as great a threat to her as the stalker.

"Understanding? You call what you are putting me through 'understanding'? Rooting around in my life, digging up pieces of what you say is my family's past, upsetting me, and tarnishing my memories of my grandfather? You act like my grandfather was some kind of unfeeling monster. Nothing could be further from the truth. I loved my grandfather. Now he's dead. Can't you just leave the past buried?"

"Wasn't it you who said we're bound by the past? I believe that. And I'm not leaving you alone for a minute until we've unraveled this mystery to my satisfaction." Nathaniel grabbed her arm.

"Your satisfaction! Who's the monster now? Is it money you want? Pieces of gold? I have money, a lot of it. I'll give you money. Money isn't important to me. Just leave me alone."

"Patience, please. It's not just about the money. You don't understand. I don't want to fight with you. I—"

"Well, you will have a fight on your hands from me. I can promise you that. Turn this boat about, and take me home right this instant. And stop manhandling me!" She pulled away from him in a huff and stormed up to the top deck. The helpless and broken-spirited girl had vanished, and a new, aggressive Patience was here with a vengeance.

"We *will* work together, you and I," Nathaniel whispered after her. "We have no choice."

Bermuda is where your destiny lies. His grandmother's dying words suddenly flooded back to him. Was he simply feeling her spirit, her nearness, out on the ocean? He couldn't rid himself of the notion that he was meant to be here, that he and Patience were meant to be together. The pull of the past was very strong. And very unsettling.

The first order of business was to lose the stalker, or maybe lure him into revealing himself. The closer Nathaniel got to the gold, the more the predator would want to question or silence Patience. The stalker had to know about the gold. Why else would he be threatening her?

Maybe he should stay away from her, but she was in too much danger. He and Patience were going to be—what was the term she had used? *Intertwined*—whether she wanted it or not. It wasn't going to be easy, because she didn't trust him. She didn't even like him. He had made the right decision when he left the Royal Bermuda Yacht Club and presented himself at her door, a *fait accompli*. And there wasn't a damn thing she could do about it. If she balked, he could always threaten to go to the authorities and reveal his secrets about her family.

Nathaniel found her up on the deck leaning against the railing, braced for a brawl, eyes swollen with tears, sensuous mouth stubbornly set in fierce determination. He wanted to go to her, to take her in his arms and comfort her, kiss the breath out of her. But it was obvious she didn't want to be touched or comforted. Certainly not kissed. Not by him. Not now. Maybe not ever.

He watched her lift the journal from her canvas beach bag, settle herself on the deck, and begin reading intently. He wouldn't disturb her now. He would let her learn the truth for herself. The words in the journal did not lie. Even if she was lying to herself.

"Let's go back in, Patience," Nathaniel said. "It's getting dark and cold." He massaged her shoulders a moment before guiding the boat to the dock and assisting her onto land. His arm around her shoulder, and they walked back into the house together.

"Have you had enough for today?" he asked quietly. "Do you want to stop now?"

"No," she said firmly, her refusal to quit punctuated by the stubborn set of her jaw.

After she had changed into a diaphanous white ankle-length dress, he settled her onto the couch, covered her with a wool blanket, and gently positioned her neck on a pillow he had brought in from her bedroom.

He left her alone in the room and wandered around the house, continuing to look for clues, looking for the fortune in gold he was convinced was somewhere on the premises. Nothing he had read in the journal had been definitive about the location of the gold. Nathaniel was certain that if Patience were to read it, it might trigger a clue in her mind about the location of the treasure. And he was going to be close to her when she had that revelation.

The prospect of staying so close to Patience, in the

same house, was disturbing. He constantly fought his unbidden attraction for her. She was a bewitching puzzle. She had haunted his dreams and invaded his privacy. And that was before he'd even met her. Half the time he didn't know whether he wanted to strangle her or seduce her. He would definitely have to watch his step around this enchantress.

Nathaniel paced the length of the residence. As comfortable as he was around Patience, her house was also casting its spell on him.

He looked over at Patience, who hadn't moved since he'd settled her on the couch.

Nathaniel looked around at the luxurious surroundings. "Things aren't that bad. The wolf is not exactly at the door, is it?"

"I'm not helpless," Patience sniffled.

"I never said you were."

"But you were thinking it."

She would probably be surprised to know he'd like to wrap her in a protective cocoon and never let any harm come to her. In that respect, he wasn't much different from her grandfather.

A study in balance and symmetry, with its steep Bermuda buttery punctuated by the large snowball-looking finial perched on top, the house was grand, yet it managed to reflect intimacy and romance. Double French doors opened onto a courtyard that led to a sheltered swimming pool and a pool house tucked away in a magnificent setting. The lush, walled formal garden bloomed quietly in a riot of color, with blue Bermudiana, hibiscus, oleander, snapdragons, day lilies, and poinsettia. Rustic cedar benches rested under rustling palms that flanked a circular stone moon gate.

The veranda spanned the length of the house and offered a magnificent view of the restless Atlantic Ocean on one side and, beyond a deep lagoon, peaceful Tucker's Town Bay on another.

The spacious drawing room featured a large, brick-lined fireplace, exposed cedar beams, and cedar banisters, and was decorated with Bermuda cedar furniture, Oriental rugs, and a respectable row of Blackburn portraits lining the wall. Nathaniel had been around luxury all his life, and he recognized it in the delicate porcelains and the Chippendale pieces.

An intriguing collection of antique maps was displayed under the stairwell. The parlor walls were painted a pale yellow, trimmed in high-gloss white, and the room was graced with antique English imports. The comfortable couch, covered in a robin's-egg-blue stripe, blended with chairs dressed in a sea green floral pattern and seemed to extend a leisurely invitation to sit and stay awhile. Beckoning floor-to-ceiling windows all opened to water views.

He was interested in exploring the bedrooms and backrooms that held the promise of unexpected treasures. Although Patience was still jittery around him, Nathaniel sensed an aura of peace settling over the house, an atmosphere he hoped would dissolve her resentment. But he knew she was desperately clinging to her anger and her fear as she steeped herself in her grandfather's past, threatened by Nathaniel's determination to dig up her family secrets at any cost.

PART TWO

The Socialite and the Spy

Bermuda 1937-1958

Marilyn Baron

Prologue

Hamilton, Bermuda, May 1937

Nighthawk worked best under cover of darkness. But on this particular Sunday morning, he was forced to come out into the light. His typical style was, in effect, to swoop down on long, broad wings, like a giant bird of prey or a sleek, shadowy vampire, and pluck up unsuspecting victims in his sharp talons.

His latest victim, Sir James Markham, hardly presented a challenge. Sir James should have been born a fish. Weekends invariably found him on the water in his trim, two-masted seventy-two-foot luxury yacht, *Guilty Pleasures*, a craft worthy of the richest and most powerful man on the island.

"James, be sure to wear your hat," his wife chided, as he skillfully maneuvered the boat out of its slip behind their waterfront estate in Hamilton. "You know how easily you burn."

Nighthawk knew Sir James had no intention of wearing a hat to protect his mottled skin. He wouldn't need it. He planned to spend most of the day in his cabin—entertaining. But he was probably already burning for his exotic mistress. When he was with Yvette, he undoubtedly fancied himself young, vibrant, and in love again. Who could put a price on such a glorious feeling?

Yvette claimed to work for the Imperial Censorship Staff handling transatlantic air mails. If there was one thing Nighthawk knew for certain, it was that Yvette, if that really was her name, was no British censorette. She *was* an expert linguist—proficient in German and French—and perhaps she *was* even engaged in the wartime censorship work being done in the colony. But she was no more British than the American-born Duchess of Windsor.

Sir James knew very little about Yvette's past. After some discreet inquiries, Nighthawk's sources had revealed that her parents, a French mother and a German father, had been labeled "enemies of the state" and imprisoned in one of the detention facilities the Nazis started in Germany soon after they took power in 1933. Yvette, some kind of German-French mutt, had narrowly escaped the roundup.

Compromised, Yvette knew she was no longer safe in Germany, so she passed herself off as French and aligned herself with the British. Sir James had arranged for her travel from England to Bermuda for an assignment in which her particular talents would be put to good use.

Sir James had no idea what that assignment was. All he knew conclusively was that they were on the same side and that his contacts and position were useful to his mistress in her vendetta against the Germans. And that she was eternally grateful for the small role he had played in arranging her safe passage to the colony.

Sir James had touched and tasted every hot-blooded inch of his petite French pastry, sometimes right in plain sight on the deck of his yacht, out in the middle of the Atlantic when there was no one around but Nighthawk to see. And what Nighthawk couldn't verify with his own eyes, his new loose-lipped friend Sir James bragged about to his brash young drinking buddy after being primed with a bottle of five-star brandy.

Yvette never asked anything from Sir James, but he would gladly have given her whatever she wanted. She claimed she only wanted to be with him, to be loved by him, for him to fill the empty spaces in her heart. He was the only family she had now. Sir James had no illusions about why she was with him. Perhaps he *was* just a doddering old fool. But if she thought of him as a father figure, he was perfectly willing to place her under his paternal protection.

Sir James had offered Yvette diamonds, money, anything her heart desired, to keep her in his bed. And, with a little coaxing, she had graciously taken what he had to give. She had told Sir James she would use it to start her new life in America, as far away as possible from the unpleasantness of the past, where she would finally be safe.

Sir James considered Yvette the perfect companion. She had the face of a goddess and managed to maintain an aura of innocence while loving him with the practiced body of a courtesan. She didn't scold or whine or nag like his aging wife. She was attentive and seemed interested in every detail of his business. Her whole purpose in life seemed to be to give him pleasure.

The wind veered to the east as the *Guilty Pleasures* docked at the Princess Hotel and Sir James stepped out to meet a smiling Yvette. Holding a bottle of Champagne and a large wicker picnic basket, Yvette looked fresh and delicious in her bright blue sundress. Even from Nighthawk's motorboat, the glint of a giant emerald on her finger caught the light—an emerald her benefactor had presented to her on their last ocean outing.

After steaming out of Hamilton Harbour and taking a brief pleasure cruise, Sir James brought the boat to anchor. Lunch would have to wait. And so would Nighthawk. No matter. He was used to waiting.

On the heels of what Nighthawk hoped was a particularly satisfying and exhausting romp in Sir James's cabin—he imagined the elderly gentleman crushing Yvette against his bloated body, kissing her greedily, then gently nuzzling her as she lay still, naked and vulnerable in his arms—he visualized a sated Sir James by now fallen into a drunken stupor. The sound of the waves rocking rhythmically against the boat would already have lulled him into a sound sleep.

As he snored loudly, a contented smile on his face, he never saw the shadow that crossed the cabin toward him with silent but deadly purpose. He never felt the curved blade that sliced his throat wide open as easily as if it were an overripe melon. He never heard Yvette's terrified but muffled screams as the predator's strong hands clamped over her mouth when she struggled at the sight of Sir James's blood saturating the sheets.

"Oh, God, James," she breathed in terror, trying to scream but never making a sound. She was probably wondering if her actions had precipitated this attack, if Sir James was just an innocent victim being punished because of her, if the Germans had finally discovered her. Tender-hearted girl that she appeared to be, she wouldn't be able to bear the thought of that. She couldn't possibly be in love with Sir James, but she obviously cared for him.

Nighthawk choked off the air to Yvette's delicate throat as he dragged her away, struggling, to the waiting launch pulled up beside the *Guilty Pleasures*. She kicked and scratched and bit and lashed out until, finally, when she had no strength to continue fighting, her body hung limp at his side. She would have been surprised to learn that Sir James, not she, had been the target of this particular foray.

****

Nighthawk's mission had been simple. Out with the old, in with the new. When the British Navy finally found the *Guilty Pleasures*, after an exhaustive search, Sir James was not on the craft. Nor was there any evidence he had been entertaining. It was assumed that Sir James had consumed too much alcohol, accidentally fallen overboard, and been eaten by a shark. Evidence of blood and some of his personal effects were conveniently discovered in the water around the boat. The sea never gave up its dead.

At the funeral, Bermuda's elite paid Sir James the proper respect, appropriate to his position. At his perch, Nighthawk stood apart as he listened attentively to the suitable eulogies from Sir James's business associates and friends, and appeared sympathetic to the tears that spilled from the eyes of the wealthy widow. Everyone wondered how Bermuda Power Company, Ltd., would ever recover from the tragic loss of its chairman. But Nighthawk knew that no one was irreplaceable.

Chapter 8

Tucker's Town, Bermuda, 1940

William Whitestone had only come to the Starlight Terrace of the Castle Harbour Hotel for a quick diversion. A few drinks. Maybe one dance. He'd heard there was a fancy coming-out party for the spoiled daughter of the new vice admiral. He'd do his best to steer clear of the vice admiral and his snobby socialite daughter at all costs tonight.

Since his arrival in Bermuda three years ago, William had attended an endless round of such boring balls, exchanging meaningless chatter about everything and nothing, so he could be in the right place at the right time. Since Britain and France had officially declared war on Germany, information was king in wartime Bermuda, and secrets were as negotiable as coin of the realm.

William had a mission, but he was still a man. He was lonely, and he craved the company of a soft woman. It had been a long time. He had been given a new identity, a new life. From the beginning, he'd understood that a new woman was part of the plan. He had resisted until now, but marriage was the next logical step. Perhaps he could find an addlebrained woman, one who could be easily manipulated, who wouldn't ask too many questions. She didn't have to be beautiful, but it wouldn't hurt if she were pleasant to look at, at least, and to touch.

In that instant, a blonde beauty danced into view, and he was lost.

The girl was a vision, flitting around the room like a hummingbird thirsting in a sumptuous garden. She was impossibly lovely in the pale yellow silk gown that molded to her body, with the flare of the full-length skirt swaying to the rhythm of the music as she moved under the bright lights with one man, then another, then another. Never left unattended, she was a much-sought-after partner.

William couldn't keep his eyes or his mind off her. With just one look, his heart had expanded and all rational thought had flown out of his head. Now he wanted—no, needed—to have his hands on her. No other woman, since Emilie, had ever caused such a stir in him. But Emilie was his past. He moved closer to the orbit of the beautiful dancer in yellow, his heart pulsing to the rhythm of the swing music.

She was heavenly, achingly young and innocent, with unruly blonde curls cascading around her head. Her green eyes flashed as her smile lit up the room. Though she was tall, she was elegant and moved with a grace and a spirit that shone like an aura around her, a butterfly who could never be captured. He knew he could never bend this girl to his will. And that made her even more attractive.

She was doing the jitterbug, imitating the latest craze from America. The Brits were wild for all things American. The girl moved tantalizingly, racing across the room to the beat of the drum in "A String of Pearls."

When the music fortuitously switched to "Change Partners and Dance," he made his move. He cut in on a tall man in dress whites, and, taking the girl in yellow into his arms, melded their bodies together until he was on fire. He didn't let her go when the music slowed to "I Had The Craziest Dream."

"I must be dreaming," he said smoothly. "Your name. I must have your name."

She laughed. "Well, if you must, then, it's Diana...Diana Hargrave."

"Like the Goddess Diana. The huntress. Do you hunt, Diana?"

"No, I could never kill anything." She looked up at him, mesmerized like a deer trapped in the searing lights of his eyes.

"But I imagine *you* are a hunter," she said, as he tightened his hold on her.

"Yes, and I'm stalking you right now." He smiled and risked kissing her softly on one side of her mouth and then the other, brushing his lips full against hers to gauge her reaction.

"Sir, please," she said, placing a gloved hand against his shoulder to steady herself. "I don't even know your name."

William could feel her warmth through the flimsy silk fabric. She stirred and trembled, and he pressed his advantage, nuzzling his cheek against hers, tasting her lips again.

"You needn't be afraid," he whispered. "I would never hurt such an angel."

When the music stopped, they stood swaying in the center of the room, and then, slowly, they moved again to the strains of "That Old Black Magic." By the time the dance was over, she had him completely enchanted.

Other men moved to cut in, but William's warning glare caused them to step aside.

"I need your name," she pleaded.

"And I don't need anything but you."

"Don't say pretty words you don't mean."

"But I do mean them. Let me show you."

He whisked her outside into the garden, snatching a drink from a passing waiter for her and another for him. The band played "Moonlight Serenade" as he continued to hold her in his arms.

"Come out into the moonlight, under the moon gate with me, Diana."

The smell of her mixed with the scent of hibiscus and pink oleander, and the sounds of jazz were punctuated by the rhythmic night music of the tree frogs.

He ached to touch her breasts, as pale and smooth as alabaster in the moonlight, but that would have to wait until they were alone. He could hardly contain his desire.

William placed a flurry of kisses across Diana's face, kisses that left her breathless. He could feel his heart beating. *Gott*, what was this woman doing to him?

****

Her partner's gravelly voice melted Diana's remaining reservations.

"Drink this, Diana," he coaxed.

She obliged him, although she'd already had two glasses of Champagne earlier in the evening. The frothy concoction, deliciously sweet and wicked, went right to her head. She felt loose and a little reckless in the stranger's arms as she sipped and then drained the glass. While she stood sheltered in his grasp, his strength and warmth shot to the bottom of her toes.

The man placed the empty glasses on the stone wall and bent her back for a leisurely, languid kiss under the moon gate, the centerpiece of the Castle Harbour's massive stone structure.

In the moonlight, the decade-old hotel looked less like a stately resort and golf club for wealthy British and American tourists and more like a fortress. In this man's arms, she was a willing prisoner.

"Did you know that an English steamship company, Furness-Withy, built this hotel in England, then had it shipped piece by piece to Bermuda?" Diana asked.

"You're intoxicating, Diana," William sighed, and she knew then her attraction to him had nothing to do with Champagne. He took his time and used his tongue to taste her. Then he massaged her shoulders and risked a touch beneath the silver heart locket in the spot where it disappeared beneath her dress.

She reached for his hand and tried to push it away, but he pressed her closer. Her back felt cool against the stone of the moon gate, but she knew his kisses were heating her blood.

When she started to move away, he captured her lips with another mind-numbing kiss and placed his heat against her.

"No, my sweet, don't push me away," he coaxed. "Let me feel you."

She moaned and sighed. "I don't think we should—"

"Sssh, don't think. I want you, Diana. I have to have you."

"This is a public place, sir," Diana pleaded. "My parents are watching us. Everyone is. People will talk."

"Let them, then," William said, kissing her again. "Diana, I don't think I'm going to be able to control myself. Is there somewhere we can go, somewhere more private?"

"I hardly know you," Diana protested weakly. "I don't think it would be right to leave my own party."

"You're not married, are you?" he asked. "Not spoken for?"

"No," Diana admitted, "but it's my—"

"I just might have to marry you myself then, to get a moment alone with you."

She pulled away from him as her eyes searched his for the tiniest grain of truth.

Shivering, she wanted this feeling never to end.

"Are you cold, my love?" He removed his jacket and covered her shoulders. "Let's go back inside."

"Thank you, sir."

****

From across the room, Vice Admiral Sir Stirling Hargrave hissed, "Who the devil is that man with his bloody hands all over our daughter? I'll have his hide for that."

"Do you not see that your daughter seems to want his hands on her? She's not exactly fighting the man off. For heaven's sake, don't make a scene. This is her coming out."

"By God, she's fairly *coming out* of that dress, Olivia. The piece of silk barely covers her. If you needed more money for extra fabric, my dear, you should have asked. I can bloody well afford it!"

"It covers her quite well, I think," Olivia said, her

eyes twinkling with mischief.

"The man looks much too old for her. I think I'll have a word with him."

"Don't interrogate the boy. He's not one of your ensigns. And, as I recall, when we first met, you were also an older man."

"That was entirely different. Look at the man, Olivia. He's blond. He looks like one of those bloody Hitler Youth."

"Diana's always had a thing for blonds," Olivia said. "He could be Scandinavian. He looks like a Viking. He's a handsome devil, at any rate. Cuts a fine figure in that white tuxedo. And he looks at her the way a man should look at a woman. The way you used to look at me."

"The way I still look at you," the vice admiral insisted, placing his hand lovingly on his wife's cheek to soothe her ruffled feathers. "But he looks as if he wants to devour her right here on the dance floor. This is war, Olivia. And that man is *not* in uniform. The island is probably crawling with German spies, saboteurs, agents, double agents, and informers, not to mention British intelligence officers. I'd lay odds he's operating at British Censorship Headquarters in the bowels of the Princess Hotel or buried with all the rest of the moles underground in any number of hotels on the island. Some of them are so deep under cover I doubt even they know which side they're on. And neither do we.

"Maybe he's Roosevelt's man on the island," the vice admiral continued, his imagination running wild as he watched the man lay his lips on his daughter's mouth. "An agent with the OSS. I know the Americans have a cadre of people here. There are so many petty rivalries between the agencies in Washington that no one hand knows what the other is doing. And Roosevelt is the puppeteer. You know how he and Churchill love their secrets. Have to mastermind everything."

"Men and their war games," sighed Olivia.

"I'll bloody well know who the cad is before he starts cavorting with my daughter."

"Cavorting with a cad? Dear, you can be so priggish sometimes. Remember when you were courting me? As I recall, your hands were doing quite a bit of roaming of their own."

"That was another matter. This is our daughter we're talking about."

"Oh, quite," she said, rolling her eyes. "But I'm coming with you, to soften the blow." She smiled. "You can be overwhelming and, at times, gruff."

"Me, gruff?" he purred, as he eased his wife to the other side of the ballroom.

The band was playing, and the blond man was still dancing dreamily with Diana, cheek to cheek, heart to heart, like there was no one else around. His hands were cupping her face, entwined in her hair, kissing her lips, seducing her. She wore a look of rapture. The vice admiral was determined to put a stop to this outrageous display of emotion.

"Ahem. Diana, aren't you going to introduce me to your…to the man who is practically draped all over you?"

"It's William, sir," William said quickly, before a flustered Diana had a chance to speak.

"Yes, William," Diana said evenly, recovering, as she breathed a sigh of relief. "I'd like you to meet my father, Vice Admiral Sir Stirling Hargrave, and my mother, Olivia Smithfield Hargrave. Mother, Daddy, this is *William*."

The vice admiral continued to direct his attention to his daughter's partner. He had always considered himself a tall man, but he had to look up at the interloper.

"You, sir. I don't like the liberties you are taking with my daughter."

****

William stiffened.

"Your daughter, sir?" Damn. He had to go and fall for the daughter of the one man on the island he absolutely could not afford to tangle with.

"Quite. I don't think I heard your last name."

"Name, last name, sir. I didn't give it, sir, but it's Whitestone. William Whitestone."

"Any relation to the Northampton Whitestones?"

"No, sir. I don't believe so, sir."

"I'll bloody well have you checked out. And I'm going to keep my eye on you."

"Checked out?" Diana wailed. "Must you investigate everyone I go out with? Daddy, he's just a man, not a war criminal. I'm only dancing with him."

"We'll see about that."

Olivia whispered some soothing words into her daughter's ear and turned to William.

"William, if you're serious about seeing our daughter, then I'd like to invite you to come around next Sunday for brunch, so we can all get to know each other," she offered.

"So I can get my hands on you," the vice admiral grumbled.

"Right, sir, Mrs. Whitestone, next Sunday. Looking forward to it. Thank you." He shook the vice admiral's hand and hoped his nerves weren't showing.

Of all the women on the island, he had to choose the pampered and well-loved daughter of an English vice admiral and the matron of Bermuda society.

"What did your mother have to say?" he asked Diana, visibly shaken after her parents walked away.

"My mother says you couldn't possibly be a spy. Your obvious blond good looks would arouse too much suspicion."

He frowned.

"Let's see if we can't manage to arouse something else," she taunted. She appeared to be more relaxed now, and satisfied that her parents would eventually come around, since they had invited William to the house.

"Diana, I do believe you're a dangerous woman. Dangerous and desirable."

"Are you, then?" she teased.

"Am I what?" he asked.

"A German spy?" Her lips curled seductively.

"Don't even joke about something like that at a time like this," he warned.

She was slowly driving him crazy. The look of her, the feel of her, the smell of her. She was invading his senses, and he was spinning out of control. He pulled her possessively back into his arms and refused to give her up for the rest of the evening.

Chapter 9

Hamilton, Bermuda
One Week Later

On Sunday, William arrived exactly on time to the vice admiral's house for brunch. He could have driven his car. Befitting his status as the CEO of Bermuda Power Company, he was one of the few people on the island, with the exception of certain high-ranking military personnel, who had access to one. Everyone else rode the train, bicycled, traveled on foot, or rode in a horse and buggy. But William sensed that the very proper vice admiral would have frowned on an obvious display of wealth from a man out of uniform.

Instead, William rode comfortably in a wicker chair in the first-class carriage of the Bermuda Railway, which had opened less than a decade earlier and stretched the length of the island from the eastern tip of St. George's, Bermuda's original capital, to Somerset Parish in the west.

The Bermuda Railway was a far cry from the swift, efficient trains of Zurich that had rushed him through the mountain passes to every capital in Europe, but the steady rhythm of the rails took him back to that earlier time.

Sometimes a rendezvous would bring him painfully close to Dresden and to his Emilie. He'd promised to leave his past, to leave Emilie, his first love, behind. He'd cut off their relationship without even a goodbye. He'd tried to put Emilie out of his mind and his heart forever and never look back. But they couldn't control his thoughts and, even after all these years, he was having trouble letting go of the memories.

Memories that haunted him at the most inconvenient times. Memories of her sweetness, of how beautiful she looked in her garden. On the day of their parting, only William had had the advantage of knowing he would never see Emilie again, not until after the war, maybe never. So he'd memorized her face. And made that last day, their last time together, count. It was selfish of him to use her that way. To Emilie, it was just another glorious day to be spent together. There would be a lifetime of others, or so she thought.

When he'd turned toward her a final time, he had whispered faintly, "There may come a time when I'll have to leave you. I may be called away suddenly, and I won't know when I'll be back."

"I'll be waiting," she assured him, "forever, if I have to."

He wondered if she was still waiting. So many times he had been tempted to go to her, surprise her and say, *"I'm back, my darling."*

And she'd ask, *"Forever?"*

And he'd answer with finality, *"Yes. This time, forever."* Then he would take her away with him where no one could find them. But that tender reunion took place only in his dreams.

The balmy Bermuda weather seemed a world away

from the snow-covered villages of Switzerland. It put him in mind of the years he'd spent away from Dresden, away from home and family, away from Emilie, establishing his new identity as a partner in a Swiss engineering consulting firm. He was a ghost, the years before his life in Switzerland smoothly erased as if Wilhelm von Hesselweiss had never existed. They could erase his past, but would he ever really be able to escape it?

William got off at the bustling city of Hamilton and headed toward the Front Street shops. He stopped at Trimingham's and noticed a tweed topcoat and a handsome double-breasted navy serge suit in the store window that would make nice additions to his wardrobe. Yesterday he had purchased a bottle of five star brandy and a bottle of Chilean wine at Gosling Brothers to bring to the vice admiral, some flowers for his wife, and some Australian raspberry jam and biscuits at Trimingham's for teatime.

Crossing over to the waterfront, William bought a ticket and rode the ferry to the stop closest to the vice admiral's house. Once off the boat, he walked the rest of the way, passing several Invest in Democracy and Victory posters that encouraged people to buy War Savings Certificates.

William admired the vast estate. He'd done his research. It belonged officially to Diana's mother, he knew, a large white stucco house set like a sparkling gem against the clear blue sky overlooking Hamilton Harbour. Despite the breathtaking views and the simple profile of its traditional lime-washed roofline, distinctive angles, architectural accents, and stone-stepped chimneys, William had the secret pleasure of knowing his own house was even more magnificent. Soon he would show them. His house would make a big impression on the status-conscious Hargraves.

****

The topic at brunch was the topic of discussion at the table in every other household in Bermuda. The island was buzzing with the news of the upcoming visit of the Duke of Windsor and his wife, the divorcée Wallis Simpson, who had been granted permission to stop over for a visit to Bermuda on their way from Lisbon to the Bahamas.

"Just think how he must feel, going from being the king of England to governor of the Bahamas," said Sir Stirling, as he dug into his toast and eggs. "No doubt he and the duchess will want to leave London and all the talk far behind them."

"I wonder what she'll wear?" Olivia said. "I'd like to get a good look at her jewelry, too."

I'm curious about how many people are in the visiting party—maids, valets, and the like," said Diana.

"They'll be staying at Government House, but I think I will have a private reception for them here," Sir Stirling continued. "And of course, Diana, you're invited, and William, too, if you'd like to join us. I think we'll arrange to be waiting on the wharf when the S.S. Excalibur drops anchor and Their Royal Highnesses the Duke and Duchess of Windsor arrive in the Admiral's barge and disembark at the public steps at Albuoy's Point. I expect there will be thousands lining the streets. The governor plans to greet them with a military guard of honor and an informal welcome ceremony." Diana's father paused long enough to swallow half a cup of tea before continuing.

"William, I've been asked to join the duke for golf at the Mid-Ocean Club. He's visited the Colony before, and he's played golf here, but the duchess has never been to Bermuda."

"I've read there will be fifty-eight different pieces of luggage and, of course, their cairn terriers," Diana interjected. "Naturally, mother and I have to have new outfits."

"Naturally," echoed Sir Stirling. "Since when have you needed an occasion to justify buying a new outfit? William, maybe you and I will each try one of those single-breasted suits, in chalk stripes or herringbone."

"I hear the duchess will be wearing a pink-and-blue all-over dress of satin-faced crepe, with a bow at the bodice and a bright royal-blue full-length coat with elbow sleeves," offered Olivia. "I wonder how she'll wear her hair."

"Don't care much for her looks, myself," said the vice admiral. "She's a bit horsey for my tastes. But the crowds adore her, apparently, and everyone she meets find her courteous and charming."

"No doubt the duke will be quite tan and fit. He's a sailor, you know," Olivia challenged, her eyes twinkling.

"As am I," the vice admiral growled.

"Of course you are, dear. I didn't mean anything by that."

"Harrumph."

"How long do you think they'll stay?" Olivia asked sweetly, trying to wriggle back into her husband's good graces.

"I have no idea how long the party will be in Bermuda," he answered. "They're waiting for orders from London. I imagine he'll feel far away from the war here. Naturally, the women's hearts are all aflutter over the man who gave up his throne for the woman he loves."

William wondered if anyone at the table was aware of the duke's pro-Nazi sympathies. He didn't think it would be prudent to bring that up. He did wonder about the former king's abdication of his throne in December 1936. What would he, William, be willing to do for the woman he loved? What would he be willing to risk for Diana? Would he abandon his mission? Such traitorous thoughts had been filtering through his mind lately.

****

While Diana's mother spirited William away to show off the inside of the house, Diana's father pulled her into the study.

"I made some discreet inquiries about your young gentleman, ran his name through channels, and it was like bumping up against a brick wall, even with my clearance, but he checks out," the vice admiral reluctantly admitted.

"You actually had the man investigated?"

"Bloody right, I did. Just a preliminary check for now. Did it for your own protection. And for Queen and Country. This is war."

"Well, that's good to know," said Diana as her stomach began to settle. She didn't like going against her parents' wishes, although she had tried their patience more than once in the past where young men were concerned. She'd neglected to tell her father she had seen William every day and night since the party at the Castle Harbour. Somehow, she'd managed to sneak out so they could be together. He had taken her dining and dancing, sailing, out for ice cream, and to see a movie at the Colonial Opera House Theatre. They had attended a soccer game and gone on a scooter ride to a secluded cove where they swam and snorkeled and, on the pink sandy beach, exchanged simmering, stolen kisses that left them both aching for more.

She spent every free minute with him. He was so romantic and sophisticated. She didn't care what her father dug up or manufactured about William, she was already in love with him. It had been love at first sight, a split-second shock, as electrifying as a lightning strike. And he seemed to be thunderstruck too. It was so exciting. All her girlfriends agreed. William was the one she had been waiting for. All she could think about when she was around William was what it would be like when they finally made love. She blushed and lowered her eyes.

"I still don't trust him," said the vice admiral.

"You don't trust anyone who's not wearing a uniform, Daddy. A *British Navy* uniform. Well, I do. And I think I might be falling in love with him. He says he wants to marry me."

"Isn't that rather sudden?" the vice admiral demanded, alarmed. "You just met the man."

"Like you said, we're at war, Daddy. Who knows what tomorrow will bring?"

"Diana, don't you know that's the oldest line in the book? I used that line on your mother."

William and Olivia paused outside the study.

"I assume your mother has had the proper talk with you," her father fumbled awkwardly, lowering his voice.

"Oh, Daddy, you're such a dinosaur."

The vice admiral grumbled. "Then you and your mother are in agreement. She thinks I'm an old fossil."

"You know I don't really think that," she said and kissed his forehead. "I adore you, Daddy."

****

"Promise me you'll be careful, and don't rush into anything," her father advised, looking nostalgically after his little girl as she ran to meet William, as if he knew he'd already lost her.

"I won't," she assured him, but judging from the longing gaze she bestowed upon the man as the young couple walked off toward the parlor, arm in arm, the vice admiral somehow doubted the sincerity of her pledge.

"I don't suppose it would do any good to forbid her to see this boy, do you?" he asked Olivia when his daughter and her suitor were out of hearing range.

"Remember what happened the last time? You forbade her to see that musician, and she almost ran off with him. She's very headstrong. I wonder who she takes after?"

"Harrumph," was all the vice admiral could muster. "Diana said the boy was already speaking to her about marriage."

"How is he going to support our daughter?" Olivia wondered.

"That's the strange part," noted the vice admiral. "The man has enough money in the bank to buy the entire island and is on his way to doing just that. He's purchased the old Gilbert estate in Tucker's Town and renamed it Marigold House."

"Impressive," Olivia noted. "That's a very desirable and expensive property."

"It seems he's materialized out of nowhere. Some type of *wunderkind*—was a partner in an engineering consulting firm in Zurich, comes from family money. Family background's rather fuzzy—the father was a wealthy industrialist, I think. Died and left his fortune, lock, stock, and barrel, to his son.

"Remember, in 1937, when Sir James Markham went missing in that mysterious boating accident and they needed someone to take his place at Bermuda Power? Whitestone's qualifications were tailor made for the top job there, so the government brought him in on an emergency basis. He's been very successful, so they asked him to stay on permanently.

"He also has ownership control of the telephone company in some kind of joint venture arrangement with an overseas conglomerate. He's already on the board of several of the banks on the island."

"I've asked some friends about him. They all agree he's very good-looking—I mean, very forward-looking," said Olivia.

"We're not arguing the pros and cons of the man's looks," said the vice admiral sourly. "It's apparent to me that he's more than forward. He's insinuated himself into our daughter's life. He's got his finger in every pie. Why haven't we run into him socially before?"

"Maybe he's trying to maintain a low profile," Olivia suggested. "You know how discreet the Swiss are, darling."

"More like secretive," the vice admiral said. "And there's something about him. His record shows minimal compulsory military service, but the way he behaves around me, I'm certain he's been under someone's command. Or had his own command. Bad business all around. Smells bad."

"Actually, he smells delicious and he looks divine," Olivia inserted. "He's just being deferential, dear."

"Harrumph!" the vice admiral said, sulking.

****

He should ignore her, William thought, looking adoringly at Diana, and chase after some insipid, less attractive, less spectacular girl. A girl he wouldn't regret leaving. A girl whose life he wouldn't put in danger. Whose heart he wouldn't mind breaking. Because, in the end, he *would* break her heart. He could hardly take Diana back to the Fatherland after the war and live with her happily ever after. Or live with her here in Bermuda after the Germans came into power.

What had he been thinking? Now it was too late. He didn't want another girl. He had developed a taste for Diana. He wanted her, even though he could barely breathe and hardly think when he was around her. And he was used to getting what he wanted—or taking it. But his feelings for her went far beyond a passing desire for a beautiful woman and crept dangerously close to raw need. She was the only one who could fill the gaping hole in his heart Emilie had occupied. He was slipping. His need for Diana went against all his better instincts.

The daughter of a British Royal Naval officer, no, *the* British Naval Officer on the island, Diana was all wrong for his plans. He had known it from the moment he laid eyes on her. And yet, she was perfect. He was never going to be able to let her go.

Luckily, she hadn't been to Switzerland. So it was

easy to play the name game with her. Not so with her father. He would want to know everything about his family, his history, his roots. So be it. He was well prepared. In fact, being married to a vice admiral's daughter might prove helpful in the years to come and provide him easy access to the military bases and the movement of Allied convoys. Smooth the way for his associates and contacts at the Princess and make his job of providing reports to the network a lot easier. His superiors would think he had planned the whole thing. Well, let them think his stroke of luck was a stroke of brilliance.

Hadn't his superiors paid him the highest compliment after he had completed training when they said he blended well, wrote, even *thought* in English? It was all those movies he saw. Movies were a great way to perfect his English, to learn the nuances of the language. His superiors had also said they only hoped he didn't make love in German, and call out something inappropriate that would give himself away during the throes of passion. Diana was certainly more than capable of making him lose control of his mind and his body.

In fact, she almost had. It had happened yesterday, barely a week after they'd met. They were on the party circuit, in formal clothing, as befitted the occasion. She'd led him out to the garden, away from the lights. She'd looked…amazing.

"Take me, William," Diana had said breathlessly.

"Take you where? We just got here."

She'd laughed slyly and gone soft and pliant against him like a pampered cat.

"Catch up to me, William. I want you to make love

with me."

He'd been shocked and surprised and unexpectedly aroused.

"Darling, here, at the party?"

"We're quite alone in the garden. Don't you want me?"

What was he going to do with this mischievous vixen? She was like a pretty pink package all wrapped up in a bow, delivering herself to him, begging to be unwrapped.

"Of course I want you," he said and desperately meant it. She gave her love so freely, how could he possibly resist her?

Her eyelashes fluttered and she stroked the inside of his arm lightly.

I've got a hot one on my hands, don't I," he teased. "I don't even think you know what you're asking me."

"I do so," she pouted. "It's all your fault. You make me crazy, William. I can't stop thinking about you, about what it might be like."

"Then we're even. You drive me to distraction, darling Diana, you little temptress."

"Is it someone else?" she asked. "Was there someone else you left behind, at home? Someone you can't forget?"

He was blindsided by her perceptiveness.

"There was. I can see it in your face. I knew it, and that's why you won't—"

"Diana, listen, you naughty little thing," he said lightly as he grasped her by her bare shoulders and set her aside. He realized he hadn't thought of Emilie once the entire week since he had laid eyes on Diana, and he felt guilty. He closed his eyes. He still had the picture of Emilie emblazoned on his mind—small, delicate, dark, passionate Emilie. The longing was still there, burning like a brand in his flesh and a chronic ache in the recesses of his mind.

"Okay. Yes. There was someone, once, a long time ago. We were young, so young."

"What was her name?"

"Emilie," he whispered, so softly that he didn't think she'd heard him, and he wasn't sure he'd even said the word. "It was Emilie."

Diana gathered her skirt and kneaded the soft material nervously.

"Was she very beautiful?" Diana managed.

Gott, yes, she was. His Emilie was very beautiful. They had grown up together, had been childhood sweethearts, and his past life was inextricably linked with hers. But he would not be seeing her again. And here, now, he could not afford to think about her, to be distracted from his mission. Emilie and Diana were opposites. Both dear, but utterly different women. Diana was tall and blonde and generated a fire that burned like a shooting star, all brightness and heat. His Emilie was tiny and precious and mysterious. Loving her was like dipping into a stream, so cool and dark and dangerously desirable, with a lot of layers to delve into.

"You overshadow her, my love," William promised. "I didn't think I would find that happiness again with anyone, until you."

"Oh, William," she sighed. She nuzzled against his neck and whispered, "Did you love her terribly?" And he could tell that she really didn't want to hear the answer.

"I hardly knew what love was, then."

"Did you and she, did you…?"

He didn't answer. Instead he soothed her suspicions and quieted her concerns with his sensitive hands and searching lips that plied her sensuous mouth with hot, searing kisses.

"No more questions. You're the one I want now, Diana."

Satisfied, she pulled away, hesitant to broach the subject, but…

"William. Daddy had some papers, important ones, go missing from his study. When I came home yesterday, he asked if Mother or I'd been in there, cleaning, rearranging like Mother sometimes does. But no, we know to stay away from his study, his personal things. And he asked if you, I mean—"

"Whether I had been there with you?" he asked in measured tones. "You didn't tell him we were alone in the house that day they went into St. George's, did you?"

"Of course not," Diana assured. "Even though we agreed not to tell my parents we were seeing each other, I did tell them we'd been together that day, but away from Hamilton, to protect you."

"All day," he reminded her.

She bit her bottom lip. "All day, most of the day, yes, but there were the hours in the afternoon when you had to go off. Remember? Where did you go, darling?"

"Diana, what are you accusing me of?"

"Nothing. I just want to know."

William frowned.

"Well, I wasn't going to tell you, and now you've gone and ruined the surprise. This isn't the way I wanted it to be, but now I have no other choice but to come clean."

Diana stared at him, wide-eyed, as if she expected a dangerous confession.

William pulled a tiny wrapped box from his jacket pocket.

"This is for you, Diana." He offered her the box.

"Oh, William, for me? A present. You know how I adore presents. What is it?"

"Why don't you just open it and see?" he teased.

Diana tore into the ribbon and bow and paper and opened the box eagerly. Her delighted eyes widened again, and her sensuous mouth flew open.

"Oh, God, William. Is this what I think it is?"

"What do you think it is, my sweet?"

"The most beautiful diamond in the world. It's so large. And sparkly. So perfect. William, can you afford this? This must have cost a king's ransom."

"I suppose I could take it back to the store," he ventured, pretending to grab for it, "if you don't like it."

"No!" she screamed. "I'm never letting it or you out of my sight again. Then this is where you were yesterday?"

"Guilty as charged."

Diana jumped into his arms and placed hungry kisses all over his face.

"Put it on my finger," she said anxiously.

"But first, Diana Smithfield Hargrave…" He got down on bended knee. "Will you marry me and make me the happiest man in the world?"

"Of course I'll marry you," Diana said, her eyes filling with tears. "I want to give you everything. I want to be your Emilie. I want you to forget. I want—"

He was touched.

"I know what you want, darling Diana," William whispered, fairly tingling with anticipation of how it would be between them. "And it's what I want too, but I want you to come to me innocent and pure and ready. We have a lifetime to be together." And, he remembered bitterly, that he had promised Emilie exactly the same thing right before he had loved her and left her. But he was resolved to put Emilie out of his mind. To hold on to her memory would be disloyal to Diana. William was nothing, if not loyal. He vowed to begin his new life with Diana with a clean slate and to offer himself fully to her without any ties to the past, as she was offering herself to him. It was the least he could do for the woman who had given him back his life.

Chapter 10

Tucker's Town, Bermuda, 1941

"Are you ready for me to transmit the message, *Herr Kapitänleutnant*?" Nighthawk asked. He waited for the order to proceed from his position in the makeshift station hidden in a secluded section of shore at the back of Marigold House.

"Yes, but do it quickly. The sub is in position. We need to keep U-boat traffic to a minimum. Radio links have become too dangerous. We need to avoid giving away our position."

From his observation post Nighthawk tapped out the code with his signal light, relaying his information to the sub that had just surfaced only a short distance offshore.

"Finished transmitting reports on anti-sub schedules for ships, and position, course, and speed of British convoys at sea. They will transmit details to Central Operations. Wait. There's another message coming. Another shipment is ready for pickup. Shall we go now?"

"Yes. I'm ready."

It was a breezy night, and both men wore light jackets to ward off the wind. They did their best to fight the powerful tidal currents, navigating cautiously as their craft slipped out of the bay and into the open sea.

"The damn coast is lit up like a Christmas tree," Nighthawk protested, noting the floodlights flashing across the island.

"Part of our island defense plan, which I instituted myself," William boasted. "Seems the electricity is not operational at the exact points where our subs are located. A pity."

Nighthawk laughed as the crew of one of the surfaced subs began unloading its golden cargo onto their boat.

"Haven't you people heard of the blackout?" joked William's old childhood friend, *Kapitänleutnant* Karl Krauss, calling his greeting from the bridge when he stepped out to supervise the transfer.

"We call it our night illumination plan." William viewed his friend's dark blue cap and overcoat with longing. It had been a while since he'd worn the uniform, and he still missed the sight and feel of it.

"You're not the only sitting ducks," Krauss joked. "German Headquarters repeats every broadcast to us at half to one hour intervals."

"In case the transmissions are garbled?" William asked.

"No, just in case the British Admiralty in London didn't get the message the first time."

William laughed. "Nothing changes."

"Not even the frequency."

Both men smiled at their feeble attempt at naval humor.

"When are we going to break the British naval cipher?"

"Probably just in time for the end of the war."

William slapped his friend on the back.

"Karl, it's great to see you again."

"You too," said Krauss. "Now, my parting gift to you, for the war effort, to keep the coffers full, Wilhelm—or should I call you Island Eagle?"

"It's William now," he corrected.

"William, then. What are you going to do with all these gold reserves? Between our night drops and the gold pouring into your bank from Switzerland, you could buy your own private island."

"I already have," said William, laughing. "In times of war, gold is the best currency. Who wants Reichsmarks anymore? Strong gold reserves will enable us to move when the time is right. We'll use it to finance our agents and subversive activities in the U.S., with Bermuda as the base of operations."

"By the way, how is *Unternehmen Seelöwe* proceeding?" asked Krauss, lowering his voice to make sure he wasn't being overheard.

"I speak only English now," William chided, admitting, "Not according to plan. Last year, I was informed that Hitler was postponing Directive No. 16, *Operation Sea Lion*, the Luftwaffe attack to destroy RAF airfields in preparation for the seaborne invasion of England, until this spring. I've been instructed to put all our plans on hold."

"The total blockade of Britain by sea and air," Krauss confirmed. "An ambitious plan. And you are Hitler's insurance policy—*Unternehmen Teufels Insel.*"

"Operation Devil's Island," William translated. "He issued the Bermuda subdirective in case Operation Sea Lion fails."

"But we all know that the Führer is infallible," Krauss managed to say with a straight face.

"Precisely, and everything must be carefully coordinated," William explained. "We must neutralize the United States before they can come to the aid of the British and resupply their allies. The British will have their hands full. Bermuda will provide a nice distraction. There is no margin for error. At my command, the lights will fall dark and the telecommunications system in Bermuda will go down."

"Our mutual friend sends his regards," said Krauss. "He would like some assurances so he can report back to the Führer on your progress at their next strategy session."

"How is Old Whitehead?"

Both men knew Krauss referred to Rear Admiral Wilhelm Franz Canaris, William's longtime mentor, family friend, and former battleship commander, also known as the mysterious "Prince of Shadows." Canaris detested Hitler, but he loved Germany and, by nature, was deeply pessimistic about the outcome of the war. He'd confided in William that he'd detected signs of madness and paranoia slithering out of the cracks of the Führer's fractured mind. He was convinced Hitler was losing his already tenuous hold on reality.

"He actually wanted to come himself," said Krauss. "You know how he is. Any excuse to get out of Berlin. He told me to tell you that if Germany doesn't hold its own in the air, then the Bermuda directive takes on even greater significance. If we strike at Bermuda now, we stop the flow of food and arms and cripple England for good. I will assure Canaris that all is in readiness, that you await his signal."

The wind had whipped into a frenzy, and the precipitation gave them a light soaking. An eerie grayish mist had set in and seemed to be clinging to the submarine. Visibility was so poor now, William couldn't see two feet in front of him. He tightened his jacket in a futile attempt to stay dry. These inauspicious conditions didn't bode well, but he was aware any mention of weather conditions on the island would be left out of Krauss's report. Everyone knew how superstitious the Führer was and how he was governed by his belief in the decree of Providence.

William tried to mask his nerves and growing sense of unease, a hint of a scowl forming on his face even before he started speaking through the strange fog.

"The mines have been laid, explosives are in place," reported William. "Our U-boats have surrounded the island and are on patrol and on alert. When Great Britain falls, Bermuda will automatically become the property of Germany. But Hitler prefers to err on the side of caution and disarm the island in advance. That will leave the U.S. coast defenseless when we turn our attention to America."

"A great deal is riding on this."

"When have I ever disappointed Germany?" William responded.

Krauss seemed satisfied for the moment.

"We may have lost the opportunity to seize the advantage, to achieve the element of surprise," William confided. "Our network is on alert again around the island. Everything is in place, waiting for our orders to move. Any word about the timing of the operation?"

"My sources say we will not be hasty. President Roosevelt is looking for any excuse to get his country in the war, so there will be no moves on Bermuda until it's prudent. But as you know, we're patrolling the island regularly. We're ready to move as soon as the signal comes. So take care, William."

Krauss hesitated before speaking again.

"You know Canaris loves you like a son, so he asked me to warn you. He knows Hitler has controls in place and that his Chief of Security Police has his own secret file on you. And they believe they have another insurance policy safely tucked away in Dresden. You know who I'm talking about, I assume? But I assured them you are now happily married to a woman in Bermuda and that there is no need to threaten old lovers."

Since his friend had brought the subject up, William cleared his throat and spoke, perhaps a little too anxiously in an obvious attempt to sound indifferent. He knew he would never find his way back to his beloved Emilie, but he had to know. "Krauss, any news of home?"

Krauss debated whether to tell Wilhelm about the new development, but that would only complicate matters for his old friend and distract him from his mission.

"If you mean Emilie, no, I haven't been back since you left," he lied. "But you've got yourself a beautiful new wife. Best to leave the past in the past. Who knows when any of us will be going home again?"

****

What good would it do to tell Wilhelm that he *had* seen Emilie on his last leave and she was lovelier and lonelier than ever? Would it serve any purpose to admit he had always harbored a secret love for the woman who had eyes only for his best friend? Or that she was still desperate for any word of him even though he had left her so abruptly, shattering her heart into tiny pieces? Could he tell Wilhelm that he had even toyed with the idea of proposing to Emilie himself, to protect her? It was so obvious that she needed to be loved, deserved to be loved. Even though Wilhelm was now a married man, he still felt a disloyalty to his friend for even considering the notion. Emilie was off limits to him. Wilhelm would always think of Emilie as his. And it would eat Wilhelm up inside if he found out how Karl felt about his woman.

Besides, tossed by the seas wherever the whims of war took him, what could he offer Emilie but his name? No, it was best for all concerned to leave things unspoken between them, at least for now. He could still care for her as a good friend. But it nearly broke his heart to leave her so alone and miserable. She had tried to wring promises from him, promises to find Wilhelm and bring him back to her. Promises he knew he couldn't keep. But it was a relief to know that Wilhelm hadn't forgotten her, that Emilie was still seared forever in his mind. She deserved that kind of devotion.

He remembered when they were still schoolboys in Dresden, with not a care in the world, not a sign of trouble on the horizon. Even then, Wilhelm had known what he wanted.

"I'm going to marry Emilie," he had boasted about the young girl who was just beginning to show signs of the beauty she was to become.

"She's the most desirable girl in Dresden, don't you think?" he posed, not even expecting an answer. He was stating a fact that needed no confirmation.

Karl never doubted then that Wilhelm would prevail in his mission. He was one of those people who could make things happen. As boys they had always dreamed of going to sea. They had been cadets together, then midshipmen. They had gone through the Naval Academy together, where William had excelled at all his classes. They trained at the U-boat defense school and U-boat Commander School at Kiel, where Wilhelm again proved to be the brightest and the best of all the candidates. They served under Rear Admiral Canaris for a number of years on the *Schlesien*. He was brave and intelligent and extremely capable. He'd already demonstrated a quick mind for codes during his tour of duty as part of his military intelligence training in the *B-Dienst*. The *Kriegsmarine* did not offer a life of comfort. But Wilhelm was disciplined and determined to succeed, while Karl just managed to keep up.

There was no question that Wilhelm would make Emilie fall in love with him before she even knew he was pulling the strings. That was when Karl had abandoned his secret dream of possessing her. It wasn't jealousy, Karl reminded himself. It was admiration. Not only was Wilhelm better looking and more charming, he was also a born leader. He was very popular with the ladies. That had already proven to be an advantage on this mission. Every woman wanted to be with him. Every man wanted to *be* him, to stand with him, to follow him, to lay his life on the line for him if it became necessary. Wilhelm had a keen analytical mind, a brilliant and clever brain, abilities that had served his ambitions well. He was capable of solving any problem and could always find a way out of any situation. Unfortunately, there was no solution to this particular problem of the heart.

****

Disappointed but resigned, William frowned and buttoned up his jacket as he tried to beat back the wind and the memories that hadn't yet stopped nagging at him.

"And William," Krauss warned, closing the gate on the past, and nodding in the direction of William's associate, "Be careful. The night has eyes. Do you trust him? We both know the man is an amoral butcher. He isn't fit to lick your boots."

"Don't let him hear you say that." William glanced at Nighthawk and then back to the sub's lieutenant commander. "Thank you for your concern, my friend, but what choice do I have? The hawk watches the eagle. I intend to watch my back."

"Well, then, I guess it's back to shadowing convoys and listening for propellers for me."

"Happy hunting!" William said with a touch of nostalgia, shaking his friend's hand as they took their leave. The chill followed William.

First and foremost a seaman, he longed to feel the salty spray of the ocean on his face again. Submerging his desires for the past, he headed for shore to quench a different kind of desire.

****

When Diana woke in the middle of the night and reached for her new husband, he was gone. She searched the house, and as she passed by the parlor window, flashes of light illuminated movement by the water. What she saw disturbed and puzzled her. She could barely make out the shapes in the darkness. But one was definitely William. He and another man were hoisting a large chest from his boat. As William opened the lid of the chest, the two were engaged in a heated discussion. Raised voices assaulted her ears. After the small craft landed, the two men proceeded to dig in the back yard. What were they burying?

She grabbed her shawl from the chair in the parlor and had started down the stone steps when she noticed the light at the bottom of the study door. Glancing into the room, she realized the large suitcase her husband usually kept on his desk was gone. She remembered him telling her about his shortwave radio. He'd said he used it to listen to historical and sporting events, news, dramas, lectures, symphonic orchestras and other programs. She was learning a lot of new things about her husband. She wanted to be the best wife she could be and share his interests. But she didn't see the shortwave radio tonight. In fact, she had never actually seen him use it.

It was really none of her business. Should she mention it to her father? There was no sense in alarming him. She loved and trusted her husband completely. Hadn't he said he would never harm her? No one who was as tender and loving as her William could ever be capable of treachery.

She supposed even married couples had their secrets. He was an important businessman with a lot of responsibilities. Of course there were things he couldn't tell her. Problems at an electric substation that might need his attention in the middle of the night. He might get upset if he thought she was suspicious of him or, worse, spying on him.

But she wasn't one to fade into the background. She would confront him on the matter. First, she'd give him an opportunity to explain himself and his midnight escapade in his own time, in his own way. For now, she would go back to bed and wait, longing to be in his arms again, to be stroked by him, loved by him.

"You were gone a long time," Diana said when William finally returned to bed, trying not to sound like a scolding fishwife, "and you smell of the sea. Where were you? I was cold and lonely." She had given him the opening.

"Nothing for you to worry your pretty head about, darling. Just had to check something out. I thought I heard a noise."

"But I saw you digging in the garden," she protested.

"Sssh," he said, putting his finger to her lips. "You must have been dreaming. Let's not waste time talking about what you *thought* you saw. It's a surprise, so I can't talk about it. We're still on our honeymoon, after all, my darling. We've got more important things to do, have we not?"

He removed her nightgown and kissed her deeply, soundly, passionately, until she forgot why she wanted to question him.

"Now what was that about being cold and lonely? I think I can manage to do something about that. Come closer. Let me warm you."

Then they made fierce and furious love, leaving Diana properly sated.

"Was I too rough, Diana?" William whispered, his mouth against her cheek. "Sometimes I can't control myself around you."

"Never, darling," Diana assured. "We are a perfect match."

"Go back to sleep, then," he coaxed.

****

William rose two hours before the sun to the brilliance of Venus, which was dazzling in the early morning sky. He walked around the garden to make sure the dirt was packed properly. Then he looked out to sea. Harbor fishing season was about to open. He was more of a sailor than an angler, but he missed being out on the water.

He returned to the bedroom, and his thoughts turned to Diana. Loving Diana was like coming home. He gathered her to him and, arms and limbs entwined with hers, fell back asleep dreaming of their wedding day. She had worn a dress of white lace over satin and carried a bouquet of yellow daffodils. The ceremony had been at the Castle Harbour Hotel, under the circular stone moon gate. William was in the process of replicating the stone structure behind Marigold House as a special surprise for Diana, built to bless their marriage and to commemorate the first time they had danced together under the moonlight. The moon gate would overlook the garden she had created especially for him as a wedding present, a garden filled with glorious, fragrant flowers and new plant species that had just been introduced to the island. What he remembered most was their wedding night, and as he did, the memory of his last night with Emilie faded.

He remembered how Diana had offered her innocence to him so sweetly and had so generously opened herself to him. He remembered the quiet tremors and sounds of satisfaction she made when they eagerly came together for the first time. And the look of surprise, the flash of pleasure, and the flush of passion on her face when she called out his name.

His feelings where Emilie was concerned were still

raw, but the more time he spent with Diana, the more the old ache in his heart began to ease. He looked down at his sleeping wife and tenderly stroked her hair. Diana was his salvation. Two great loves in one lifetime. That was more than any one man deserved. Choked with emotion, he looked out the window at the rising moon, thanked the stars, and wondered what stroke of divine providence had landed him in this paradise with this woman.

Chapter 11

Bermuda
1940-July 1941

In another place and time, William and his father-in-law might have been good friends. They were both naval officers, despite their opposing allegiances. Sir Stirling Hargrave was a worthy adversary, one William had come to admire and respect. And they had something else in common. They both loved Diana. William could hardly expect the vice admiral to become his greatest confidant and champion just because he had slipped a wedding ring on his daughter's finger. He could not assume that all the vice admiral's suspicions would miraculously melt away and the icy reception with which William was initially greeted to thaw. But he was determined to get Diana's father to trust him.

He was prepared to work hard to gain his father-in-law's respect and was ready with money, information, contacts and connections, whatever it took to soften the crusty old vice admiral's heart toward his new son-in-law. It was a relationship he was carefully cultivating and counting on. If he were honest with himself, what he really wanted was for the vice admiral to become the father he had lost.

The vice admiral stretched after a satisfying meal and relaxed to enjoy tea and dessert in his daughter's new home. Diana had confided that her father was impressed with Marigold House and the comfortable life his new son-in-law was making for them. His father-in-law seemed to be in the mood to pontificate, one of his favorite pastimes, and William was sure he was parroting Prime Minister Winston Churchill's words.

"I fear that this little outpost, this speck in the middle of the Atlantic, is all that stands between England and certain destruction," the vice admiral said, referring to the fishhook-shaped landmass that was Bermuda, the island William had grown to love.

"You know how important Bermuda has become as a Royal Navy port. Bermuda serves a critical function as a communications intersect point for transatlantic traffic, a refueling base for our ships and planes, and a theater for battling the U-boats that are attacking our convoys. It's a life-or-death fight for us.

"Great Britain is in a perilous state," the vice admiral continued. "Not many know this, but we're on the brink of bankruptcy and starvation. I don't know how much longer we can stem the tide of this Nazi onslaught. It's only the tenacious spirit of our people and the bravery of our fighter pilots that allows us to survive. We must be vigilant in these dangerous times.

"The fate of the entire war may be in our hands. Right now, Bermuda seems far removed from the venues of war. But Bermuda may be our last bastion of hope if we are to control the Atlantic and survive this threat. Bermuda and the Americans are our lifeline in the critical war at sea."

"Control of the seas at all costs," echoed William.

"You have been invaluable in arranging for loans

for armaments and your involvement in dozens of other projects on the island have helped pave the way for us here," the vice admiral acknowledged. "The prime minister is eternally grateful."

William was uncomfortable being portrayed as a hero and despised himself for deceiving Diana's father in this little give-and-take game they were playing. Sir Stirling had welcomed him into the family, a pit viper among defenseless rabbits. He wondered how long he could maintain his current illusion, and what Diana would think of him once she learned of his traitorous deeds.

"Did you know that in the first six months of 1940, German U-boats sank 900,000 tons of Allied shipping?" Sir Stirling remarked, thumbing through *The Royal Gazette*. "The Secretary of the Navy said that if England should go down—and he prays to God that will not happen—America will not have a friend in the world."

William shifted uncomfortably in his seat as his father-in-law shook his head.

In 1941, the tide had turned. From William's perspective, it was the frequent Royal Air Force attacks on Nazi submarine bases and Atlantic nests that were problematic. The *Kriegsmarine* was losing its best U-boat commanders to British convoy escorts while William was dying a slow death in Bermuda waiting for action.

How I wish I could feel the salty sting of sea spray on my face again. I would have loved to stand with them. Or sink with them if it came to that.

"I can't figure it out, son," said the vice admiral. "How did the Germans manage to sink those ships? It's almost like they had a line into us. Like they knew every move we were going to make, before we made it."

"Father, is that all you care about?" Diana cried. "Cargo? Think of all the lives lost. The Atlantic is a graveyard. Imagine those poor boys, wounded, gasping for their last breaths of air, drowning and dying alone at the bottom of the cold, dark ocean."

William took a deep breath, closed his eyes and willed away the image that had haunted him since he was a child. His own father had lost his life in a stormy sea battle and rested at the bottom of the Atlantic along with his crewmen. There had been no survivors. But of course Diana didn't know about his past.

"I have heard stories about the Germans, that they shoot survivors in the water instead of rescuing them," accused Diana. "What of the poor souls who can never go home to their families, to their wives, their lovers? Oh, William, it's so horrible. I'm so glad you're not a sailor. I'm so glad you're safe here with me. That's selfish of me, I know."

William felt as if Diana had slapped him. No self-respecting sailor would ever shoot a survivor—a fellow seaman—in the water. The world acted as if all Germans were monsters. If Diana were ever to discover the truth about him, she would never understand. She would look at him differently, think of *him* as a monster. He couldn't bear to see the light of her love for him extinguished. He'd lost the first love of his life. He still had deep regrets about the way he had hurt Emilie when he left her. Losing his greatest love all over again was his worst fear.

"That's an insult to your husband," the vice

admiral said. "Every man worth his salt wishes he was in the fight. Those boys who drowned were heroes, but your husband has other skills, necessary skills he offers to the war effort. He does his part even if he's not in uniform."

"No need to defend me, sir," William said. "But I appreciate the sentiment."

"Oh, William, I didn't mean anything by that," Diana recanted. "I was just distraught." She turned to him with tears sparkling in her eyes.

"Try not to think of it, my darling," William said solicitously. "I can't bear to see you this upset. Come, maybe you'd better lie down. Sir, Mrs. Hargrave, if you'll excuse us."

"Nonsense," barked the vice admiral. "You coddle the girl too much. Diana's always had a tendency for the dramatic. You think the loss of lives doesn't bother me? Let's put the blame where it lies, with the bloody Germans!"

William flinched.

"Diana, why don't you lie down on the couch for a while," Olivia recommended, hoping to separate herself and her daughter from the fray. "William will settle you in with a nice pillow and a warm blanket. I'll bring in some tea. Don't worry about cleaning up, sweetheart. I'll handle that. You'll rest here for a while so your father can finish his conversation with William."

"Okay," Diana sniffled, allowing her husband to lead her into the drawing room and place a tender kiss on her forehead.

"The girl's sprung another leak," the vice admiral mumbled when his son-in-law returned to the table. "Did you manage to plug it?"

"She's resting comfortably, sir," William replied tactfully.

"William," the vice admiral said, "the girl needs to develop some backbone. Work on that, son."

"Yes, sir," William said, secretly disagreeing with the vice admiral's assessment of Diana. Did he even know his own daughter? Diana had backbone and spirit to spare. "She's just overly sensitive, sir."

"Perhaps she has strained nerves," Olivia pointed out. "The ads say that undermines your efficiency and that drinking Ovaltine will help by building up nerve strength and physical fitness."

"That's utter nonsense, Olivia," the vice admiral said, turning to his son-in-law. "William, you're making excuses because you love her. I understand."

"I think it's all that talk in the papers about the murder of that censorette," William suggested. "It was a violent fight. And there have been no new developments."

Olivia shuddered.

The vice admiral had warned Diana and her mother not to go out alone during the day or at night, especially where the victim's bludgeoned body was found, near Prospect Railway Station.

"I know the constables are on alert, but you'll see to my daughter's protection, won't you, son?" the vice admiral asked as he pulled William aside. "Ever since that censorette was murdered, Diana and her mother have both been jittery. Can't blame them. Most of those poor girls on the Imperial Censorship staff are worked to death. I'm surprised they don't keel over from heat exhaustion down there in the basement of the Princess Hotel. Not exactly the glamorous jobs they signed up for. But to be clubbed to death with a sawed-down softball bat and foully murdered—no English lady, no lady, deserves that. Police Headquarters have hinted that a sex maniac was responsible."

"The police have raised the reward that will hopefully lead to the apprehension of Miss Stapleton's murderer," William volunteered. "Until they solve this crime, all our residents and visitors will remain alarmed."

"Regardless, we can't be too careful with our women until the killer is found and he's swinging from the end of a rope," said the vice admiral. "Poor woman probably took up with the wrong man or inadvertently discovered something she shouldn't have. Nasty business. No doubt it's one of those German spies who did it."

William pursed his lips. He suspected Nighthawk was somehow involved. It was his style. But he'd never admit it. And his mistress *was* a British censorette. William was convinced Nighthawk was a dangerous madman. Volatile and very unpredictable.

"Diana's been so emotional lately," Olivia began. "You don't think she's…"

"Pregnant?" the vice admiral finished her sentence. "So soon? That would be wonderful, wouldn't it, William? A grandchild. Son, do you suppose that's the reason she's been so teary lately?"

The color drained from William's face. It was unthinkable. A child in these uncertain times would be disastrous. He was doing everything he could to protect his wife, but a child? A helpless child? He couldn't let that happen. William couldn't speak.

"Sir, Mrs. Hargrave…I…I mean, I…I don't know

what to say," William stammered, feeling sick.

"Don't scare the boy, Stirling," Olivia said. "He's just become a husband, and now to learn he might be a father on top of that? But William, a child! There's no greater joy in life, and it would be such a blessing at a time like this."

At a time like this? The war isn't going well. This is no time to bring a child into the world. Not his world.

Of course he and Diana had talked about a family.

"My life would be complete if only we could have a child," Diana had said.

William would rather cut out his heart than deny his wife what she wanted more desperately than anything else. But that was the way it had to be.

"But we have each other," he would always say to coax her out of her doldrums. "I love you to distraction. That's all we need."

"But a child would be a celebration of our love," Diana pleaded.

"We can't in good conscience bring a child into a world at war," William had countered. "It wouldn't be fair." And then he had manufactured other excuses to placate his wife.

He had been a child alone. He had known what it was like to grow up without a father. His father had been a hero, a submariner killed in the war twenty-five years ago, before he really had a chance to know his son at all.

What was the going rate for a dead hero? How different would his life have been if he had grown up with a regular father like the other boys had? Instead, he had grown up with a ghost—a picture, placed on a table over a lace cloth, of a man he had never known.

His mother had presented him with his father's medal, the Iron Cross, and he had left it with Emilie to assure her of his return.

What he remembered most were his mother's tears. The medal was a poor substitute for a flesh-and-blood man. William himself had been awarded the Knight's Cross of the Iron Cross for successful leadership as a submarine captain of the German Navy. He was proud of it but didn't dare wear it.

He was not going to let Diana be a war widow. He didn't know what the future held for him, and there was no way he would let Diana raise his child alone. No child of his was going to go to bed lonely every night, missing his father's guidance, his praise, his love. If things were different, he would love to have a son. But no. Even after the war it would be impossible.

Loving Diana was out of his control. But he couldn't knowingly bring into the world a child who would be the target of a threat. Maybe not today or tomorrow. But one day. He didn't know when it would come. Or from whom. He was only sure that it would come eventually. He would spend the rest of his life looking over his shoulder, watching his back. And that was not the kind of life he wanted for any child of his. A child was simply out of the question. It had never been in the plans.

William made his apologies and said his goodbyes to the Hargraves. Checking to see that Diana was still resting comfortably on the couch, he locked himself in his study to update his war diary and review the highs and lows, the ups and downs in the dangerous and volatile game he was playing.

Chapter 12

Bermuda, December 6, 1941

With sixteen shopping days until Christmas, William did his part to get into the holiday spirit by buying Diana a tweed skirt, a new English camel-hair topcoat, a Shetland cashmere pullover, and an angora sweater to keep her warm on the cool Bermuda nights. He picked up some trowels, rakes, forks, and spades, as well as a watering can, for when she puttered around in her garden. He planned to surprise her with diamonds from Crisson Jewellers on Christmas Day, sure to make her smile.

Diana insisted he try on a tweed topcoat and some of the new khaki for men, which she called "knockabout" clothes, suitable for soldiers or civilians. She said she loved the way he looked "in clothes and out of them." He couldn't help noticing the unwrapped boxes from Astwood-Dickinson in the bedroom closet. When he peeked, he found a felt hat and a new watch. He'd act surprised. Diana had trouble keeping secrets. He didn't have that problem.

William and Diana attended the annual ball of the Bermuda Branch of the Over-Seas League at the Belmont Manor Hotel and a dinner dance at the New Windsor Hotel, where, to the casual observer, all seemed right with the world.

The next morning, the news in *The Royal Gazette* was all about Tokyo and reports of Japan saying America had "misunderstood" her. A Japanese government spokesman made it clear that Japan had no territorial ambitions. The spokesman expressed his opinion that both the U.S. and Japan would continue with sincerity to try to find a common formula for a peaceful situation in the Pacific.

Journal entry *7th December 1941:*

The headlines read: Japan attacks U.S. bases and declares war on America and Britain. The inside pages report about "The Japanese Stab in the Back." While Japanese envoys were still at the State Department, the White House broke the news of the aggression and, unable to substantiate reports of a second attack on Army and Navy bases in Manila, Roosevelt hoped that the report of the bombing was "at least...erroneous." Amid reports that RAF bombers will set a new pace in attack, and unidentified planes were approaching San Francisco, the San Francisco Bay area was blacked out and radio stations were ordered off the air.

In the same vein, the governor of Bermuda asked all householders and the public generally to make every endeavor to obscure their lights, particularly outside lights and naked lights shining through unscreened windows. "Absolutely Light Proof" blackout paper is for sale and there is a rush on the flashlight business.

U.S. base workers' Christmas leave is cancelled. Bermudians are instructed in emergency procedures. Should an attack be considered imminent, a two-minute blast on public "Syrens" will signal danger.

After they hear the warning, Bermudians are instructed to take the following actions:

- *If you are in a building, stay there.*
- *If you are in the streets, or in the open, make your way quietly to your homes and take shelter in the nearest available place.*
- *Close shutters.*
- *Leave windows open.*
- *Keep calm.*

Carriage drivers were instructed to unhitch horses and tie them up.

What not to do:

- *Don't use the telephone.*
- *Don't spread rumors.*
- *Don't stand near glass.*

Amid efforts to formulate a civil defense plan, the governor declared, "I do not want people to become hysterical, but we cannot sit back and say it cannot happen here. That idea is fast disappearing. We can no longer bury our heads in the sand."

With the Americans electrified and united, and Britain and the U.S. declaring war on Japan, the strength of American forces stationed on Bermuda would undoubtedly increase after the invasion of Pearl Harbor. If ever there was a time to move, it was now.

Chapter 13

Bermuda, December 7, 1941

Journal entry 7th *December 1941:*
Bermuda has been plunged into darkness, and the cause is not inclement weather. The world is at war. Our time has come. Telephone lines across the island have been cut. The power has stopped humming. Commercial planes have stopped their crossovers. The island is virtually paralyzed.

I cannot help but think that the High Command is acting out of desperation. When Operation Sea Lion never surfaced as scheduled, I assumed all related plans had been scrubbed. Now, when I got the unexpected signal from the sub this afternoon outlining the advanced timetable, I headed straight for home, quickly gathered my wife, prompted her to pack a bag, and rushed to install her at her parents' house in Hamilton. Hamilton Harbour is exposed, but at least Diana will be with her mother. I don't know how safe they'll be there. I am no longer able to reach Diana after dropping her off.

By now everyone on the island has heard about the "Japanese treachery" at Pearl Harbor and the hostilities perpetrated against American and British forces in the Pacific.

****

The women were stunned but frantic, and Diana wouldn't let go of him.

"What does it all mean, William?" she asked anxiously, holding hard to his arm.

"Everything will be fine, darling Diana, I promise," he said, as he bent to kiss his wife on the lips and fold her tightly into his arms.

Trying not to convey his alarm, William futilely struggled to overcome his need to clasp Diana desperately against him and kiss her roughly, maybe for the last time. He was wondering whether he'd ever see her again, and whether, after today, she would ever *want* to see him again.

"You act as though we will never see each other again," Diana whispered, echoing his thoughts and his worst fears.

"Of course we will," William assured, smoothing her hair and rubbing her back in what he hoped was a calming, circular motion. "I just miss my wife."

"But I'm here, William. I'm here with you now."

"I know you are, sweetheart."

Diana was used to his amorous ways, but she detected the edge of desperation in him, and her face telegraphed her fear.

"I just want you to stay with your mother until things can be worked out. I need to get into the office to handle this emergency. I'm a businessman, darling. Not exactly a dangerous profession. I'll be with you soon."

"When will you be back for me?" she demanded.

"I can't say exactly. I really can't say."

"William!" she screamed in alarm as he broke out of her arms and dashed to the car. "I'm frightened. Please be careful."

While the vice admiral rushed to his base, William's car swung by the Princess, the massive pink waterfront resort hotel on Pitts Bay Road in downtown Hamilton, to pick up Nighthawk on the way to their appointed emergency station. Nobody was out on Front Street, with the exception of a few sailors cycling by. A Fire Evacuation Practice was scheduled for today, so William left the car parked at the hotel's entrance and paid the attendant to watch it. He took the elevator to the second floor and pounded repeatedly on Nighthawk's hotel room door, behind which he was no doubt comfortably cocooned with his French mistress.

When Nighthawk finally answered the knock, William peered into the low-lit room and inclined his head toward the bed, where Nighthawk's woman was shamelessly sprawled, voluptuous breasts bared, the rest of her luscious body only lightly covered. Her lustrous, slightly mussed long, dark hair swung sinfully over one eye, and she resembled an American film star. And *Gott*, she was pregnant. It had been a long time since he'd seen her. He couldn't tear his eyes away from her swollen belly. She met his eyes and placed a protective hand on her stomach. The flash of an emerald on her finger nearly blinded him.

Posed like a satisfied cat, she affected a sleepy stretch, moistened her sensuous lips, flashed back an inviting smile, and fixed William with her smoldering green eyes. What was her name? Yvette, Claudette, Rosette? Something like that. He could never remember. A man could lose his head around a woman like that. A woman like that would certainly test a man's resolve.

Personally, he didn't have much use for the French.

However, he imagined Nighthawk was finding plenty of uses for his longtime lover. He had seen Nighthawk's paramour fully clothed, had conversed with her on the few occasions his associate had allowed her to venture out of their hotel room. She was clever and she was stunning, the incarnation of perfection itself. So much so that it would have been difficult to determine who was taking advantage of whom in this unorthodox arrangement.

William often wondered what would have happened if he had met her first. What dark power did Nighthawk hold over this beautiful woman that would cause her to remain imprisoned for so many years in what seemed, on the surface, to be a very depraved relationship? It certainly didn't resemble any form of love he was familiar with. William half suspected she might be a double agent. But he assumed Nighthawk had the situation under control. Where did Nighthawk's loyalties lie? He was not quite certain. But that was a matter to be pursued at a later date.

"Excuse me, *Herr Kapitänleutnant*," Nighthawk whispered smugly. "As you can see, I was just taking care of business."

William could see from the advanced state of Nighthawk's arousal that his business had not yet been concluded.

"Well, yes, the war is hard on everyone," William said dryly.

"The bitch is insatiable," Nighthawk explained with his back to his lover. "She's always in heat." Yvette/Claudette/Rosette flinched, and for a minute, from his vantage point at the door, William detected a flash of pure hatred, immediately replaced by a steely resolve. But other than the daggers shooting from her eyes, and a wayward tear that slid down her cheek and was quickly brushed back, the girl betrayed no emotion. At that moment, there was something so sad, so vulnerable about her, that William was tempted to reach out and brush the drop of moisture from her face. She seemed to be imploring him with her eyes. And then, just as quickly, she lowered her lids and a look of resignation replaced the fear.

He thought he might have imagined the wild look of helplessness he had seen there. If Nighthawk wasn't more careful in his liaisons, William suspected the man would one day find himself washed up on the shore with a knife in his back.

"We were just reenacting the exact moment when Germany entered Paris," Nighthawk recounted in an amused voice. "It didn't take long. She just lifted her skirts, spread her legs like a French whore, and let us right in."

"Your remarks are crude," William stated with disgust, "and your behavior careless." It was becoming increasingly obvious that Nighthawk's recklessness would have to be dealt with.

"You're just jealous," Nighthawk sneered.

William was in love with his wife, but he could see how a weaker man might be sorely tempted by the woman who now appeared to be waiting obediently on the bed for her lover's return.

"What you do with your seed is your own business," William warned in a harsh whisper. "What you do with your secrets is mine." Then he nodded his head toward Yvette/Claudette/Rosette.

"*Je m'excuse de vous interrompre, mademoiselle.*"

William apologized for the interruption as if they were making polite dinner conversation. Continuing in perfect French, he added, "It was nice to see you again." She never lifted her head, and he didn't bother to wait for her acknowledgement.

"Finish it, then, and meet me in the car," William said sharply to Nighthawk before he turned to leave.

"I'd be happy to share, *Herr Kapitänleutnant*," Nighthawk said slyly before advising over his shoulder, "When I return, *cherie*, we're going to practice the armistice and the occupation."

William turned to leave, and Nighthawk observed, "Women are capricious. If she had seen you first, I've no doubt you would be the one in her bed now. She has a weakness for powerful men."

William didn't have a clue how to respond to that revelation. "Don't be long," he admonished darkly and disappeared down the hall.

Chapter 14

Bermuda, an hour later

"The Princess is in chaos," Nighthawk relayed with satisfaction when he slipped into the passenger seat of William's car. "Everyone is running around like ants without a queen. Sailors on a sinking ship. A headless hydra. The attack on Pearl Harbor has blindsided them. All they can do is wait helplessly for instructions."

"You've got blood on your shirt," William observed irritably, "and a nasty gash on your face."

Nighthawk smiled and answered, "The lady likes to play rough."

"This is insanity," William grumbled to Nighthawk, expressing his frustration at his associate's tardiness and unconscionable behavior, as well as the latest war news. "You know, as well as I do, they couldn't have picked a worse time to move. Germany will be declaring war any day now, and after we attack, the United States will unleash its wrath on Bermuda like an angry tiger just released from its cage."

"As I see it, this is our only window of opportunity," Nighthawk maintained. "The Americans won't be able to mobilize fast enough, and we are not yet at war with them. They won't stand in our way."

"A month ago we could have waltzed right in, and now we'll be forced to fight," William pointed out as they reached their destination and left the car.

"Are you saying we should not follow orders?" Nighthawk challenged.

William calculated the odds before speaking.

"Are you doubting my loyalty?" William seethed, raising himself up to his full height.

"Of course not," Nighthawk retreated gingerly.

"I've already cut off all communications to and from the island," William acknowledged. "Everyone is in position. But according to Vice Admiral Hargrave the British are now on full alert because of Pearl Harbor. Once they get wind of our plans, they will request America's help. The U.S. won't be able to refuse. They'll dispatch destroyers. We can still put a stop to this."

"Our subs will act as a buffer," Nighthawk argued. "Once they land their troops on the island to temporarily secure the airfield, they can go back out to sea and greet the British and American destroyers before they ever reach us."

"Do you think a small contingent of subs surrounding a tiny island will stand up to the lethal force of the American fleet?" William countered. "The Americans will be rendezvousing with the British, and our U-boats will be crushed in the middle. Bermuda will be caught in the crossfire. We don't have the manpower in place to handle the onslaught that's sure to come."

"We have the element of surprise," Nighthawk reminded his superior. "Our transport planes have already taken off from the landing strip on the coast of Spain with enough men and equipment to handle any challenge. Once we've taken over the airstrip here, our reinforcements will be able to land and offer support. It's a brilliant plan. It was your plan, if I remember correctly."

"I don't like the odds now," William muttered.

"You have a lot to lose," Nighthawk observed perceptively. William's objections were masking a fear that went straight to his heart. Nighthawk wasn't questioning William's bravery or loyalty or even his fear of defeat. "You don't like the personal consequences. Your new identity fits you like a second skin, but I gather it's getting a bit snug."

Nighthawk was right.

"You can't stop it now," Nighthawk said simply.

William was at a crossroads. He didn't doubt the operation would be successful. It was success that he most feared. Once the Germans occupied Bermuda, he would be in charge of the operation. There would be no hiding his identity. When Diana learned who he was, what he had done, she would never forgive him. Her father would want to break him apart with his bare hands. The man he was just now beginning to regard as a father would look on him with disdain. William rubbed his fingers across his throat, trying to erase the sensation of an ever-tightening noose.

From his vantage point, William could see a great deal of the island. He studied the sparkling sea at the Hamilton waterfront. It was quiet now, but soon the island would be rocked with explosions. He surveyed the sun dancing on the waves as they crashed to shore and lapped at the pink, sandy beaches. He scanned whitewashed roofs that topped colorfully painted houses high on the hills. His eyes followed the slow progress of a ferry on its way to its first stop at

Somerset Bridge, skipped over the fishermen hauling their pots against the wind, and the sails of sleek pleasure boats. And he knew things in his world would never be the same again.

In an earthly paradise where there were normally no worries, people would soon be burrowed in, frightened of the unknown, with visions of Pearl Harbor overshadowing their every thought. These were strong, independent people, born of pirates and seafarers. People he had come to admire and respect in a land he had come to love. They weren't just statistics anymore. How many people would have to die to secure this strategic toehold in the mid-Atlantic for Germany?

In war, William knew, all bets were off. He couldn't protect anything or anyone, not even his beloved Diana. He had spent his entire time in Bermuda preparing the island for readiness, reviewing military strategies, and perfecting plans. He hadn't really stopped to consider the personal consequences of the action he was about to take and how that would affect his relationship with Diana. Now, thoughts of Diana clouded his mind. He desperately needed her in his life. But now she would slip away. And he was powerless to do anything about it.

"Should I signal the subs?" Nighthawk asked. He was greeted with stern silence and William's stiff back. "We're wasting time, and soon we'll be losing the light. The subs will be waiting for our orders."

In a flash, William made up his mind and rushed to act on his decision before he could change it.

"You continue to monitor the situation," William instructed, ignoring the anger building in Nighthawk's eyes and registering on his face. "I have somewhere to go."

"Now?" Nighthawk was outraged. "Your presence is needed here. Give me the order!"

William ignored him, jumped into the car, and drove toward the Royal Naval Dockyard on Ireland Island. The afternoon traffic was starting to build. People were apparently beginning to panic and going out to get emergency supplies when they should have been staying off the streets. Military and civilian traffic was starting to clog the highways. It was a long drive to the far side of the island. He knew he was racing against the clock.

"I need to speak to Vice Admiral Hargrave," William barked to the guard as he drove up to the fortress forty-five minutes later. William had been there numerous times, and he was recognized at once.

"Is the vice admiral expecting you, Mr. Whitestone?"

"No, but I must speak to him. It's urgent."

"Certainly," the guard responded, handing him a pass.

William rushed though the gate as soon as it creaked opened. Several times he had thought about turning around. But he was here now, and he would follow through with his plan.

He was escorted to the vice admiral's outer office. His secretary smiled and told William that his father-in-law was deep in a meeting with his staff.

"It's an emergency!" William insisted.

"It's not Diana or Mrs. Hargrave, is it?" the secretary's face registered alarm.

"No, but I must speak to him now!"

She had never seen William look so rattled, and he

was a man with a forceful personality, so she stepped into the conference room and signaled her boss. The vice admiral came right out.

"Sorry to interrupt, sir, but I need to talk to you, privately," William apologized.

"Of course, William," the vice admiral greeted him warmly, pounding him on the back. "I'm right in the middle of something, but—"

"This won't take long. It's a rather delicate matter."

"I'll be right back," the vice admiral called to the gathering of uniformed men in his conference room as he led William into an outer office and shut the door.

"How are the women holding up? I thought you'd be holed up in your office trying to get the lights back on."

"They were fine the last time I saw them, and my very capable staff is attempting to do just that. We're having a bit of trouble restoring the power."

"Have you determined the cause yet?" the vice admiral asked.

William paled before he spoke.

"It was undoubtedly sabotage," William responded. On alert, his father-in-law began pacing, clasping his hands behind his back.

"I was afraid of that, son. And the source? Japan?"

Sweat was pouring from William's brow. He clenched a fist at his side and plowed forward.

"Germany," William stated.

The vice admiral's eyes narrowed.

"Have you alerted the police?"

"My own security team is handling it," William assured him. "Sir, when I went into the office this afternoon, I came across some sensitive information, vital communiqués that I thought you should be aware of. The intelligence came in earlier, before the telephone lines went out. When I put them together it painted a rather grim picture."

"Where did you get this information?" the vice admiral wanted to know.

"As a practice, for national security purposes, in times of war, we…uh…have been monitoring phone calls," William continued.

"And you'd just as soon no civilians know about that," noted the vice admiral.

"Precisely," William breathed in relief. "People naturally might be concerned about privacy, their rights."

"I completely understand," said the vice admiral. William wondered if his father-in-law was aware of just how flagrantly rights were already being violated in the basement of the Princess Hotel. Any suspicious letters coming in by plane from Europe or America were inspected, decoded, resealed, and sent back on the plane before it left for its final destination. The data was then transmitted to Berlin. The British were doing the same thing, transmitting their information to New York.

"Sometimes, subterfuge is necessary in times of war," stated the vice admiral. "Individual freedoms sometimes have to be sacrificed to achieve the overall goal of protecting the country from aggressors from within and without."

"At any rate, regardless of how I came across this information, I've learned that, at this very moment, a squadron of German transport planes, carrying troops and equipment, is winging its way from the coast of

Spain and is due to arrive in Bermuda in a matter of hours."

The vice admiral stared at William.

"Are you sure?"

"Positive, but I'd prefer it if you didn't press me for the source."

"Strange, but we've just received the same information from one of our operatives at the Princess Hotel. She called it in an hour ago and requested to be picked up. She said she was in trouble."

William rubbed his jaw.

"We've found several caches of explosives, set to go off at critical points around the island," William said. "My team is dismantling them."

The vice admiral was astounded.

"And there's more."

Now it was William's turn to pace.

"German U-boats are positioned in a tight circle around the island, locking us in."

"Why wasn't I aware of this?" the vice admiral fumed.

"I imagine it just happened as a result of the attack on Pearl. And I don't think the timing was coincidental. There's no doubt the Germans are working in tandem with the Japanese. They strike at Pearl, and the Germans follow by taking Bermuda on the same day, effectively choking England off."

William hoped his father-in-law believed the blatant lie. He had indeed been monitoring communications and had intercepted the *B-Dienst* message, dated today, informing Hitler of the surprise attack. So he knew with certainty that the German leader and his high command had been stunned at the treacherous Japanese action at Pearl Harbor. He also knew that Admiral Karl Dönitz, commander in chief of U-boats, was even now suggesting to the Führer that he deploy a U-boat strike on the doorstep of the east coast of the United States. His rationale was that the superior German submarine fleet could deliver a solid blow to the unprepared and vulnerable Americans with their fleet of obsolete warships. Hitler was still pressing for Bermuda as the first choice for a planned attack.

"This is disastrous," yelled the vice admiral. "We're being invaded! It's another surprise attack."

"It appears that way," William agreed. "When I put everything together, the pieces seemed to fit. I thought you would be the best person to tell, since it's not my area. I knew you could handle it."

"I appreciate that, son." The vice admiral shook his son-in-law's hand. "William, you just may have saved Bermuda."

"I would be grateful if you wouldn't tell anyone about my involvement," William said, feigning modesty.

"Of course not, if that's what you wish. But I am indebted to you."

"Sir, what are you going to do about this?"

William could see the wheels spinning in the vice admiral's head.

"We'll need a coordinated plan of action," his father-in-law said. "I'm going to contact the other branches."

"This is not my purview, but the transport planes?" William interjected, trying not to be too obvious, as he imagined the formation of Heikel 111's, Germany's "Secret Bombers," speeding toward Bermuda.

Produced in Spain, modified for increased range, and specially outfitted for transport, the former airliners carried enough troops to complete the beginning stages of the mission.

"German transport planes don't have the range to make that trip," the vice admiral reasoned.

"I'm not exactly sure of their range, but why take the chance?" William continued, trying not to appear too eager. "I doubt if they'll have enough fuel to return to Spain if they get much farther. They'll have to land in Bermuda, unless you can get them to turn around *now!*"

"Excellent point, son."

"I assume you're going to alert the United States, have them dispatch all the battleships they have in the area," William prompted.

"I've got my work cut out for me. I'm going back to charge my staff. We're going after some U-boats."

"I'll get out of your way, then," William said, turning to leave. "I'll have my hands full at the power plants."

"Thank you for your contribution. I'm proud to call you my son." The vice admiral embraced William. In William's mind, Sir Stirling Hargrave could not have paid him a greater compliment. Or made him feel so utterly unworthy.

William's heart pounded in his chest, and he hoped his father-in-law couldn't hear it. He got into his car and headed out of the complex. He had done his part. Sir Stirling and his team would have to handle the rest. If his hunch was correct, by the time he made it back to St. George's, the German subs would be alerted to the presence of the British and American destroyers in the area. Once they realized they were exposed and vulnerable, they would radio a message to their contact, who would in turn redirect the transport planes. It was just too risky for the operation to go forward now.

William didn't speed on the return trip. He wasn't anxious to get back to Nighthawk, but he had an urgent need to see his wife. He needed to hold her, be with her, and let her know that everything was all right now. That she was safe with him.

As he stared out to sea, he imagined himself in one of the *Unterseeboots* when the alarm signal sounded from the *Zentrale* ordering an emergency crash-dive. He wished he were with them. He loved the thrill of the chase. He sincerely hoped he hadn't jeopardized the lives of any of the crews, especially his friend Karl, and that they would slip away before they ever had to hear the call to battle stations, "*Auf Gefechtsstationen!*" He could breathe easier now, confident he had saved lives on both sides.

"Where have you been?" Nighthawk demanded furiously when William returned.

"I had some business to take care of."

"At such a critical time?"

"It was related to the mission."

Nighthawk sneered before he announced, "The mission has been aborted."

"What?" William shouted, feigning anger and surprise. "When?"

"A few minutes ago. I got a message from *Kapitänleutnant* Krauss. They were forced to break radio silence. The U-boats are on their way out to sea. They've been redirected to patrol the U.S. east coast. The transport planes from Spain have been ordered to turn around in mid-flight. I'm having the team dismantle the explosives. We are instructed to have our people restore communications and electric service to the island."

"And the operation?"

"Delayed indefinitely, according to the message transmitted from Herr Krauss," Nighthawk informed his superior with disgust. "Essentially, we're dead in the water."

William breathed a sigh of relief at the message from the radioman but tried his best to appear disappointed.

"All that work, all that planning," William sighed. "We'll never have another opportunity like this one."

"You've changed your tune now that you're out of danger," Nighthawk said. "You're not fooling me at all, *Wilhelm.*"

William didn't bother to respond to his subordinate's insolence. He hadn't asked for this assignment. Hadn't wanted it. It had been thrust upon him by Canaris. He had been lured into it, courted, charmed by his former commander. Neither of them had much respect for Hitler, but William had not refused what he clearly saw as his duty to his country.

"I'll be at home if you need to reach me," William said, dismissing Nighthawk before he walked away.

"Wait." Nighthawk stopped him, but seemed to hesitate. He knew something about Wilhelm von Hesselweiss. He was the keeper of secrets, and this secret had been carefully safeguarded, but now was not the time to reveal it. It wasn't his place to set the emergency plan into motion. He nearly choked on the information, but he would follow orders.

"If you think your hands are clean, you are naïve, Wilhelm. Do you think it was an accident that the man you replaced when you first got to the island was lost in a boating mishap? Oh, yes, I forgot, it *was* an accident. A very *fortunate* one, for you. They never did find the body, did they?"

"I had nothing to do with Sir James Markham's disappearance!" William protested.

"Disappearance?" Nighthawk scoffed snidely, rubbing at the spots of blood on his shirt. "If it makes you feel more respectable to think of it that way. But you've got blood on your own hands."

"What do you mean?"

"It seems that my delicious little French pastry is spoiled," Nighthawk remarked.

"Am I supposed to understand your crude references?" William asked, anger bubbling to the surface.

"While she was masquerading as a British censorette, and playing the role of the seductive French mistress, a role she played very well, I learned she was about to reveal the identity of the German spy known as *Island Eagle*."

William's face paled.

"But how did she—how could she have known?"

"She had us under surveillance; she was a British agent," Nighthawk sneered. "It seems the British helped her escape after her parents were transported to the detention center to be 'reeducated.' She was eternally grateful to them."

"You compromised our operation?" William seethed. "What if she talks?"

"I assure you, she won't be talking to anyone

anymore," Nighthawk said dryly.

"What did you do to her?" A growing sense of dread had the bile rising to William's throat.

"You interrupted us at a most inopportune time. I was just beginning to question her. But you seemed to be in such a hurry, you took all the sport out of it. No matter, it will be taken care of by the end of the day. She'll be found in the nude, with her throat slit, in the basement of the Princess Hotel. In all the confusion of the day, it won't even warrant a mention in the papers. Not like that other British censorette. Yvette, or whatever her real name is, is a spy. I doubt anyone will even acknowledge her. It's a risky business." Nighthawk smirked and shrugged. "Of course, I shall miss her very much—in my bed."

"How can you make light of this?" William tried to recall Yvette's beautiful face and the vulnerable swell of her belly and knew it would haunt his dreams forever. Evil emanated from the monster beside him. "The woman is pregnant—with your child, I assume."

"That's no matter to me, nor should it be to you. I'm saving you and our whole operation at a most critical time, and all you can do is berate me?" Nighthawk railed. "You don't have the stomach for this business. They put the wrong man in charge."

Nighthawk never saw the punch coming. When William's fist connected with his subordinate's jaw, the crack reverberated and the lightning-like blow toppling Nighthawk like a solid oak. William lifted Nighthawk by his shirtfront, willing him to gain consciousness so he could finish the job. He flexed the sore hand that had felled his nemesis. One punch wasn't enough. Like a lava flow, William's molten rage saturated the crevices of his mind and the raw intensity of his anger searched for an outlet.

William realized he had to get away or he would kill his associate with his bare hands. Captaining a U-boat required nerves of steel, but perhaps Nighthawk was right. He was growing weary of all the killing on both sides of the conflict.

His stomach churned. He needed to feel clean again. He needed to see Diana. He would pick her up at her parents' house, take her home, and coax her into bed, so he could pretend this whole episode had never happened. A man and a woman could lose themselves in each other, and the sounds of love could surely block out the sounds of war. He was anxious for the familiar feel of his wife.

But first, there was the matter of the French woman—British spy or whoever she was. One word from her and their cover would be blown. Everything he had worked for would be destroyed. He would lose Diana forever. But the woman was pregnant! How could he have her blood on his conscience? If he did, he'd be no better than Nighthawk.

William jumped into his car and drove to the Princess Hotel. He'd decide how to handle matters when he got there. Nighthawk would be suspicious, and he could be a problem in the future, but he couldn't prove anything. Whatever else he was, he would remain a loyal soldier. He would follow orders.

With any luck, William's role in undermining the German plot and compromising the mission would never be revealed. He had averted a certain catastrophe for both sides. One day he would have to pay a price for that. But he couldn't worry about that now.

Chapter 15

William arrived at Nighthawk's hotel room and pounded on the door. Greeted by silence, he tried the lock.

"Yvette, are you in there? It's William Whitestone. Let me in." He thought he heard a muffled reply. "Stand away from the door," he shouted. Looking up and down the hallway, assured that no one was loitering there, he pulled out his gun and shot several times around the door handle. He reached his hand in and turned the knob from inside, stepped into the room, and closed the door behind him.

The scene that greeted him made his stomach lurch.

Yvette was bound and gagged on the bed, still only half dressed, tears staining her cheeks, struggling to get free. When she saw him she cringed in fear.

He untied the gag.

"Please, don't hurt me," she whispered. "My baby." Tears stained her cheeks.

"Do you think I'm an animal?" William asked bitterly. He untied her. She rubbed her hands and feet to restore circulation.

He handed her a robe. "Here, put this on." He picked up the telephone and couldn't tear his eyes away from the bruises on her face. Nighthawk had beaten her bloody.

"Yes, I need an ambulance at the Princess Hotel. Room 205. Emergency. Immediately."

Yvette screamed.

He slammed down the phone and turned to her.

"I think I'm in labor! Please, help me," she sobbed.

He rushed into the bathroom, grabbed some clean towels, and soaked a washcloth with water, thinking that this woman needed more help than he could give.

At her bedside, he tenderly patted her face to remove the blood.

"Hush, now. I'm here. Everything will be okay."

She grabbed his hand and squeezed it.

"The pain...my baby... It's coming!"

"How long have you had these pains?"

He knew nothing about childbirth. He was a sailor, for *Gott*'s sake. Not many occasions to deliver babies on a ship.

"All morning," she replied, "since he left. The pain is worse now."

"The ambulance is on its way," he assured her. "It should be here soon." He hoped he was right. In all the confusion, it was unlikely that any ambulance would respond. In a few minutes he would have to drive her to the hospital in his own car.

"Will you help me?" she pleaded.

He smiled and nodded his head, hoping he could provide some comfort to the poor woman.

Her pains had subsided for a moment, but she still held his hand in a death grip. "He means to kill me when he returns."

"He admitted that to me."

"You've got to get me out of here," she said anxiously. "He will be back for me."

"He won't hurt you. That I can promise you. I'll kill him before he lays another hand on you. He shouldn't be a problem right now. What is there between you?"

"He fed me lies," she began. "I sifted through them and reported half-truths. It was a game we played."

"A dangerous game," he frowned. "Is it true you were going to expose me?"

"Then you know who I am? Yet you're still helping me?"

"Whatever you think of me, I am still a human being," William said. "Where's that damn ambulance?"

"You were never in danger. I was going to expose Nighthawk as the Island Eagle. When my baby and I are safe, I'm going to have him hunted down like the dog that he is."

"He'll go underground," William said.

"He can go to hell," Yvette answered, screaming again. "It's coming, my baby's coming!"

"Can you wait for the ambulance?"

He got his answer when she sagged back on the pillow, spread her legs and clamped down on his hand as she pushed. He could see the head crowning.

"I see it. I see the baby's head." *What in the hell do I do now?*

In the next minute, out came the shoulders, and the rest of the child slipped out in a whoosh of fluid onto the towel he had placed at the foot of the bed.

"He's here." William smiled widely. "It's a boy."

Yvette started crying, tears of joy. "A boy?"

"A bruiser." William laughed.

"Is he…?"

William stared at the child in wonder.

"He doesn't have horns, if that's what you mean. He has the requisite number of fingers and toes."

Yvette choked back her laughter.

"Then he doesn't take after his father."

The baby cried.

"I want to see my—"

Suddenly she sat up on her elbows.

"William, I have to push again."

"The afterbirth?" William wondered.

In another minute, smooth as a slippery eel, another child slipped out of the womb behind her brother.

"It's a girl," William marveled. "Twins. Madam, you've just delivered twins."

"A miracle," Yvette said, awed. "Let me see my children, William."

Suddenly the ambulance driver and his associate swept into the room like bats and brought chaos with them. Too soon for William. He wanted to savor the moment, share it with Yvette.

"What's the emergency?"

"Henry, look," the other worker said. "She's just delivered. Two babies."

They scurried about, cutting the cords, washing the babies, while William looked on in wonder.

"The babies, they're so tiny," William whispered. "So beautiful, like their mother." He took a step toward the babies and then back, hesitant, dropping Yvette's hand.

"Is this the father?" the taller worker asked, wrapping one baby in a towel and handing the bundle to William.

"Oh," William said, startled as the baby shifted in

his arms.

"No," Yvette laughed, looking at him wistfully. "Not the father, a friend—I think, yes?"

"Yes," William said strongly, fascinated by the tiny boy he was holding.

The workers lifted Yvette off the bed and onto the stretcher. Then one of them took the bundle from William. Yvette was cuddling her daughter against her chest.

"Well, then, I guess I'd better go home and get cleaned up."

"William," she breathed. "Don't leave me, please don't leave me alone now. I need you."

"I'm right here with you, then," he said. "The babies, they'll be okay?" William asked one of the emergency workers.

As if on cue, both infants wailed.

"You can hear 'em, can't you?" the man replied. "They're madder'n hornets, wanting to be fed, no doubt."

William turned to Yvette, who was already coaxing her nipple gently into her little girl's mouth. William blushed when he saw the baby nursing furiously, her tiny fist nestled against her mother's breast.

A tear spilled out of William's eye.

Yvette smiled.

"I think we have been part of a true miracle, William," she sighed.

William caressed Yvette's cheek.

"You were very brave," he said.

"And so, William, were you."

"Okay, we're going to get mother and babies to hospital," the ambulance driver announced.

"Will you follow us?" Yvette asked.

"Just let me clean up a bit here, take care of a few things, and I'll be right behind you," he assured as Yvette and her children were wheeled out the door.

The room was a bloody mess. It looked like a murder scene. In a few minutes, it would have become one.

The splintered door would be hard to explain. He rinsed his hands, threw the bloody towels into a bag, and sanitized the room, removing any evidence of Yvette's ever having lived there.

Then he walked down the hall, took the elevator, and danced down the steps of the Princess. He called for his car and drove home. But he couldn't go to his wife, not yet. He went to Marigold House and removed a pouch from his safe.

Chapter 16

When William arrived at the hospital, he tracked down Yvette and hurried into her room, anxious to see her and the babies again. They were so beautiful, so tiny, so new. His heart filled just to see them. Yvette was feeding the boy now, and the little girl was sleeping soundly in a bassinette by the bed.

"Are you well?" he asked.

"Sleepy, but fine, thank you. Thank you for coming back. I wasn't sure you would."

"I promised, didn't I?"

"You're a man who keeps his word, I could tell that right away about you." She smiled, looking at him in rapture.

"Have they fed you?" William wanted to know.

"I've been able to eat a little."

"I brought you something. A sweet pear from our garden." He held it up to her mouth so she could taste. The juice dribbled down her cheek and he wiped it away.

"That's delicious, William. Thank you."

"And I've brought you something else. Something to help you, for your future."

"I don't understand."

"Some insurance."

"What?" Yvette asked, puzzled.

"Don't ask questions. Just take this. It holds

diamonds. They're yours." He thrust the pouch toward Yvette. "You deserve this and much more."

"I don't know what to say."

"I want you to have it." His words, spoken with force, left no room for objection. "For the children. And if you ever need anything, you know you can come to me."

They left the rest unspoken between them. William pulled up a chair beside the bed and held Yvette's hand, closing it around the dazzling emerald.

"I wish…" He paused. "I wish that I could do more for you." There was a look of longing in his eyes, matched only by hers.

Then the nurse came in and took the children from their mother so Yvette could rest.

He stayed for a while, until Yvette fell asleep, and then he whispered, "I must go now, but I will see you soon."

When he returned to the hospital the next morning, all trace of Yvette and her babies was gone. It was as if the new family had disappeared off the face of the earth. He used every available channel but could not determine what had happened to the three of them. It haunted him for days, weeks, months. He was frantic that Nighthawk had come for them in the middle of the night, and his mind went wild imagining all the cruel things he could do to the woman and her innocent babies. But he couldn't ask Nighthawk. His associate had disappeared also.

Chapter 17

Bermuda 1943-1945

31st May 1943. "Black May." Forty-one of our U-boats have been sunk in the Atlantic. The Allies' achievement of naval supremacy effectively marks the end of our sustained U-boat campaign. The Allies are beginning to employ new radar technology, thwarting Wolf-pack attacks, and the Ubootwaffe suffers a heavy death toll. Canaris tells me 863 U-boats have gone out on operational patrols, and 754 have not returned to their bases. Of the 39,000 men who put to sea in U-boats to date, 27,491 have died.

****

"Thank God the worst of it is over," Sir Stirling said to William over drinks at Marigold House. "The Germans came dangerously close to starving us out and forcing Britain to come to terms with Germany."

William wondered if he had even made a difference in the war effort and whether he should have stayed in the *Kriegsmarine* and fought to the death with those daring men with nerves of steel. While *Grossadmiral* Dönitz, head of the *Kriegsmarine*, proclaimed, "You have fought like lions!" William had done nothing but struggle with paperwork and record his "exploits" in a journal.

****

June 1944. Sir Stirling has just returned from England with grave news about heavy attacks on the city of London. The vice admiral and his wife came for dinner, and we caught up on the news.

"I was in London the day the first B2 bomb hit," recalled the vice admiral. "It was a 3,000-mile-an-hour missile—and it didn't make a sound. Not like the scream of the Stukas, but terrifying in its own right. One minute I was leaning against the Red Cross building and then, without warning, the bloody thing dug a hole about 40 feet deep. Nobody heard it coming.

"The city has been bombed so badly, you can hardly find a place to live. People can climb a set of steps and there's no house left at the top. All the glass is gone. To replace windows, they're smearing brown paper with shortening to let light in. How our people can manage to live under the bombardment I don't know. The spirit and the fortitude they display is remarkable. The Blitz has killed more than 40,000 people, including thousands of children."

****

1944. The right to vote was given to all eligible Bermuda women.

William continued to follow his instructions to record all events in his shore-based war diary, or *Kriegstagebuch*, no matter how insignificant they seemed at the time. It amused him to think that this particular milestone, women's right to vote, would probably have longer-lasting repercussions than the Third Reich's fading dreams of world dominance.

"Diana and Olivia are over the moon because land-owning women have been given the right to vote," the vice admiral said. "My wife and my daughter are suffragists. What is the world coming to? Diana told me you put Marigold House in her name so she could receive a vote. I know you have properties all over the island, but signing over the house meant the world to Diana."

"And she means the world to me," replied William, who continued more and more in love with his wife each passing day.

William didn't know how well that move would sit with his superiors, but the way the war was going, he didn't know how much longer he'd be in Bermuda. If he were to be pulled suddenly, he wanted to leave Diana well protected and cared for. He had already begun placing his other assets in her name. To hell with his handlers. She was the most important thing in his life. The only thing he valued.

He had built an entire operation here, waiting for word of an invasion, for his people to smooth the way for the waiting submarines, and still the word never came. It had been years. Did they think that overseeing and maintaining such an intricate network—facilities, supplies, resources, operatives—had not been difficult or risky? Bermuda was a gem, ripe for the picking, and still no word to move the plan forward. He knew German subs were still out there, lurking off the island. He had seen them with his own eyes, boarded them on occasion, communicated with them regularly, and still no one had issued the order to proceed or dismantle the operation. His operatives were growing impatient. And so was he. The information he reported was becoming sketchier. In truth, he had learned some damaging information from his father-in-law that he didn't bother to report to his superiors.

He was losing his appetite for the game, especially once he'd heard the distasteful, nasty, actually revolting rumors about the Jews and their inhuman treatment in the concentration camps—the "KZs."

Bermuda was his home now. He had been here seven years. What if he were pulled back, his cover compromised? The way the war was going, where would he be pulled back to? It was apparent to him that Germany was going to lose the war. What would become of his operation? Of his wife? He had amassed a fortune, and to what end? Who else knew about it? Could his subordinates be trusted? What was he supposed to do with the gold and his properties if the operation was permanently torpedoed?

The Third Reich was imploding with typical German precision—folding on every front. Desperate, William had even toyed with the idea of turning, becoming a double agent. Going to his father-in-law and revealing all, offering to help the British war effort and seeking his protection. But it was much too late in the game to play both sides of the fence. Either they would hang him or his own agents would seek retribution. And then what would become of Diana? Every move had to be made with her in mind. She was his world now, his lifeline.

He heard rumors that Canaris had attempted to change sides but his peacemaking posturing was ridiculed in the Foreign Office. Everybody knew Hitler was already doomed.

William had been receiving conflicting reports. He knew that between February 1942 and October 1943 German U-boats sank 17 ships off the Florida coast. He wondered if Germany was still in control of the sea. He had his doubts. He was isolated here, dangling precipitously. Not knowing the final outcome of the conflict was tearing him apart, preventing him from moving on with his life with Diana.

The first sign of a chink in the German armor came little more than a month later.

****

20th July 1944. I was shocked to learn of Colonel Claus Count von Stauffenberg's putsch at Wolfsschanze, Hitler's secret headquarters in East Prussia. The bomb killed four people, wounded more, but the target escaped. Hitler went on air the next day to assure the German people that all was well. He was unhurt and the plot against his life was foiled. Stauffenberg and his aides were immediately convicted of high treason and shot by a firing squad.

23rd July 1944. Admiral Canaris has been arrested, three days after the attempt on Hitler's life! I will never believe the admiral was involved in the conspiracy to kill Hitler, although it was no secret he didn't hold Hitler in high regard.

William recalled the last time he saw his friend. He had been surprised, shocked really, by the appearance of Canaris himself standing on the bridge during a recent submarine rendezvous in the waters outside Marigold House late in the war. He had personally come to Bermuda to warn his protégé so he wouldn't be left out in the cold.

"How did you manage to get out of Germany?" William wondered as he saw his mentor standing in the moonlight. "It's much too dangerous for you to be here. You shouldn't have taken the risk. Karl should never have let you come."

"He couldn't have stopped me. I had no choice, Wilhelm. I had to get away. Germany, at least the Führer's glorious vision of Germany, is crumbling around us. I've been in touch with the Americans and the British to negotiate for myself and an unnamed associate."

Canaris put his arm around Wilhelm's shoulder.

"I promised your father I would protect you, and I have tried to honor my pledge. You've been like a son to me. But it's too late. They weren't interested."

"I see," William said, deeply touched. "Are you going back? You could escape now, go to South America, where you'd be welcomed."

"I'm a loyal soldier. Our leader is mad, but I won't desert my country. I had to see you one more time. I wanted to tell you I'm sorry things didn't work out but that I'm proud of you. I know your father would have been, too. He's been in my thoughts a lot lately. You are so like him. Brave, fearless, and intelligent, with an open heart and always a willing hand out for a friend. There are some who would say we Germans are unfeeling. That's the way the world will brand us. I just wanted to tell you there is much of his goodness in you."

William's heart swelled. The two embraced.

"Don't come back," Canaris warned. "There's nothing left for you in Germany."

William had no intention of returning to his homeland.

"You've lost a lot in your young life," Canaris said. "Have you built some happiness here?"

"I have," he said, grateful for his mentor's concern. "And I've been blessed with love again."

For a moment Canaris seemed poised to impart some additional information, but he reconsidered, and the opportunity passed as their talk returned to a discussion of the grim statistics of war.

****

13th/14th February 1945. The American Air Force and Royal Air Force conducted firebombing raids on Dresden, killing thousands, perhaps hundreds of thousands of people, and destroying much of the city.

Dresden. Although William hadn't seen his hometown in years, he could still recall the beautiful medieval city on the Elbe River, the city of his heart. A major center for European art and culture, with its historic monuments reduced to rubble; its helpless, hopeless people reduced to dust and ashes. Germany was on the verge of surrender. With no major war production or industry in the city, Dresden was of questionable military value and clogged with refugees fleeing the Red Army. So why punish Dresden and annihilate civilians? It was outrageous! Barbaric! Senseless!

When he was finally able to contact Karl, he was almost afraid to ask, and he had to have his friend repeat his words.

"They're gone. They're all gone. Your mother... Wihelm, I'm so sorry."

He thought of his mother. He hadn't been able to contact her for years. She'd perished not knowing if her son was dead or alive.

"Are you sure?"

"Yes. I went there myself. You would not recognize our city anymore. Or our street."

"And Emilie?" William whispered.

There was a long silence on the line.

"Yes," Karl said quietly. "I'm sorry. And Wilhelm, there's something else..."

Suddenly the line went dead and the connection was lost.

"Karl, Karl, are you there?"

But he was not able to reach his friend. What else had Karl been trying to tell him? It sounded urgent. No matter, his mother and Emilie were gone. There was nothing else to say, nothing more he cared to hear.

William couldn't face Diana right now. One look at him and she would be able to read his grief. And that would give him away. He couldn't go home yet. He left work and drove to a bar in Hamilton to drown his sorrows and lament the life he had been denied. Celebrate the blessings.

The papers were full of Dresden; the story ran for weeks. Eyewitness accounts of the firestorm from the two days of saturation bombing and the subsequent days of burning. Explosions that wouldn't stop. Fire. Scorching heat, hot enough to burn the human hair and tender flesh of innocent women and children. Smoke so thick you couldn't see or breathe through it. Screaming from the wounded. Collapsing buildings. Mutilated corpses. The darkness of the night, the darkness nightmares are made of. Dresden, a burned-out shell, a hell on earth. He conjured up his mother's angelic face. And Emilie's perfect, porcelain one, cool and still as a marble statue, now horribly, painfully, burnt. He only hoped they hadn't suffered overlong.

8th April 1945. On Hitler's orders, Admiral Canaris was executed at the prison in Flossenbürg. He was like a father to me. I will mourn his loss greatly.

Chapter 18

Bermuda, 1958

William picked up the telephone. This was not a conversation he relished having. He hadn't come into contact with his aide since the end of the war, when their association had ended abruptly and awkwardly. Everything had fallen apart. No instructions had been given, no contingency plans made. No one expected to lose the war. He was on his own, isolated on an island. Wrapped in riches, but nevertheless isolated. When he noticed his papers were missing, he wanted to take action. But he was helpless to do anything until their inevitable phone conversation. He had finally tracked the monster down.

"I believe I may have lost something of value," William began when he heard what sounded like Nighthawk's voice.

"Misplaced?" Nighthawk virtually sneered through the lines.

He wished they could have met in person, so he could see Nighthawk's eyes. Then he would know for sure.

"No," William said, detecting a hidden message in the silence that followed.

"Could these items you're missing possibly compromise you?"

William paused. He had not mentioned the fact that more than one item was missing. So, that was the way the game was being played.

"Yes," William said simply.

"There's something I find very curious. You kept such complete records during the war years. But the entry for 7 December 1941, which should have been the culmination of our years of hard work and planning, was scant. No detailed notes, no mention of the failure of our operation. It was glaring in its absence."

William couldn't breathe.

"Hopefully these items weren't too valuable, Herr Whitestone. I assume you had the proper insurance?"

The message came through loud and clear.

"They're uninsurable, irreplaceable, as you well know."

His journal and the other missing items could potentially blow his cover, ruin him, and bring harm to his wife. Now he was being told that his survival hung by a thread, that he could be exposed at any moment. He was well pleased with his wife, his home, and his life on the island, and he had no intention of jeopardizing them.

He'd always known his former associate was dangerous, that when a dirty job had to be done, Nighthawk had been the one to call. He should have killed the man when he had the chance. He could seek out Nighthawk and threaten his life unless he revealed where the missing documents were. But he could not afford to kill him until he knew the whereabouts of his property. It was too risky. That was Nighthawk's insurance policy. Nighthawk could fly at any time. He lived among the shadows. William was prominent and visible on the island, and therefore vulnerable.

And Nighthawk didn't pose the only threat. How many of Nighthawk's shady associates had known about his past? His double identity? His buried fortune?

If he required any evidence of Nighthawk's capacity for violence, he need look no further than Yvette. The man certainly had held a great affection for her, yet he had planned to kill his pregnant mistress without hesitation. Murder his own children.

William's sexual appetite was as deeply developed as the next man's, but he had experienced only two true loves in his life, and he was loyal, at least in his heart, to both of them. But he could hardly blame his associate for falling under Yvette's spell. He had been a little in love with her himself. The birth of her twins had created a bond between them, even though he'd never seen Yvette again once she disappeared from the hospital. Watching the miracle of a baby's birth softened his heart and made him yearn for a child of his own, a child with Diana.

Perhaps Yvette had first turned to Nighthawk for protection, alone in the world as she was, although that notion was utterly ridiculous. Nighthawk was the kind of man you sought protection *from*. She had used *him*. What secrets had he accidentally revealed to her or to the others who came after her? What secrets had they shared? And what had happened to that brave woman?

The past was catching up with him. But what of the future? He wondered if he would ever know the extent of Nighthawk's betrayal.

PART THREE

The Treasure

Bermuda 2013

Chapter 19

Bermuda 2013

Patience's eyes were blurry from reading the handwritten journal entries and from plain exhaustion. Tears from her swollen eyes splotched the already delicate pages. Waves of nausea threatened to drown her. Her head was splitting apart. Shame and disappointment threatened to choke her. There simply wasn't any doubt about where her grandfather's loyalties had lain. Nathaniel must hate her. She rubbed her neck and sank back onto her pillow.

She didn't have the resolve to read much more. Her grandfather's spirit was noticeably sagging, especially after the death of his champion, Canaris. He was demoralized and depressed. After that his ramblings detailed a series of defeats, crumbling pockets of resistance on all fronts, cessation of operations, occupations, Victory-in-Europe Day, a stunning defeat for the *Kriegsmarine*, and suicides—Hitler's and Eva Braun's soon after they had married, the Goebbels family, and others. Dönitz, who had assumed the duties as the new German head of state following Hitler's death, was ordering maximum resistance on all fronts, hopelessly followed by unconditional surrenders and war crimes trials. The last gasps of the dying Third Reich. Her grandfather's legacy. Reading his words was tantamount to watching him die all over again.

There were also tears over everything William Whitestone had lost, over Emilie and everyone else who had perished in Dresden or lost their lives in the world conflict, and over the death of his daughter, the mother Patience never knew.

She swallowed hot, bitter tears as she reread the traitorous passage. Her grandfather had lied to her about many things. He had called her his *little miracle.* But he never even wanted a child. Never wanted her real mother. Never wanted her. Oh, he had accepted his responsibility, was even great at playing at being a grandfather, but in the end, he had tried his best not to have a child. She wondered what else he had lied about?

"He never loved me," Patience said, not realizing she had spoken the words aloud or that Nathaniel had returned to the room and was sitting right beside her on the couch. Chewing on her bottom lip, her hand clung to the material of her dress, balling it up in her fist. Her breath sailed out in a painful whoosh. Her entire life had been an illusion, a beautiful but cruel illusion.

Nathaniel placed his hand over hers and slowly unclenched her fist, opening one finger at a time.

"Of course he loved you," Nathaniel said gently. "His actions proved that. Why do you think he worked so hard to keep you close and safe? He had lost one daughter. He couldn't protect her, so he was ferocious about protecting you."

"Protecting me?"

"If William Whitestone's true identity were discovered, his life and the lives of those he loved would be in danger because of what he did during the war. His way of protecting you was to keep you locked away in the safety of his compound, on a rock in the middle of the Atlantic, where no harm could come to you. If I'm sure of anything, it was William's love for Diana and for you. Come here, Patience," Nathaniel said as he took the diary from her hand and gathered her up in his arms.

She dissolved into him, her arms reaching out to hold him tightly. They sat there in silence on the couch, not saying a word, until she fell asleep against him and he carried her into her bedroom.

****

Nathaniel settled himself on the couch and pored through Wilhelm von Hesselweiss's last journal entry, trying again to find clues that would reveal the identity and whereabouts of Nighthawk—the man he believed was threatening Patience.

Nathaniel reread William's journal entries with interest and the dispassionate eye of a historian. He thought he could almost understand the spy known as William Whitestone. Patience's grandfather as a young man had been caught in a new world order where orders were to be followed and love sacrificed.

Nathaniel read about the man who had followed his own father to the sea. For all his wealth, for all the respectability he had achieved in the business world, William Whitestone was, at heart, still a seaman. He did not consider himself inherently evil, though he provided regular reports on Allied shipping activities, enabling his counterparts to pursue and massacre enemy merchant ships in the mid-Atlantic. Like Canaris, William's allegiance had been to the German Navy, not the Nazis. He would have given his life for his fellow

U-boatmen.

He had also written about his respect for the Allied submariners. As fellow men of the sea, he felt a special kinship with them. Just as he would never have sanctioned the killing of survivors in the water by his crew, he could not fathom how Allied Air Force crewmen could kill innocent civilians in Dresden, even from their anonymous heights.

A picture arose of a man who had managed to rise above the cutthroat competition that existed in the *Kriegsmarine* and was more comfortable in pitching seas than in petty politics.

William had written a lot about life on his submarine before he was dispatched to Bermuda by way of Switzerland. He did not feel confined by the U-boat. The close quarters only heightened his readiness for action, highlighted his recklessness, and hammered home his hunger for danger in his role as submarine commander.

In the months following the assassination attempt on Hitler's life at Wolf's Lair, William had known that some five thousand people associated with the plot were rounded up and executed. Nathaniel wondered if Patience's grandfather had felt the noose tightening then, if he had realized suspicion would arise in the inner circle of power, questioned how long it would take before they wondered whether Wilhelm von Hesselweiss, protégé of Canaris, was a threat to them? Whether he could be trusted, or if he would have to be *handled* as well?

Nathaniel was familiar enough now with the words and thoughts of William Whitestone to know that his first fears would not be for himself but for his wife, whom Nathaniel was convinced he'd loved deeply and to whom he'd given his greatest allegiance.

Nathaniel's only regret was that Patience finally knew undeniably who and what her grandfather was. That's why Nathaniel had taken to rereading sections of the journal just before Patience did so he could anticipate her moods. He placed the journal on the coffee table, stretched, and decided it was time to wake up his princess, perhaps with a kiss.

Nathaniel padded into her bedroom in his socks so as not to startle her. But she was already awake.

"Are you okay?" he asked.

She shook her head. "It's in the past. It's all in the past, Nathaniel."

"Of course," he said, in an attempt to comfort her. "Patience, I think you were born too late, into the wrong time, even the wrong century."

Nathaniel had known the effect the journal passages would have on the woman he was growing to love. And there was no way to protect her from that. He'd wanted to rip the pages out of the journal because he knew the words would destroy her. But he could no sooner destroy those pages of history than rip apart the spine of a reference book. He would have given anything to spare Patience from the grief she experienced when she discovered the love she took for granted was an illusion.

In Nathaniel's mind, Patience was a miracle. *His* miracle. Had her grandfather ever really appreciated what he had in her?

Chapter 20

While Patience puttered around in the garden, Nathaniel decided it was time to open his grandmother's letter. The one he had promised on her deathbed to hand deliver to William Whitestone, along with the diamonds. Perhaps the answer to his and William's questions could be found there. William Whitestone was dead. Nathaniel's grandmother was dead. What could it matter now if he read the letter to finally discover what had passed between them? Nathaniel brought the crumpled envelope out of the pocket of his jeans and began reading.

To William Whitestone at Marigold House,

William, perhaps you will remember me. Maybe you have even thought of me since we last met. Or perhaps I flatter myself that you would even be interested in what happened to me after all these years. You certainly made quite an impression on me, one I'll never forget. If you're reading this, then I am no longer alive. But before I leave this earth, I want you to know that I owe you my life and the lives of my children and grandson. So I am writing to finally thank you properly. A mere letter must seem inadequate after all this time. But your offer of help at such a desperate time in my life meant everything.

When you returned to the hospital and found me missing, I cannot imagine what you must have thought and how you must have worried. But I think you knew who I was and that I had no choice but to leave. My life and the lives of my babies were in danger.

We once guarded each other's secrets although we were on opposite sides. I could have betrayed you with just one signal. You could have taken my life to save your own. Or you could have left me in the hotel room to die. For certainly our mutual "friend" would have killed me. Or I would have died in childbirth before he got there. But I saw something in you, something good. It was easy to recognize after I had been immersed in evil, literally sleeping with the devil. And that goodness caused you to respond to me when I needed you most.

I had the advantage of knowing what happened to you. It was easy to follow your career. You are a legend in Bermuda. You have done well in your life and done good with it. I hope you found some happiness along with your fame and fortune. It was with great sorrow that I read about the death of your daughter Gwyneth. I cannot even imagine how you must have felt. From the way you cared for my babies, I know you must have been a wonderful father.

I also know the great love story of William and Diana Whitestone. I was fortunate to find love with a wonderful man when I came to

America and settled in Virginia. But now I can admit, because I would never have had the courage to say it to your face, I was a little in love with you myself. Maybe it was the bond we forged when you delivered my children.

My daughter and my son were always restless and unhappy and never at peace. I think the twins might have had too much of their father in them. When my daughter abandoned her son, I raised him. My grandson, Nathaniel Morgan, was the real joy in my life. He has brought me so much happiness that all the rest was worth it. I hope your granddaughter has brought your life as much fulfillment as Nathaniel has brought to mine.

I know you will like Nathaniel, and I would like him to meet you. He is at loose ends right now, and I feel that his destiny lies in Bermuda.

So I have asked my grandson to deliver this letter and to return the diamonds you gave me, along with the trunk my son found containing your private papers. Having them helped me find my way through the darkest hours. I have hopes that Nathaniel will find his way, too.

I never knew what became of Nighthawk. That is still a great mystery. Maybe you know his whereabouts? I certainly have wished him in hell often enough, even though he was the father of my children. But there was never any love between us. Thank God he never found me after he left me there in that hotel room. I think he may have been in touch with my son. I fear that he was. Otherwise, why would my son have possession of your trunk with documents that could compromise you? I don't, for a minute, believe my son's story about how he came to find the trunk at the bottom of the Atlantic. I will go to my grave hating that man and hoping he never hurts Nathaniel.

I know what you must have thought of me, how my relationship with Nighthawk must have looked to you back then. But there was a purpose in everything I endured. I did what I had to do. I made my choices for my own reasons, hoping that some good would come out of it for the world.

So, my dear William—I hope I can take the liberty of calling you that, because that is how I think of you whenever I think of you, which is often. And I thank God you came to me when you did. You were the answer to my prayers.

> *Eternally, Gratefully Yours,*
> *Simone (My real name. I'll bet you never*
> > *knew. I reclaimed it when I came to*
> > *America.)*

So, his grandmother was the Yvette in William Whitestone's journal, a British spy and Nighthawk's mistress. It all began to make sense—the French lullabies, the secrecy surrounding his heritage, and now the proof in her own handwriting.

Would he share the letter with Patience?

Then she'd know his provenance was just as evil as

hers. He wasn't quite prepared to do that, not while there was still a threat against her.

She would banish him from her life and he couldn't protect her.

Chapter 21

Bermuda 2013

The blood of William Whitestone was on his hands. He could still feel it seeping out of the body of his enemy. He had tried to wash it off dozens of times, to remove all traces, but still it remained to haunt him.

The man called William Whitestone had cried clever tears and uttered words that had almost taken him in. He had looked at William Whitestone with contempt, prepared for the fear, but he was staggered by the love and understanding that shone back at him from the eyes of the nearly dead man. Whitestone had invoked the name of his wife and his child, but he had ignored his victim's pleas and shown no mercy. He had waited too long for revenge.

But the girl, Patience, had come home unexpectedly, and he'd had to finish it sooner, much sooner, than he had planned, or risk being caught.

Then the damn sea captain from America had sailed in on his strange pirate ship and threatened to ruin everything. What was his connection to Patience, and why did he have to show up here now? He'd have to be dealt with. They both would. And he was looking forward to it.

Chapter 22

When Nathaniel answered the door at Marigold House the next morning, Cecilia breezed in, pulling him into the foyer.

"Where's Patience?" she asked.

"Still asleep."

"Good. Because we need to talk."

"To you, anytime, sugar," he said, trying to get a rise out of her.

"Why, Cousin Nathaniel, are you flirting with me?" Cecilia purred.

"Do you want me to?"

"Under any other circumstances, you'd already be in my bed."

He raised one eyebrow.

"But I sense you are attracted to Patience. Would I be correct in that assumption?"

"What makes you think that?" he asked warily.

"Oh, I don't know. Maybe the way your eyes follow her whenever she enters a room and ache with longing when she leaves it."

"Am I that obvious?"

She smiled and nodded. "Whatever you're doing, you seem to be good for her. She's laughing and smiling again. You're helping her heal. But if I find you've hurt her, in any way, I'm going to have to boot your adorable buns back across the Atlantic. After I've skinned you alive. I'm just here to warn you to be careful with her." Cecilia had turned serious. "You strike me as a man who likes women, lots of women. Patience is special. She's in a very fragile state now, with the loss of her grandparents. I'm the only one looking out for her now. And I won't have anyone taking advantage of her vulnerability."

"What's wrong with her?" Nathaniel asked. "Has she always been so fragile?"

"It's called mourning," Cecilia said sarcastically. "She's had a lot of experience with it lately. So, yes, she is fragile, and she is breakable, and if you mess with her mind or anything else, you'll have to answer to me. It would be a mistake to underestimate her, though. Because she's a hell of a lot stronger than she looks right now. In fact, she's one of the strongest women I know, very anchored, very true, and extremely intelligent," Cecilia emphasized. "She can handle herself in most any situation. But when it comes to men… She's very romantic, old fashioned. She hasn't had much experience. She's a dreamer. And at the moment, she's all dreamy-eyed over you. I wouldn't want to see her dreams shattered."

"She's a beautiful woman. I'm sure she's had her share of men."

"Now, that's where your thinking is off course, sailor," Cecilia explained. "Patience doesn't have a vain bone in her body. I doubt she thinks of herself as attractive. But anyone can see what a great beauty she is, just like her grandmother was. And she carries herself like a princess. Most men don't get her. She's proper and refined, and that tends to put some guys off. I guess she told you she was raised by her grandparents, so she is a little old-fashioned. She's a rare and complicated woman. Certainly, many men would like to possess her. She's the best catch in Bermuda. She has looks and money on both her mother's and her father's side. Quite a lot of money, in fact." She stared at him suspiciously. "Are you after her money, *Cousin* Nathaniel?" Cecilia asked pointedly.

"I have enough of my own," he answered smoothly, not skipping a beat, but almost choking on the guilt. He *was*, after all, chasing her gold, or rather, her grandfather's gold.

"Well, then, what's your game? What are you really after? Because I'm not buying this cousin business."

"That's between Patience and me. Our business doesn't concern you."

"I'm making it my concern," she challenged.

"If men are lining up at her door, why haven't I seen any of these suitors?"

"Patience posted the *No Trespassing* sign herself. They're just respecting her wishes."

"If they really cared about her, they would know that the last thing she needs is to be alone right now," Nathaniel pointed out.

"Agreed. That's why she's lucky to have you here."

"When you said she hadn't had much experience…" He broached the subject tentatively.

"What are you asking me?"

"You know what I'm asking. Has she ever…been with a man?" He held his breath.

Cecilia eyed him carefully.

"That's getting rather personal. Are you sure you

shouldn't be asking Patience that question?"

"I'm asking you."

Cecilia hesitated only a moment, apparently deciding she could trust him.

"If you thought not, your instincts would be correct."

Nathaniel's stomach stopped pitching and settled before he focused on Cecilia.

"What about you? What's your story?"

Cecilia was only too happy to talk about herself.

"Patience and I couldn't be less alike in that department. I've been married three times."

"At your age?" He was incredulous. "What happened?"

"The first time I married too young. The second husband left me cold. He was not hot enough for my blood. The third husband was too hot. He left me for a younger woman."

"Have you given up on men, then?"

"Heavens, no! I'm like Goldilocks. I'm looking for a man that's not too hot and not too cold. I'm looking for *Mr. Just Right.*"

"What do you know about Patience's grandfather?" Nathaniel asked. "What kind of man was he?"

"He was devoted to Patience and her grandmother." Cecilia shrugged. "Loved them both to distraction. So much that he would have given his life for them. He cherished them. It was sweet, really."

"How did he make his living?"

"He was a private investor, I guess. At one time he owned half the land and businesses on the island or was connected to them in some way. He ran the telephone company and the power company. He was on the board at several banks. He didn't go to an office on a regular basis, not in recent years. He didn't have to. He conducted business out of Marigold House. He was an astute businessman. They say he had the Midas Touch. Everything he handled turned to gold."

"Interesting choice of words," Nathaniel commented. Nathaniel surmised that with the lines of credit available to William Whitestone through Swiss banks and the capital he had been provided to set himself up initially, he had probably amassed a fortune many times over, thanks to his own business savvy. He might not even have needed the untraceable shipments of gold to maintain his lavish lifestyle. But in Nathaniel's experience, it took money to make money. His solid gold foundation had given him an advantage.

"My parents said the Whitestones were devastated when they lost their daughter, Patience's mother," Cecilia continued. "Mr. Whitestone thought he should have been able to prevent the accident somehow. He was used to controlling everything. But after it happened, they never talked about it, like it hadn't occurred. In fact, they never told Patience she wasn't really their daughter until she was old enough to figure it out for herself. As far as Patience and the world were concerned, she was their daughter. They were as close as any parents and child could be. He spent most of his time and attention on Patience and Diana, and that's why his death and her grandmother's have left such a vacuum for Patience."

"Was he a kind man?"

Cecilia mulled that question over before answering.

"He had a dangerous edge to him," she acknowledged. "He was very cool, calculating, very controlling. He was overly protective, I guess, because Patience was his only child and a daughter. He hardly let her out of his sight. Either of them. He wouldn't even let Patience go away to school or travel. He had tutors brought in to supplement her education. She's never left the island. I always thought it was a bit unnatural. But Patience would never have questioned it or disobeyed her grandfather. She loved him. And she loves Bermuda. She says she never wants to leave. But was he kind?" Cecilia paused a moment. "He had a good heart, I think. Otherwise Patience would not have adored him so. She is a very good judge of character."

"Sometimes love can blind you to the truth," Nathaniel observed.

"Who's a very good judge of character?" Patience asked sweetly, as she sailed out of her bedroom clothed in a white terrycloth robe. With that tousled look and the sun shining just so on her yellow hair, Nathaniel thought she looked like an angel, a fallen angel. The thought had his blood boiling. He could gaze at that face forever. A good night's sleep had done wonders for her disposition. She wasn't the same girl who had looked like she wanted to murder him right there on the deck of his boat.

Cecilia planted a kiss on her friend's cheek. "Feeling better?" she asked solicitously.

"Much better, thank you. What brings you by so early?"

Cecilia glanced at her watch. "Honey, it's almost noon. You overslept, big time."

"She needed it," Nathaniel said irritably.

Cecilia looked at him and shook her head. Then she stood on her tiptoes and whispered into his ear,

"You're acting like a protective mother hen, Cousin Nathaniel. You have it bad, and you don't even know it. Well, good for you. I love it when a man suffers."

Nathaniel shot her a venomous look.

"What are you two whispering about?"

"The menu," Nathaniel said, ignoring Cecilia. "We were just discussing the menu. I've fixed us a traditional Sunday breakfast, Patience."

"My cousin is not only a sailor, he's an excellent chef," Patience pointed out.

"I aim to please," Nathaniel answered. "Now, come into the dining room. I've already set you a place."

Cecilia flashed Patience a knowing smile. "I guess my work here is done. I'll leave you two lovebirds alone."

"Cecilia!" Patience objected.

"Bye. I'll call you, and I'll let myself out."

Patience followed Nathaniel into the kitchen.

"You chased her away," she challenged.

"I didn't want her here," he said simply.

"What a spread!" she said, forgiving him as she looked around the kitchen, savored the smells, and lost her taste for argument.

"We have boiled salt cod, eggs, boiled Irish potatoes, and Bermuda onions, of course, with sliced bananas and avocados, and a sauce of onions and tomatoes," he listed.

"A traditional Bermuda Sunday codfish breakfast." She clapped her hands in delight.

Nathaniel beamed as his heart turned over. He was already in love with the woman. And he was wondering how it had happened so suddenly. He was just sailing through life when she surfaced and somehow reeled him in. He was caught in her net, and he only hoped she wouldn't throw him back.

But there was a very real barrier between them. Her grandfather's past and the gold. And, love or no love, he was determined to find the treasure he had come for. No woman was going to run him off course.

After breakfast, Nathaniel offered to clear the table and clean up the dishes, so Patience went into the parlor and picked up where she'd left off with her painting.

When he crept up behind her later, he thought he could watch her for hours. He had grown so used to watching her sleep, watching her read those history books of hers, and paint.

The small watercolor on the stand against the window caught Nathaniel's attention.

"Did you really paint that?" he asked with sincere interest, approaching the painting.

"Yes," she said proudly.

The scenic watercolor on the easel was brilliant. She had captured the mood and unique charm of the island. The play of light on the calm turquoise seas, dotted with sailboats and caressed by the curve of a pale-pink sandy beach; the pastels of the limestone cottages; the distinctive white-tiered stone-slate roofs ready to catch the rain water; and a graceful, snowy white, black-tipped Bermuda longtail in flight. The array of yellows, greens, blues, and pinks presented a calming effect that soothed his restless spirit and spoke to his lonely heart. He had to have it.

"It's wonderful," he said and meant it. She had signed it with her initials, PKW. "You make the scene come alive."

"It's the scene I see from my window. My little window on the world. I'm calling it *Sanctuary*."

"Yes," he observed, because he understood and felt the pull of the place too. Nothing had prepared him for his reaction to the watercolor or the woman who painted it. "You should really take up painting professionally."

"It's just a hobby," Patience dismissed, flustered. "An outlet. It helps me to relax, calms my nerves."

I'd like to buy this, if it's for sale," he said.

"You want to buy one of my watercolors?" Patience asked, a smile of pure delight spreading over her face. "That's the highest compliment anyone has ever paid me. But I don't sell my paintings. I could give it to you as a gift, since you like it so much."

Nathaniel seemed touched by her reaction and by her generosity.

"But I couldn't possibly take it away from you. You've put so much of yourself in it."

"How did you know?" she whispered. "I can paint another one. The scene has taken up residence in my head, and it doesn't seem to want to leave."

Later that night, his heart shifted when he saw the subject of her latest painting. She'd kept it hidden in her room behind a canvas cloth. But he was determined to unveil it and discover what she was hiding from him.

He came up behind her and placed a soft, wet kiss between the curve of her shoulder and the gentle slope of her neck. He was tempted to take a bite out of it. She turned, startled, and fixed him with those unwavering green eyes.

"I thought you were asleep," she said, attempting to throw the canvas cloth back over the painting.

"And you're supposed to *be* asleep," he chided, "but instead you're painting." He stopped her hand and threw back the cloth.

She was painting him, dressed like a swashbuckler, with his ship, the *Fair Winds*, in the background.

"What will you call this?" he wanted to know, riveted, as he stared at the painting.

"'Swept Away,'" she said, and blushed, turning her back to him to study the painting.

He moved his hands down her shoulders to her fingers, where their hands connected.

"It's me, isn't it?" Nathaniel whispered, trying hard to catch his breath.

"Yes. I can't help painting you. It was just an urge."

"Well, that's a very fortunate coincidence. Because I have an urge too. To do this."

He turned her around and kissed her until the paintbrush dropped out of her hand.

"Nathaniel," she said huskily. Her arms went around his neck in unrestrained passion, and he answered with a deeper kiss.

"Patience. I can't help myself when I'm around you. I want you. Please."

She held her hand to her forehead like she was in pain.

"Nathaniel. I don't think we... That is... I don't think it's smart for us to..."

"You feel it too, don't you? I know you do."

Shaken, she broke the connection.

"What I feel has to be tempered with what I think," she answered slowly. "And what I think is that you are deliberately trying to soften me up and wear me down.

That you're not interested in me at all but only in how I can help you get what you want. I'm just the shortest route to the gold."

He opened his mouth to speak.

"Don't bother lying to me. I can see it in your eyes. Don't worry. I'll help you, but it's only to clear my grandfather's name. To protect him and my family. And then you will leave and whatever we feel will be over between us. So it's better that we don't let it begin. Suddenly, I'm feeling very tired. I want to be alone now."

"I'm going to start digging tomorrow morning," Nathaniel announced. "I've studied the architectural drawings. I've decided to start in the garden."

Patience turned and fixed him with a frigid stare.

"If you pull up one flower in my grandmother's garden, I will have you arrested!"

"Patience," he pleaded. "Please be reasonable."

"It's all I have left of her!" she protested. "My grandfather wouldn't have buried anything in her garden. It was too important to her. And he knew that. But you wouldn't understand that kind of devotion. Now get out." When he had walked through her bedroom door, she locked it behind him.

****

Patience lay on the bed. Her head sagged back on the pillow and she wept. She heard Nathaniel hesitate at the door, then walk away.

Was she crazy? Nathaniel was a complete stranger who had barged into her home uninvited. A stranger who didn't seem to be in any hurry to leave. So why was she willing to share her precious paintings with him, to give away her heart?

Sometime later, she slept and dreamed.

She had come home from a morning shopping trip in town, and when she wandered with one of the grocery bags into her grandfather's study to show him a special treat she'd brought home for him, she'd found the blood on the rug. Dropping the bag she ran wildly around the house.

"Grandfather, Grandfather, oh God, Grandfather! Where are you?" She followed the trail of blood that led into the parlor, through the kitchen, and out to her grandmother's garden, where she saw her grandfather struggling to reach the moon gate.

The sun was beating down on him from high in the sky.

"Grandfather, you're bleeding! Have you been shot?"

"It's nothing."

"I'm calling 9-1-1," she said and had started to run inside when he called her back.

"No," he said. "No time."

"Who did this to you?" she screamed.

"It's not important. Your grandmother. Where's your grandmother?" She could barely hear him now, his voice had grown so faint. "Is she safe?"

Patience was confused. "Grandmother is in town at a meeting. She'll be home soon. I've got to call for an ambulance." She headed for the house.

"Don't leave."

"Grandfather," she cried, running to him, and held him against her, the thick, dark blood soaking through her yellow sundress.

"Diana," he whispered. "You're wearing your special dress for me." Now the lights in his eyes were fading, glazing over, and she could tell he had gone back in time and thought she was her grandmother.

"Under the moon gate, my love," he whispered and smiled.

How many times had she seen her grandparents dancing together, wrapped in each other's arms, swaying in the moonlight under the moon gate? The one he had built for her after their marriage. A replica of the moon gate at the Castle Harbour Hotel where they had kissed for the very first time.

Then his eyes grew dim, and he reached for her hand. Her hand turned cold in his.

"Sun, sun," he said, struggling to speak, so she did her best to shield his eyes from the glare.

"Please forgive me. Goodbye, *Liebchen*."

She screamed and pulled herself away to get to a phone.

By the time she'd returned from calling emergency services, he had crawled away and was lying face up, dead eyes staring into the sun, smiling, under the moon gate.

It was too soon. She needed more time with him.

Patience was crying in her sleep, and something was pounding in her head. The police, were they pounding at the door?

"Patience, Patience, open this door. Let me in. Let me in now or I'll break down the door." The pounding was getting louder, and suddenly Nathaniel was there and she was in his arms.

"Just a dream," he soothed, smoothing one hand rhythmically up and down her back and gently stroking her hair with the other. "You were having another bad dream. I'm here now, sweetheart."

Almost hypnotized by the motion and the soft words he murmured, Patience leaned closer into him.

"Under the moon gate. Under the moon gate," she sighed. "Kiss me."

And he did. Even though he knew she was half asleep, barely conscious. He kissed her, not just because he wanted to, but because he *had* to.

When she blinked, she looked up at him.

"The door. I locked the door."

"I broke it down," he smiled crookedly. "Sorry. I thought you needed me."

She did, she thought. She did. More than she wanted to admit.

"The blood," she said. "You'll need to clean up the blood, Nathaniel. There's so much of it."

"Blood? Are you hurt?" Anxiously examining every inch of her shaking body, he could find no blood.

"In the study. It's in the study. I can't go in there."

"It's the dream again. I was just in the study, and there's no blood there." He held her tighter in his arms. "What did you mean when you said 'under the moon gate'?" Nathaniel asked.

"The moon gate at the entrance to the garden. My grandfather built it for my grandmother right after their wedding. She planted the garden for him as a wedding present. He said it reminded him of home, of his past, but that the moon gate was also a symbol of his new home here in Bermuda and their future together."

Nathaniel was deep in thought. "Do you suppose, Patience, that he buried the gold under there? It makes sense."

"Under the moon gate? He'd never have buried anything there, because he'd never dig it up.

Desecrating it would be sacrilegious to him. That was their sacred spot. He died there, crawled there so he could be closer to her in the end."

"Yes, but you said he didn't finish it until after they were married. Maybe he meant to bury something there and cover it over."

"But why would he bury it in a place he would never access?" she said, puzzled.

Patience bit her lower lip and twisted her nightgown. Then she broke into a smile. "Nathaniel, what if it is true what you said? What if he did bury the gold under the moon gate? He'd never have dug that up. So that would mean he never intended to use it. And we know the move against Bermuda was never actually made by the Nazis. Maybe he left it there because he changed his mind about what to do with it."

She was desperate, he knew, to believe the best about her grandfather.

"Maybe. Maybe it happened just that way," he said. "But if we're ever to find out, we're going to have to do some digging ourselves. So get some sleep. We have a big day ahead of us tomorrow. You'll have to bundle up. Even though it's warm outside, you always get so cold. You don't have enough meat on your bones. I'll make you breakfast in the morning, and then we'll get started."

"I'm not going to help you dig under the moon gate." She frowned.

"I don't expect you to," he countered. "You're a featherweight. The shovel probably weighs more than you do. You're going to settle yourself into a nice comfortable lounge chair, under a warm blanket, with a nice thick history book or a racy romance, and watch me dig."

"You make me sound like a frail little old lady," she pouted. "I'm not a featherweight. I'm stronger than I look. But I'm not going to help you nail the lid on my grandfather's coffin or sully my family's reputation."

"That was never my intention," Nathaniel objected, and, trying to get her mind off more serious matters, he added, "But I *could* knock you over with a feather."

He picked her up and whirled her around the bedroom. "That book you're reading weighs more than you. Featherweight, featherweight."

She beat her fists against his chest.

"Take that back."

"Featherweight," he teased, tossing her onto the bed. Then they took one look at each other and moved together.

"Oh, Patience," he sighed, and kissed her as she came into his arms.

"Nathaniel."

He gave her a deep kiss, and she brought her arms around his neck.

"Hold me, just hold me," she murmured.

"You're scared, aren't you? Of what we might find."

"Yes. A little. Although I don't really think we'll find anything." *And if you find the gold, after you find it, you'll leave. I'm scared of that most of all.*

He rubbed his lips against hers and nuzzled his face in her neck.

"Whatever we find, Patience, I won't let it hurt you. I would never hurt you."

If you leave me, that will hurt me.

"And what about my family?"

211

"They're a part of you," he whispered.

Nathaniel brought his hand up to her face and stroked her cheek. "Patience, about what's happening between us—"

"I've already forgotten it," she said, as she turned away so she wouldn't have to face the hurt and confusion in his eyes.

Chapter 23

The next day dawned bright and beautiful. Today was going to be the day, Nathaniel thought, if his luck held. The weather portended excellent prospects. Part of him didn't want to find the gold. But his reluctance wasn't going to stop him.

After Patience came out of her bedroom, wearing shorts and a body-molding T-shirt, Nathaniel fixed some tea and baked some biscuits. He broke apart one fluffy biscuit, smothered it in marmalade, and fed it to her.

"I could get used to this, sailor." She laughed, and he realized she'd been doing more and more of that lately. He hoped it was because she felt good, natural, with him and had begun to trust him and stop suspecting him. He had come here for the gold. That hadn't changed, but somewhere along the way perhaps she had captured a piece of his heart. He hoped the reverse was true, as well.

"And I could get used to you, in those shorts," he said, raising an eyebrow and looking at her appraisingly, "and that T-shirt."

"You like the way I look?" She smiled.

"More and more each day," he replied softly.

After breakfast, they were headed outside when the doorbell rang.

"Damn," Nathaniel fussed. "Who the hell could

that be? We can't afford to be disturbed. Whoever it is, send them away."

"Calm down, Nathaniel. It's probably just some delivery person with more food or a condolence note."

Nathaniel listened, even peeked around the corner as Patience answered the door. Standing before her was a tall, lanky man, attractive with his curly blond hair, dreamy blue eyes, and poet's face. He had the look of a Greek god—Apollo incarnate in a banker's suit.

"Patience Whitestone?" he queried.

"Yes, that's me. May I help you?"

"No, but I hope I can help you," he said, bringing from behind his back a magnificent arrangement of yellow roses and presenting it to her. "Guaranteed to lift your spirits."

"Yellow roses!" she gushed. "My favorite! Are they for me?"

"Of course." His smile revealed perfect teeth.

"Yellow roses are so hard to get in Bermuda, especially this time of year. Who sent them? Is there a note with the arrangement? Let me get you something for your trouble."

"Oh, no. I think you misunderstood. I'm not the delivery boy. And there's no note. I'm delivering them in person. They're from me."

"Do I know you?" she asked, puzzled, trying unsuccessfully to place him.

"Not exactly, but your grandmother did."

"My grandmother?" Her shock was evident. "But my grandmother is…"

"If you will just invite me in, I'll explain."

"Of course." She was obviously flustered but thought this man was no threat as she ushered him in and closed the door behind him.

"Let me just get a vase to put these in. They're lovely. I'll be right back."

Holding the mammoth arrangement in front of her, her view was blocked, and she collided with Nathaniel.

"What the hell are those?" Nathaniel demanded.

"Yellow roses."

"I can see that, but who sent them?" Nathaniel allowed suspicion to fill his words.

"A friend of my grandmother's."

"And does this friend have a name?"

"I…well…I didn't think to ask."

"You didn't think to ask?" he repeated. "Where is this person now?"

"He's sitting in the drawing room."

"Really." He fixed her with a glare. "And are you in the habit of letting strangers into your home?"

"I let *you* in, didn't I?" she replied sweetly.

"You think that's funny?"

"Yes," she said, her eyes twinkling.

"I don't think it's funny when you let a stranger in the house, a stranger who might be connected with our stalker or may be the stalker himself," Nathaniel fumed.

"Oh, I hadn't considered that. He looks harmless."

"You hadn't considered… No, of course not. Now I will have to deal with him."

"Nathaniel, lower your voice. He'll hear us. You're being rude. He's just given me roses. No one has ever given me flowers, except Grandfather. I need to get them into water." Her voice nearly broke, and he thought he detected a tear in her eye.

Damn it all! Why hadn't he thought of giving her flowers? Women loved flowers. And there was a whole garden of them right outside the door. The least he could have done was pick one of them for her. Imagine that. No one had ever given her flowers before.

Nathaniel strode into the drawing room, spoiling for a fight.

The man he was ready to do battle with stood up from the couch.

"Who are you?" Nathaniel demanded, sweeping the man with a glance. Damn, the man was...*pretty*. That was the only word for it. He had the kind of dreamy looks women swooned over.

"Allow me to introduce myself," he said, offering a hand that Nathaniel refused to shake. "I'm Hamilton Farnsworth, from London."

"What are you doing here?" Nathaniel asked gruffly.

"I'm here to call on Patience," he answered, unflustered.

"Why?"

"I'd rather discuss it with Patience. It's a private matter."

"Private?" Nathaniel was steaming. "I'm her cousin, and you can discuss it with me."

"Nathaniel!" Patience protested, sailing into the room with the vase of flowers. "Get away from my guest and try to control yourself."

"I'm perfectly in control of myself. I was just about to show this man to the door."

"Just take a seat and let me handle this."

Nathaniel grumbled as Patience placed the flower arrangement on the sideboard.

"Allow me to introduce myself, *again*," the man said pointedly, turning on his charm as he reached for

Patience's hand. "I'm Hamilton Farnsworth of the London Farnsworths."

She held out her hand, and he kissed it. Patience blushed.

"You're even more beautiful than your grandmother led me to believe."

Nathaniel sat down on the couch, slouched, and rolled his eyes. *This guy is a major bullshit artist.*

"How did you know my grandmother?"

"We corresponded for a time, and then she invited me for a visit. But by the time I could get here she had already passed away."

A cloud of sadness passed over Patience's face.

"What was your business with my grandmother?" she asked.

"You," he stated simply.

"Me?" she asked, confused.

"We corresponded about you. Didn't she tell you about me?"

"No. I don't understand."

"I knew this was going to be difficult," the man said. "You see, your grandmother intended that we…I mean… How shall I put this delicately…"

"Just spit it out," Nathaniel growled from his place on the couch. "We don't have all day."

"Nathaniel, please!" Patience pleaded. "Behave yourself."

Nathaniel crossed his arms and glared at Hamilton.

"I think she had in mind some sort of arrangement," he began.

"An arrangement? What sort of arrangement?"

"A flower arrangement, obviously," Nathaniel sputtered.

"You're such a juvenile," Patience said.

"An arrangement of a more permanent nature," Hamilton said, interrupting their sparring.

"You'll have to speak plainly," Patience said. "I don't understand what you're trying to say."

"You see?" Nathaniel barked. "That's what I was trying to tell him. Speed it up. We're not getting any younger."

Patience shrugged at Nathaniel and turned back toward Hamilton Farnsworth.

"Kindly get to the point, Mr. Farnsworth, if you have one."

"That is exactly the point, Miss Whitestone. We're not getting any younger. Your grandmother realized that, and she…hand-picked me for you."

"She hand-picked you? You mean like you would pick a flower in a garden?" Patience was still trying to comprehend his meaning. This man was making no sense to her.

"No, Miss Whitestone, Patience. You see, your grandmother knew she was dying, and my grandmother, Lady Carolyn Farnsworth, was a longtime family friend, and your grandmother was deathly afraid of leaving you alone. She wanted someone to care for you when she was gone. So she sent me your picture and wrote me about you and arranged for us to be, I mean…"

Nathaniel began howling with laughter. "I don't believe this!"

Patience looked at Hamilton and back at Nathaniel in confusion.

"Will someone please tell me what's going on here?"

"For God's sake, Patience," Nathaniel said. "You don't get it, do you? Let me translate. Your grandmother arranged a match for you. She intended for you to marry this man. It's a done deal. Signed, sealed, and delivered. She bought him for you, lock, stock, and barrel. Your gentleman caller is a suitor, isn't that right, Farnsworth?"

Patience was rendered speechless for a moment.

"You can't be serious," she stammered. "An arranged marriage? Is this true, Hamilton?"

A whoosh of air escaped from Hamilton's lungs. "Precisely. But I assure you, no money changed hands."

Patience took a step back. "This was what Grandmother meant when she predicted someone would come for me? Not serendipity? She decided to give fate a helping hand, did she? Well, I don't need any handouts. I'm not a charity case, so I don't know what to say."

"Say yes," Hamilton said, hopefully.

"Are you crazy?" Patience spit.

"Crazy about you," Hamilton said. "I know this is a bit unorthodox. But when I saw your picture and read your grandmother's letters, heard the way she described you, I thought you were an angel. Now that I have seen you, I know she wasn't exaggerating. Your picture doesn't do you justice. Patience, do you believe in love at first sight?"

Her response came with a touch of impatience. "Well, yes, I mean, it happened that way for my grandparents."

"Patience, can't you see he's a fortune hunter?" Nathaniel objected.

"I am most assuredly not a fortune hunter. I am

very wealthy in my own right. In fact, I'm in line for a title. I am looking for a wife, more precisely, a wife who can produce an heir. And you need a husband. We're both alone. Your grandmother thought we would have a lot in common. She simply reasoned that if she put you in my path, events would proceed according to plan."

"According to whose plan?" Sarcasm hardly suited Patience.

"Did I mention that I have excellent references? My credentials are impeccable. Would you like to see them?"

"Do you have a bank statement?" Nathaniel posed seriously, eyes narrowing.

"As a matter of fact, I do. I brought my entire portfolio."

"I don't believe this is happening," Patience muttered.

Nathaniel choked and tried his best not to laugh. He thought this man seemed familiar. He was a male version of Patience, a clone. They looked alike, both with the same blond, angelic features. They talked alike. They were both dreamers, both prim and proper. Her grandmother was exactly right. They did have a lot in common. And the man she had selected for Patience was exactly the *wrong* man for her. How did he know this? Because *he* was the right man, the *only* man, for her. He would just have to convince her of that.

He noticed Hamilton trying his best not to leer at Patience's legs and failing miserably.

"Patience, go and change into something less— revealing," Nathaniel ordered.

"You liked what I was wearing a few minutes

ago."

"Well, I changed my mind. Go cover yourself with something more respectable-looking."

"You're nuts, Nathaniel Morgan. I'm perfectly comfortable in these clothes. They're entirely appropriate for working in the garden."

"Uh, Patience," Hamilton interrupted, trying to get her attention.

"Are you still here?" Nathaniel remarked.

"Yes, and I'm going to stay here until I claim the woman I am going to marry."

Patience turned on him. "I can't believe my grandmother thought she had to find a man for me. I'm perfectly capable of finding a man on my own, if I want one. As a matter of fact, I have a perfectly fine man living right here in my house."

Hamilton's eyes bulged.

"For heaven's sake, Patience, this man is your cousin! He's hardly suitable. Have you looked at the man? He's a bloody pirate, for God's sake, and a rather hairy one, at that. I think what your grandmother had in mind was a gentleman, someone refined, with the right sensibilities."

"What's wrong with my sensibilities?" Nathaniel demanded with a mock-injured look.

"You're missing the point. This was your grandmother's dying wish. She only wanted your happiness. I've even written a poem to you. I call it 'Ode to My Beloved.'"

Nathaniel could see that Patience was about to fold. She was a sucker for romance. "I'm sure we don't want to hear it," he piped in.

"Mr. Farnsworth, Hamilton, this really isn't a good

time," Patience said. "I'm sorry for the misunderstanding. And I'm sorry you had to travel all this way for nothing. I know my grandmother meant well, and I know your intentions are honorable. This just comes as a shock. I'll need some time to process it."

"I completely understand," Hamilton conceded.

"Maybe you should come back later," Patience suggested. How long will you be in Bermuda?"

"I'm here for as long as it takes. I'm prepared to wait. I waited for what I thought was a respectable period of time before I approached you, in consideration of your feelings. I see it is too soon. Once you get to know me, I'm sure you'll find us quite compatible in *every* way."

Nathaniel bristled at the less than subtle message.

"I'm sure," Patience said mildly, blushing.

"And you're going to love London," Hamilton assured her. "Your grandmother especially wanted you to see England. She said you'd never been off the island."

"England?"

"Well, yes. That is where we'd be living. That's my ancestral home."

"And Bermuda is my home," she reminded him. "I'm perfectly content here."

"Sounds like a dealbreaker to me, Ham," Nathaniel interjected, a grin pushing at the corners of his mouth.

"We couldn't possibly live here," Hamilton protested. "Bermuda is so—remote."

Patience sighed, and Nathaniel beamed.

"Hamilton, this whole notion is utterly ridiculous. I think you're getting ahead of yourself. I'm not going anywhere with you, now or ever."

"If she wants to go to England, she can call a travel agent," Nathaniel said smoothly, tasting victory. "Or I could take her. Patience, why don't you meet me in the garden? I will help Mr. Farnsworth find the door."

"But Patience, we have a lot to discuss," Hamilton pleaded. "Our marriage, all of our plans…"

"It was lovely to meet you, Hamilton, and the flowers are beautiful, really," said Patience as she backed out of the room into the kitchen. "Thank you. We'll talk later…much later."

"You heard the lady," Nathaniel said, hustling Hamilton to the front door. "It's time for you to go."

"Now see here," Hamilton said angrily. "Patience needs me."

"No, you see here," Nathaniel growled, grabbing Hamilton's suit jacket by the lapels. "You don't know a thing about what Patience needs."

"I resent that."

"You can resent it all you want—on the other side of the door," Nathaniel said, releasing the man. "I'll bet you don't even sail."

"Well, no, I…I have chartered a yacht before."

"Let me guess. Golf is your game."

"Yes, how did you know?"

"Just lucky. Now you listen to me. You can't have Patience."

"Why not? Who's going to stop me?"

"I am," replied Nathaniel, fixing Hamilton with his most menacing glare. "How's your swing?"

Hamilton looked puzzled. "My golf swing?"

"I'm going to start practicing mine in about ten seconds if you're not gone," Nathaniel challenged, pounding the knuckle of one hand into the palm of his other.

The man looked unsteady on his feet. "Perhaps I should come back when emotions aren't running so high."

"I think that would be a smart idea," Nathaniel said, slamming the door shut right after adding, "Better yet, don't come back at all."

Who does the man think he is, barging in like that, trying to steal my girl? His girl? Did he just call Patience his girl? But that's how he thought of her. He was beginning to feel comfortable in this home, in his surroundings, with this woman. She would fit perfectly in his home at Fair Winds. He could almost imagine her there.

When he walked down the back steps to the garden, Patience was beaming.

"What are you looking so smug for?"

"You were jealous," Patience said.

"Of Lord Byron?"

"Of Hamilton Farnsworth."

"Even his name sounds pompous. He wasn't right for you, and you know it. He's just a boy. You need a man. We could always introduce him to Cecilia. He wouldn't last one round with her."

"He brought me flowers," Patience said simply. "And he composed a poem for me."

"You want flowers?" Nathaniel said. "Look around you, you have a garden full of them."

"Yes, but he *brought* them to me, *for* me. It's different."

Resigned, Nathaniel turned away to roam the gardens. He stopped when he noticed a single yellow bloom standing in a carpet of green. It was delicate, graceful, glorious, just like Patience. Its aroma invaded his senses; the smell overwhelmed him like her fragrance. The blossom's vivid color was the shade of the sun, but it didn't come close to matching the luster in Patience's hair. He bent down to pick it.

"Here," he said, thrusting it toward her unceremoniously, almost knocking her over. He didn't have the flowery words. "I draw the line at poetry."

"Thank you," she said as tears glistened in her eyes.

"Damn it, Patience, if I had known how much you would get off on a simple flower, I would have picked one for you sooner." It didn't take much to make her happy—or not, he thought as he noticed the tears starting to flow.

He looked alarmed. "If you don't stop, your tears are going to flood the ocean," Nathaniel pleaded. "No more tears, please. It's just a flower. What's wrong? What did I do?"

"I don't know," she sniffed. "It's not you. It's everything. It's my grandmother thinking she could organize my life from the grave, that she had to find someone to take care of me. Thinking that no one would want me, that I could never find someone on my own."

"You found me, now, didn't you?" Nathaniel said gently, as he pulled her into his arms, holding her close. "We found each other." She deserved special treatment, he thought. She deserved a title. But not if it meant taking Hamilton Farnsworth in the bargain. In fact, the thought of Lord Byron's hands on Patience, his mouth claiming hers, was suddenly very disturbing.

After a while Nathaniel kissed the tip of her nose possessively and released her.

"Why don't we start digging?" he suggested.

"I think there might be some shovels in the garden shed," Patience said, leading the way. They discovered several large shovels there, and Patience handed the most sturdy one to Nathaniel. She removed her grandmother's gardening tools from the shelf.

"I'll watch, but I will not participate," she said. "I'm going to weed the garden."

"That's fair."

He worked half the morning, sweating profusely, shoveling dirt, trying to dig around flowerbeds while he was digging up her family secrets.

She sat close by, pulling weeds, adding nutrients to the soil, lovingly tending the garden while she watched Nathaniel out of the corner of her eye. She remembered her grandmother's firm hands on her little ones when she was small, helping her pat the soil, plant the seeds, and nurture new life in her favorite place. She had lavished the same special attention on her family. Patience and her grandparents were close. They found everything they needed on the island with each other. She wanted to feel that closeness, that true happiness, again and was afraid she would never find it. She felt her grandmother's presence most in the garden. She could feel herself regaining strength among these living things. For the past week she had existed in a ghost world, summoning up fleeting shadows of the past.

She wanted to turn toward life, toward Nathaniel. He could be controlling, demanding, even arrogant, and he posed a very definite threat, but she wasn't intimidated. Instead, she was drawn to him. Her head told her to be cautious, but her heart was painting a different picture. She was responding to his kindness, the way he seemed to care for her and sense her every mood, meet her every need. She was falling in love with him. It was happening so fast. But hadn't it happened exactly that way for her grandparents? The way her grandfather told the story, it had taken only one look and he belonged to Diana forever. They were engaged within a week. But that was the 1940s, and there was a war on. Naturally, events proceeded at an accelerated pace.

When she found herself staring into Nathaniel's eyes and caught him staring back, she wished she could divine his thoughts. Her fingers longed to touch his face, a pirate's face. She wanted to touch his lips with her own, feel him against her. It was a strange but oddly exciting feeling. She had never felt that way about a man before.

"I could use something to drink," Nathaniel hinted, wiping his sweating brow and interrupting her daydreams.

"All right. I'll fix us some lemonade."

"I imagine you're really thirsty after the tough morning you've put in playing in the garden and haranguing me."

"I try to do my part." Patience smiled. "I told you there was no gold here. All those lies you fabricated about my grandfather are just that, lies."

"I didn't fabricate the journal, did I?"

Patience stomped up the steps to the kitchen.

When she came back thirty minutes later with a snack for the two of them, she was more composed. The sun was shining, and she planned to enjoy what was left of this glorious day. If Nathaniel wanted to dig around in the dirt like a schoolboy, let him. She was going for a swim in the pool.

She had put on the flimsiest excuse for a bathing suit she could find, one Cecilia had brought for her the last time they'd been swimming. Nothing was left to the imagination. She filled out the skimpy black bikini like a dream, she knew—she'd checked in the full-length mirror. Thanks, Cecilia. Was she borrowing trouble, Cecelia style?

Nathaniel was hot, sweaty, and thirsty. And not for lemonade, she saw when he looked at her. He wiped his brow and lifted off his T-shirt.

Patience tried not to focus on Nathaniel's nearly naked body and the beads of sweat gathering on his broadly muscled shoulders and hairy chest and dripping down to his fit waist. He had tied his long dark hair back out of his face. A face, she noticed, that was focused intently on her, like a fearless hunter stalking its helpless quarry.

"You know, pirates have always had a longing eye for these islands," Nathaniel said suggestively, as his eyes roamed the length of her body.

His reference to the speech by one of Bermuda's earliest governors, Nathaniel Butler, didn't escape Patience, and she picked up on his challenge by responding in Butler's own words.

"Let us, therefore, so provide for ourselves, that come an enemy…we may be able to give him a brave welcome."

Nathaniel continued to fix her with a sultry stare.

"Maybe you should start building some forts to protect your…coastline," he said provocatively, alluding to Butler's words again.

"I'm not afraid," Patience whispered warily, chewing on her bottom lip.

"Maybe you should be. I haven't decided what to do about you yet." His blue eyes twinkled, then bore into hers as he inched closer and reached out over the tray she held to take her chin with his fingertips.

"You have roving hands," Patience said, unnerved and angry, trying to back away from him. He refused to release her.

"You mean for a pirate?" He laughed again.

"For a person who pretends to have manners," Patience said.

"I don't pretend anything," he replied.

Patience placed the tray with drinks and sandwiches on the stone table nearby and turned, still dangerously close to Nathaniel. He reached out for her, and she slipped away from his groping hands and into the heated pool, looking over her shoulder to make sure she had achieved the desired effect.

"What are you wearing?" Nathaniel called out to her.

"It's called a bathing suit," Patience replied.

"Is it new?"

"No, I've had it for a while. Why do you ask?"

"You forgot to cut off the price tag," he drawled, and she frowned, felt around for the tag, found it, and tried to tuck it into the scant material. "And it doesn't look like something out of your closet."

"How would you know? Have you been snooping around in my closet?"

"I don't need to snoop around your closet to know that's not your style."

"Maybe you don't know me as well as you think you do."

"Where did you get it?" Nathaniel demanded.

"I'm sure it must have come from one of the shops in town," she said demurely.

"I was right. You didn't pick it out yourself."

"It was a gift," Patience admitted.

"Who was the gift from?" Nathaniel asked evenly.

"Cecilia," Patience said, pouting.

"Why am I not surprised? That suit should come with a warning—dangerous when wet. Or dangerous swells."

"Don't you like it?"

"I didn't say that."

"You don't think it looks good on me?"

"It would look better off you," he said dryly.

Patience laughed. "Why don't you stop digging in the dirt and come join me?"

"You're trying to distract me. You just want me to stop digging, don't you?"

"That thought had occurred to me. Is it working?"

"Do you really think you can tempt me to give up on my goal?"

"I can try," she said with a grin.

"You look like a damn mermaid…or a siren," he muttered. He took several long swallows of lemonade and pressed the icy glass against his brow. "You really want me to come in there after you?" he drawled dangerously.

She wet her lips with her tongue and stretched suggestively in the water. "Suit yourself," she said.

"I don't have a suit," he said, skewering her with his eyes as he slowly stripped off his shorts and his briefs, "but I *am* coming in after you."

She shrieked. "Nathaniel, you're naked. Don't you dare come near me!" Nathaniel was grinning like a schoolboy. "What is it? Why are you looking at me that way?"

The next thing she heard was a splash, and she dove under the water to escape. He raced around the pool after her, and for a few seconds she managed to dodge him and stay just a length ahead. Her heart was racing and her adrenaline pumping.

Then she made the mistake of looking back and saw that he was almost on top of her. Alarmed, she flipped and tried to speed away, but he caught her by the heel and slowly reeled her in, inch by inch, foot by foot, leg by leg, until he'd reached her waist and had her pressed so firmly against him she could barely breathe.

Trapped in his arms, Patience was never so aware of the masculine feel of Nathaniel's body, the hardness of him, pulsing through the warm water of the heated pool.

"You're as slippery as an eel, Patience, but it seems I've found your Achilles heel," Nathaniel said smoothly, scooping her up easily so her bottom was balanced snugly on his palms. He was tall enough to stand in the water; she wasn't.

"I thought you didn't like sports," she said nervously, trying not to focus on the fact that she was in the pool with a naked man.

"I said I didn't like golf. I was captain of my swim team in college."

He brought his lips tantalizingly close to hers.

"You want me to let you go?" he said quietly.

She didn't answer.

"I didn't think so." His lips began to taste hers, and she moved restlessly in his arms.

"One of us is wearing too many clothes," he said in a husky voice, as he lifted her bathing suit top over her head and sent it flying onto the pool deck. He palmed her breast and rubbed his thumb over her nipple till it hardened, then replaced the thumb with his tongue.

"Nathaniel," she sighed. "I can't, we can't…"

"Yes," he answered firmly. "We can. And now the bottoms," he whispered against her breast. He started to slide the fabric off, and as she became agitated, he stroked her slowly, gently, with his fingers until she quieted, whimpering.

Panting, she felt herself responding to his raw need, to this new sensation.

"Kiss me, Patience," he whispered, his breath ragged.

She wound her arms around his neck and tested his lips, then dove into him as he plied her with drugging kisses, until she felt weightless in the water and breathless in surrender.

He teased her tongue and ravished her mouth, dragging her into an undertow.

"Feel me, Patience," he groaned. "Can you feel how much I want you?" She was frozen, motionless. And then his body began to shift.

"Now wrap your legs around me," he instructed, as he lifted her from the waist, and positioned her, "like this. Please, now. Let me in, please, my sweet Patience."

She could feel him moving urgently against her, and she panicked.

"Nathaniel," she gasped, struggling as she pleaded, "No, not like this. Not here."

"Ssh, we're all alone, it's just the two of us," he said crushing his mouth to hers again. "It will be okay. There's nothing to be afraid of. Trust me."

"I can't do this. I don't understand what's happening to me, Nathaniel, this is my first…I want—"

"I know what you want," he said insistently. "I want the same thing."

****

Suddenly it dawned on him what she was trying to tell him. This was the first time for her, and he had practically attacked her in her own swimming pool. Hadn't Cecilia tried to tell him? She was expecting this to be a romantic experience, and he was acting like a dog in heat that couldn't control his hormones or his urge to rut. No wonder she was so frightened. Could he have been any less sensitive? He should have taken more care with her.

Apologizing, he held her body away from his, and she tried to cover herself, but that only embarrassed her more because she wasn't wearing any clothes. Why? Because, he had stripped them off her like a horny teenager.

"Please forgive me, Patience. I don't know what came over me. I just wanted you, and I acted, well, like a jerk. I'm sorry." He wanted to kiss her, hold her, give her some comfort, but he was afraid that would make things worse.

"Your clothes… I'm so sorry. Let me get them." He deposited her at the shallow end of the pool and fished her bathing suit bottom from the water. The wet tag had practically disintegrated. Then he hoisted himself out of the pool and found the top of the bikini, which he also returned to her. He found her towel and stood sheepishly at the edge of the pool.

"You can come out now. I promise I won't look." He laid the towel where she could grab it and turned his face away. She emerged from the pool, wrapped the towel around herself, and walked up to him.

"It's not your fault, Nathaniel. I wanted to. It's just that—"

"You don't have to say anything," Nathaniel assured her. "I understand. I do. I want it to be...special...the first time, you know, for you, when you're ready."

She breathed a sigh of relief and, dripping, walked back into the house.

Nathaniel walked back to the moon gate, gathered up the rest of his clothes and put them on, and started digging with a vengeance to release some of his pent-up energy. He stayed out there for hours, mostly because he was afraid to go back into the house and face her.

At one point his shovel hit something hard, a metal container of some kind, and he wiped away the dirt. He was sure this was only the first container. Judging from the number of kilograms listed on the receipt, the whole backyard was probably filled with containers of gold bars and coins. He had done the calculations. In the 1930s and 1940s, the value of one ounce of gold ranged anywhere from $20 to $37, about $14,000 for a full bar. Today's price for a standard bar of gold was $640,000. If all the gold was accounted for, at current market prices he estimated he was standing on tens of millions of dollars.

"Well, the first thing you know, old Nate's a

millionaire," Nathaniel sang, hijacking the opening tune of *The Beverly Hillbillies*. He was just plain giddy. Maybe it was all that digging, or overexposure to the sun.

He lifted one of the bars in his palm, moved it from hand to hand. It was standard Swiss issue, untraceable, sanitized as only the Swiss could do. The exact purity and weight was stamped and sealed on each gold bar— 24-karat gold purity, weighing 400 ounces.

Nathaniel liked the substantial feel of it, the hypnotic shine of it. This was what he had come for, what had drawn him here in the first place.

But then he thought of Patience. What he had originally considered a liability now turned out to be an unexpected bonus. But would she still want to have anything to do with him after the incident in the pool and after he confronted her with the evidence of her grandfather's duplicity? There was a reason she had turned away from him. How could she trust him after what he was trying to do to her family?

He walked into the house and called out her name.

"Patience, where are you?"

She had obviously been painting feverishly. She had showered and dried her hair, but there were streaks of watercolor all over her face, similar to the way she looked when he had first seen her.

He tentatively rubbed the watercolor off her cheeks with his thumb.

"It's okay if you touch me," Patience said. "I won't break."

"You were painting again."

"Yes, I told you, it helps soothe my nerves."

"Will it do any good if I beg your forgiveness?"

"You did nothing you have to be forgiven for. You acted on your emotions. I seem to have trouble acting on mine."

"No, Patience, that's not true. I just came on too strong."

"Maybe that's what I need," she reasoned. "I feel like a complete fool. I wanted to be with you. I don't understand it."

"Don't start second-guessing yourself. You'll know when you're ready. When the time is right."

"I'm twenty-seven. You must think I'm a—"

"What I think is that you're a beautiful, sensitive, caring person who acts on her instincts and trusts herself to know her own mind. I can be very patient. You're worth waiting for."

"Thank you, Nathaniel," she said. "For making it so easy for me. What are you hiding behind your back?"

"Nothing," he lied.

"You are. You're hiding something, and I want to know what it is. You were out there a long time. Did you find something?"

When he didn't answer, she tried to grab for the object he was shielding, but he transferred it to his other hand.

"What is it?" she insisted.

"I think we've struck gold, mate," he announced proudly, unable to help himself. He brought the heavy bar out from behind his back and presented it to Patience.

"Oh," she said, deflated. "Oh." She held it in her hands. "It's real, then." He knew she was trying to accept what that meant—that everything else was real too. The journal. Her grandfather's lies. Emilie. Her identity.

"Maybe it's just one bar," she ventured.

"Patience, this is just the tip of the iceberg. It's going to take a hell of a long time to unearth it all. We're going to need some heavier equipment."

"You can't be serious."

"Of course I am. You don't think I'm just going to leave it buried here?"

"It's not ours. It doesn't belong to us."

"Yeah, it belongs to a nonexistent government, the Third Reich. They're buried even deeper than this gold. And odds are they probably stole it from the treasuries of some of the countries they occupied. To the victor belong the spoils. Finders keepers. Those are the rules of the game in a salvage operation. Patience, this is what I came for. Half of this is yours, you know."

"Is that what you think of this as? A salvage operation? I don't want the money. You take it. Just get it out of here. I'm going to lie down."

"Patience," he called after her and placed the bar of gold on the coffee table, where it lay shining like a gulf between them.

"Don't walk away from me," he pleaded. Was she insane? Turning her back on a fortune? But he realized what finding the treasure meant to her. A confirmation of her worst nightmares. He seemed to be making a habit of being insensitive today.

He caught up to her before she reached the bedroom.

"You're filthy and you're sweaty," Patience admonished. "Don't come into my bedroom before you wash up."

"You're going to hear what I have to say," he said, taking hold of her hand, more roughly than he had intended. But he had to make her see reason.

"Patience, I'm sorry. It was inconsiderate of me to be so…happy. Just because we found the gold, it doesn't mean…I mean… He was still your grandfather. You loved him. I get that. But that's no reason to turn your back on this. Be practical."

"Oh, I'm nothing if not practical," she said, turning away and trying to close her bedroom door. The lock was still broken from when he had kicked in the door.

He held the door open, but something about the way she looked at him, disappointed, devastated, held him back. He didn't have the heart to burst her illusions.

"I'll take a shower and then we'll talk," he conceded. "This conversation isn't over." He walked away.

****

When Nathaniel was clean again, he approached her bedroom. She was lying on the bed, arms folded stubbornly, face blank, but she wasn't asleep.

"I was thinking," Nathaniel began. "I'll bet that when we finish digging we'll find all the gold accounted for. Do you know what that means, Patience? It very well could mean that your grandfather didn't use a cent of it for its intended purpose. He purposely kept it buried so he couldn't use it."

She brightened a little. "Yes, yes, it could mean that, couldn't it?"

"Yes, I believe that's exactly what this could mean."

"But we can't keep this money. It's not ours."

"Sorry, but I don't think we'll be able to ring up Old Adolf and give it back."

"Can't we just leave it there, pretend we never found it?"

"Do you know how much this is worth in today's market?"

"You take it," she repeated dully. "Will you report what you found?"

"No, I wouldn't do that to you."

"Thank you. Will you be going, then, as soon as you've found some way to get the gold out?" She dared not breathe, waiting for his answer.

"Go, well, of course I'll be going, eventually. It will take me some time to move this stuff."

"Yes, well, then, I'm tired," she said, trying to maintain control of her emotions. "I'm going to go to sleep now." He was leaving. He was going to leave her. She had thought maybe something was starting to happen between them. Now there was nothing.

****

"Patience," he coaxed. "It's dinnertime, not bedtime. Come here." He pulled her into his arms and sat on the bed, cradling her, when what he really wanted to do was shake her or kiss her out of her stupor.

"I think I've done enough damage for today, to you and to your yard. My body is so sore, even my aches have aches. I'm closing down. If you're tired, you just rest here with me now and sleep. I'll be here when you wake up." He kissed her forehead and settled himself on the bed, covering her with a blanket and rocking her until she was asleep.

She seemed so weak and limp in his arms. All the

illusions that had shored her up were gone in a whoosh that left her deflated. All she did was sleep. It wasn't right.

And if he were being perfectly honest with himself, most of the blame lay with him. He'd have to do something about it.

Chapter 24

When Patience walked into the kitchen the next morning, Nathaniel's eyes widened and his jaw dropped. He couldn't believe the dramatic change in her. Dressed to conquer in a banker's blue pinstriped business suit, with a tasteful but sexy button-down cream-colored silk blouse, her executive ensemble was complete with sheer stockings and heels that showed off her long legs to great advantage. Her lips were painted a glistening red. Full and sensuous, they seemed to scream out, "Taste me." The combination of power and sin knocked him back with a sucker punch to the gut.

"Patience, you're dressed," he managed.

"Of course I'm dressed. I'm going to a meeting."

He'd never seen her in much more than a robe or the lounging clothes she wore around the house. She'd never worn makeup; she didn't need it. Apart from the funeral and their brief sailing trip, she hadn't even been out of the house since he'd come to Bermuda. He wasn't sure he was entirely comfortable with this new Patience emerging before his very eyes. Had she been there the whole time?

"I didn't know anything about a meeting," he said, eyeing her with suspicion.

"You heard me talk about it with Cecilia," she reminded him. "It's our weekly meeting of the

241

Rediscover Bermuda committee on St. George's. I had to miss last week because of the funeral. This week's too important to skip. We're selecting the ad agency for the campaign. That's my specific area of responsibility."

"Well, you are *my* specific area of responsibility. I'm driving you. And I'm going to stay with you the entire time."

"You'll just be bored."

"That's *my* business."

"No, that's the point. What I do or don't do is none of your business. I don't need a babysitter."

"I'm making it my business," he countered. "You don't know what you need."

"If I could just point out a few things you might have overlooked. A, I'm not your responsibility. B, you don't have a license to drive in Bermuda. And C, you don't have a car. And that's just for starters. I can't ride on the back of your scooter, because I have presentation boards, tapes, and notebooks to bring."

"The hell with that. You're not going anywhere without me."

"For your information, Cecilia is picking me up."

"Oh, that's just great. If you think I'm letting you out of the house with that man-eater, think again. Your friend is a shark. If I leave you alone with her, I'd have to drag you back from some pick-up bar. You'd never make it to your meeting."

"You're losing it, Nathaniel."

"This argument is over!" Nathaniel retorted, raising his voice. "If you fight me on this, *you'll* lose. And, besides, you're too weak to go out."

"Do I look weak to you?"

Before conceding her point, he protested, "What I meant to say was, you're too delicate."

"My grandmother was delicate. I can take care of myself. Don't look at me as though I were about to have an attack of the vapors."

He bristled. "The first time you saw me, you fainted, and you slept through most of the first week of my visit. What am I supposed to think?"

"You drugged me, for God's sake. I buried both my grandparents in the space of a month. They left extensive holdings that still have to be sorted out. I'm exhausted, and I'm entitled to fall apart once in a while. I lost my grandparents, not my ability to function. And, for your information, my grandmother was also a very capable woman. She only let my grandfather take care of her because she knew it gave him pleasure to fuss over her. It was easier than resisting him."

"Your grandfather was a control freak, Patience."

"Oh, really? I don't see anyone else around here who fits that description, do you?"

Nathaniel chose to ignore that remark. "I'm sure your grandmother didn't have a choice in the matter."

"My grandmother had my grandfather wrapped around her little finger. It was quite endearing."

"I simply won't allow you to leave this house without me."

"You won't *allow* me?" she accused, leveling her gaze at him as she repeated herself. "Are you listening to yourself?" Her simmering temper had reached the boiling point. "You don't even know me. You must think I'm some kind of simpering idiot."

"Then use the brain you claim to have. Your grandfather's murderer is out there somewhere and it's not safe. What if he follows you? Corners you? You'll be helpless without me."

"I don't recall asking for your help. And I certainly don't need it. I can defend myself."

"We're in this together. And I'm genuinely concerned about your safety."

Patience looked like she was about to relent. "Look, I can't afford to be late. If you insist on going with me, you'll have to put on something more presentable," she said, tilting her head and eyeing his shorts and his hairy legs. "Do you by any chance own a suit?"

"Of course I do."

"Then go put it on. I'll cancel with Cecilia."

"Don't dismiss me!" he ordered.

She snickered. "If you want to go to my meeting, you'll have to follow my rules and behave yourself."

Nathaniel walked off in a huff. When he returned, he had calmed down considerably.

He caught Patience's eyes assessing him and registering approval of his flatteringly cut Italian suit.

He crossed the room and closed the distance between them. He reached for her hands.

"I apologize. I'm not usually like this."

"Stubborn and pig-headed?"

"I'm just worried…about you."

"I know."

"You look good," he said, "really good."

"So do you."

He wrapped his arms around her and kissed her several times lightly on the lips. As she sank into him, he wanted to dive into her, to keep her here, safe, with him, forever. Now he knew how her overprotective grandfather must have felt. Instead, he reluctantly broke the embrace and shifted away to lift her briefcase and the stack of presentation boards.

"Let me help you with some of these things," he offered.

"I knew you'd come in handy for something." She laughed as they headed for the car. "You make a pretty good pack horse."

She was a good driver, Nathaniel observed, steady and competent as she maneuvered her late model BMW through a series of bridges and winding roads linking the parishes that eventually led to the historic Town of St. George. Patience pointed out landmarks and places of interest on the way. He tried to concentrate in case she agreed to let him drive back. He imagined what it might be like to live here.

Restaurants, shops, and pubs lined the streets as they entered King's Square and parked at the Visitor's Service Bureau.

"I ought to lock you in the stocks and pillory," Patience chided as they walked toward the nineteenth-century restored Town Hall.

Nathaniel liked the harbor-front town, felt comfortable there with the open sea all around him.

She noticed him looking toward the sea.

"There's a lot to do here. Really. I'm not trying to get rid of you, but I'm going to be tied up for a long time. I can recommend some attractions. You can go to Ordnance Island and see the full-size replica of the original *Deliverance*. I know you'd enjoy that."

"No way am I letting you out of my sight," he warned.

"Maybe if there's time after the meeting, I'll show

you around. It's what I do best."

Nathaniel touched his lips to hers and gently but insistently stroked them with his tongue.

"I don't think that's what you do best, Patience."

"Nathaniel," she pleaded, stirred, as she tried to twist away from him. "We're in a public place, and you are supposed to be my *cousin*. There are a lot of very important people coming to this meeting—bankers, businessmen, *the mayor*. My friends. Someone might see us."

"I forgot," he said, smiling. "We must keep up appearances, at all costs. Okay, I'll be on my best behavior. I'll try not to embarrass you."

"We're meeting in the theater, where they show *The Bermuda Journey*. It's a thirty-minute movie about Bermuda's history and culture. Sometimes I help out as a guide at the Visitor's Center. It's low season, so that's why the space was available. It's up on the top floor."

They passed a photo gallery featuring portraits of previous mayors. No doubt most of them were Patience's ancestors.

Cecilia was waiting outside the theater.

"Cousin Nathaniel," she simpered, extending her hand to be kissed.

"Cecilia," he answered, obliging her.

****

"What is he doing in here?" Cecilia whispered as she took Patience aside. "I thought you were going to leave him outside."

"He's my self-appointed bodyguard, watchdog, jailer, take your choice. He's imposed himself on me, and it seems I'm stuck with him."

"He's more like your lapdog," Cecilia answered.

"Have you seen the way he looks at you? It's positively steamy."

"I haven't really noticed. I'm too busy watching him micromanage my life."

"It looks like he's been doing more than looking at you. You'd better go fix your lipstick."

"Darn," Patience said, taking out her compact to check. "Is everyone already in there?" she asked.

"Yes. You're on. Are you going to be okay? I mean, everyone really appreciates you being here so soon after, well, you know."

"I'm fine," Patience assured in a voice that sounded more confident than she felt. "Do me a favor and deposit my *cousin* at the back of the room for me, and then you can help me with all this stuff."

"My pleasure." Cecelia marched back to Nathaniel. "Come along, Nathaniel. I'm going to take good care of you."

Nathaniel rolled his eyes.

Patience swept into the room with Cecelia and Nathaniel at her heels. Everyone made the proper condolence noises. And their sentiments were genuine. Diana Whitestone had been head of this committee, well-loved and respected by everyone in the room. Patience's grief was still fresh, and reminders of her grandmother just made it harder to bear. But this was an important meeting and she was running it, so she held up her head, took a deep breath, and plunged ahead.

****

Patience took control of the crowd from the moment she approached the podium. She was spellbinding. Or maybe it was just that Nathaniel was under her spell. Everyone listened attentively as she spoke. There was nothing tentative or delicate about this Patience as she moved competently through the agenda, introducing ad agency representatives, making presentations herself, leading the discussion, heading off disputes. She was brilliant. It was hard to believe she was the same person who had dissolved so easily in his arms.

He was mesmerized by her voice and her face. He couldn't stop looking at her. He knew she was communicating something important, but he couldn't focus on what she said, only on how she said it. He tried to pay closer attention.

"So that's why I like the local agency's campaign so much."

She put the presentation board on the easel.

"Here's one of my favorites."

Tea Time or Tee Time?
Bermuda. We Cover All the Angles.

"And this one," Patience continued.

Whether Dark and Stormy or
Sunny and Bright
Rediscover Yourself in Bermuda.

Patience held up the photos of a couple lounging by the pool, sipping their Dark 'n Stormy™ cocktails, and another couple basking in the sun on a sailboat, to illustrate her choice.

"Most visitors already associate us with shipwrecks, hurricanes, and the Bermuda Triangle, so we may as well confront those issues, meet those challenges head on and turn them to our advantage," she said.

"This campaign, by our very own Bermuda agency, demonstrates their knowledge of the island, and that counts for a lot. And I love their Bermuda Connections series, which highlights all the well-known painters, writers, and others who have made Bermuda their home or visited our island over the course of our history. I'm not in favor of giving away our business to a New York or London agency when we have such wonderful talent right here at home," she concluded.

Everyone in the room stood and clapped. At that moment, Patience could have asked for anything and it would have been hers.

When the group broke for lunch, Nathaniel approached her.

"I don't know what to say," he began. "You were magnificent. Not exactly a damsel in distress. You ran the whole show. Impressive."

Patience blushed. "Thank you."

"Don't take this the wrong way, but you look a little tired."

"Does it show?"

"Not much, but I can tell. After lunch, let me take you home."

"That sounds wonderful, really," Patience said. "Cecilia said she would take care of bringing me all my material, so we wouldn't have to stay and collect it."

****

The truth was Patience did feel bone-tired, and her feet hurt. She was proud of her performance, and she knew her grandmother would have been, too. But she might have been a little too ambitious to think she could bounce back so quickly. What she wanted to do now was get back home, get out of these clothes, and snuggle on the couch with Nathaniel. He placed his hand at the small of her back in a supportive gesture, then stepped back as her colleagues came up to congratulate her.

When they left the building, Patience had a final request before they left for home.

"If we could, I'd like to stop at St. Peter's Church for a moment."

"Of course," he said. He took her hand and this time she didn't object or pull it away. They walked the several blocks to the church where she had buried her grandmother. This time he stood beside her as she bent down first to her grandmother's grave, then her grandfather's, arranging the flowers to make sure they were fresh and appealing.

"My grandmother loved flowers," she said, choking on the words.

"I know. Her garden is beautiful."

She couldn't say anything more as the silent tears flowed. Ready to collapse, she let him gather her in his arms and hold her while she grieved, grateful he was there with her.

"Now I have no one," she whispered.

"That's not true, Patience. You have me." He held her tighter. And she leaned her head against his chest.

Then she broke away and he followed her, maintaining a discreet distance. As she knelt at a weathered marker, beneath the shade of a magnificent cedar tree, she clasped a tarnished silver pendant to her heart. He was close enough to hear her sigh with what he keenly felt was sorrow and longing. He attributed her reaction to the strain of the last few weeks of her mother's illness and the stress of the funeral.

Though the sun shone brightly, when Patience bent to the ground, the light was blotted out momentarily by a turbulent cloud that seemed to have appeared out of nowhere. The air around them grew cold. Patience grabbed her arms and rubbed them. Nathaniel felt the chill down to his bones and a tangible connection to an otherworldly, sorrowful presence. Then, the sun skimmed easily from behind the cloud and light poured back into the hallowed space as if it had never been absent.

When Patience stood up, he moved closer to the gravesite and experienced an intense feeling—a centuries-old longing—a feeling he had been to this particular place before. He dismissed it as nothing more than déjà vu, since he'd never been to this cemetery before, other than for Diana's funeral. Glancing at the marker, Nathaniel noted that the woman buried there had died when she was just about the age Patience was now. In fact, she had died only a year after the Anglican church was originally erected. No doubt she was one of Patience's ancestors, one of the early settlers of Bermuda.

Year 1593-1620
Elizabeth Sutton Smith
Wife of Richard
Mother of Anne
I will wait forever.

At that moment, Nathaniel felt bound to Patience.

They stared at each other, electrified by their tangible connection.

Chapter 25

Nathaniel sauntered into Patience's bedroom and wasn't surprised to find her still asleep. He lifted the large heavy volume from the bed where it had fallen out of her hands.

It must be some serious history book, Nathaniel thought. He held it up to the sunlight beginning to stream into the room. *Historye of the Bermudaes or Summer Islands*. A small, dog-eared paperback fell out. He smiled when he glanced at the half-naked pirate and scantily clad, amply endowed maiden in a clinch on the worn cover. He leafed through the romance paperback and noticed it was bookmarked to a particularly steamy passage. Apparently Patience wasn't as serious as she pretended to be.

"My, my," he chuckled, his eyes narrowing as they paused over words that would make a sailor blush. He hoped she was getting some ideas they could later put into practice.

Patience tossed restlessly on the bed like a ship roaming rough seas.

"What are you dreaming about, darling Patience?" he whispered before he pulled the covers down from her chin. He tucked the paperback into his pocket. This novel could bear further investigation. But now it was time to awaken his sleeping beauty. He planted a chaste kiss on her forehead.

"Let me take you out to breakfast, this morning, Patience," offered Nathaniel cheerfully as Patience surfaced from slumber. "I've been practicing on the scooter. I think I've got my hand signals down."

"I think it might be safer to take my car," she laughed. "Otherwise, we both might end up in hospital with a bad case of road rash or worse."

Then the light left her eyes and she asked, "What day is it, Nathaniel? I've lost track of the time. I look back and the days are all jumbled together."

He reached for her hand. That's how he had felt since she came into his life. Was it truly only days, or weeks or hours? It felt like forever, yet not long enough.

"It's Sunday," he answered. "I've been hearing a lot about the brunch at the Fourways Inn. Could we try it?"

Patience squeezed her eyes shut.

"Do you have another headache?" he asked, touching his hand to her forehead and rubbing his thumb gently over her eyes.

"No, I just don't think I can summon the energy to go out again. I still feel like I'm in a fog."

"Of course. I understand." Last evening, he had seen her rustling through the clothes in her grandmother's closet, feeling them, smelling them, and he knew she was imagining Diana was still there. And he had caught her crying. He hadn't wanted to intrude on her grief, so he'd passed by the room in silence.

Perhaps she was wondering why the flowers in the garden were still in bloom, why the ocean continued to beat against the shore, why the sky was so bright and blue, and why nothing had changed even though the light had gone out of her life? He had wondered that too, once, a long time ago, when his mother had walked out of his life. But his mother had left him of her own free will. She hadn't been taken from him, like Diana Whitestone.

"Well, then, I'll just have to make you one of my famous Morgan omelets."

She laughed. "I'm almost afraid to ask what's in it."

"That depends entirely on what you have in the galley."

"All manner of things, I imagine. Cecilia and Sallie make sure the kitchen stays well stocked. They know I won't shop."

Nathaniel took her hand in his again. He couldn't seem to stop touching her. Her hand was limp and lifeless, like the limb of a wounded bird. She didn't even have the strength to run a brush through her hair. He left her for a moment to walk into the bathroom and returned with an antique silver hairbrush. He went to work on her hair, and the steady movement of the brush through her scalp seemed to soothe her, while it aroused him. If he continued, they'd never eat. He placed the brush on the end table by the bed.

"Now, come with me to the kitchen," he urged, and guided her off the bed and all the way to a chair in the kitchen. "You'll keep me company. This omelet demands an audience."

He rattled around the kitchen, clanging and banging pots and pans, trying to get a reaction. He loved it when she laughed.

"You're a strange girl, Patience," he said, as he paused, waiting for the butter in the frying pan to melt.

"Strange in an odd way?" she ventured.

"No, strange in a wonderful way," he replied. "You're a throwback from another time. So formal. Old worldly. You're also sweet and funny and endearing and strangely familiar."

Nathaniel set about making the omelet.

"Well, we really do have a big selection here, don't we?" he commented. "Mushrooms, and cheese, and—surprise—*Bermuda onions.*"

"You're teasing me."

"I suppose I am."

"You know something?" Patience mused. "You're just a big fraud, Nathaniel Morgan."

"What do you mean?"

"You're not at all what I expected." Patience gifted him with a smile that brightened the whole room. "You blustered into my life like a dangerous pirate, roaming the seas, wild and free, making demands and taking control. But you also have a softer, domestic side. You nurture me, mother me. You seem to be as at home in the kitchen as you are on the sea."

"Never had much mothering, myself," Nathaniel said and stared off, lost in his thoughts. "Except for Gran."

"Your Gran? Is she still alive?"

"No, she's gone. They all go." But he didn't offer an explanation. Instead, he made a show of fussing over the plates and the table settings.

"I thought we'd sit out on the veranda, facing the sea," he said.

"Do you miss the sea?"

"Well, how can I miss it when I've got it right outside my door?" They listened to the waves crash wildly against the rocky shore as they sat down to breakfast. "It's so beautiful here, with the pink sand beaches."

"Do you want to know why the sand in Bermuda has that wonderful pink hue?" Patience asked, her eyes twinkling.

"No, but I'm sure you're going to tell me." He laughed.

"Now, I know you're teasing me."

He tweaked her nose. "Maybe just a little."

"It's composed of shell particles, calcium carbonate, and bits of crushed coral mixed with sand, and it never gets hot, even in the summer."

"Is that a fact?"

"Yes, and we have thirty-four beaches. We've a private beach down the steps at the back of this house, and so many other wonderful beaches. I want to show you my island."

****

If she occupied Nathaniel with enough activities, he wouldn't leave the island, or her, Patience thought. There was certainly enough to do and see in Bermuda to keep him here a lifetime. And she realized she wanted that.

With delight she spoke of her beloved island, gesturing rhythmically, contagious enthusiasm in every phrase. "I'll take you for a swim at Warwick Long Bay, and back into St. George's. There's a lot of history there. Remember I told you about the replica of the *Deliverance II*? We can go on a walking tour. That would take a whole day. And you've hardly seen any of Hamilton. Then we can go over to the Dockyard, and later have dinner at the Waterlot Inn at Southampton.

That's my favorite restaurant. Being a sailor, you'll love it. It's an old converted warehouse on the water's edge. It's got old paintings of ships, gourmet food, and lots of charm. We've also got some great galleries and terrific local artists. I want you to love Bermuda as much as I do. You could spend a lifetime here."

"Whoa," Nathaniel said. "I thought all you wanted to do was languish here at the house—not that you don't have a lot to occupy yourself here."

"Well, now that I've got some food in me, I feel more energetic. Mmm, this omelet is so delicious, so delicate, so flavorful. I guess I was hungry after all. Thank you."

"Just make sure you eat every bite. You need your strength. I'm worried about you."

"You are?" she asked hopefully.

"Of course, we're cousins, aren't we?"

They ate in companionable silence.

"Have you ever been in love, Nathaniel?"

"That question came out of left field."

"Well, have you?"

"I thought so, once," he said irritably.

"Do you have anyone to go home to?"

"Not anymore," he said with finality, in a manner that suggested further discussion of the subject was off limits.

"Nathaniel," she started, and he turned to face her. "Would you think I was crazy if I told you I knew you would come?"

"You knew? How?"

"I was expecting you."

"You were waiting for me?"

"I know it sounds funny, but you've been in my

dreams."

His attitude serious, he looked into her eyes.

"Since we met?"

"And before. I can't explain it."

He reached over the table for her hand.

"Tell me."

"You were just what I'd hoped for. Dark and dangerous and daring. A wild sea captain."

"And…" he coaxed seductively.

"And terribly tender and unbearably sweet."

****

Nathaniel's heart constricted. He found it difficult to breathe. But he kept hold of her hand. Against all better judgment, he was falling deeper in love with this woman every day.

"Patience," he whispered, wondering if she could hear him above the din of the ocean.

"Yes?"

"I'm going to kiss you now."

They stood at the same time. She smiled shyly, closed her eyes and lifted her face expectantly to his eager lips. As his lips brushed hers, she eased into him, and his tongue took possession of her mouth. She shivered and clutched Nathaniel's shirt. The delicious feel of her, exciting and thrilling, pulsed through his body like a primitive jungle rhythm. He felt almost feverish against the cool breeze off the ocean, which steadily, comfortingly, lapped to shore. Moaning, she wrapped her arms around him and didn't let go.

****

She wanted him, wanted to be with him, though she did not quite understand exactly what that entailed. She only knew that being in his arms felt right, new and mysterious yet somehow safe and familiar. She was eager to explore the body she held against her. And she wanted to stay there forever, bask in his warmth, and make this glorious feeling last.

"Patience!" He seemed to have difficulty breathing when they finally broke apart. "I must tell you. I've been avoiding it all morning. Somebody's been on the *Fair Winds* again."

"How can you tell?" she asked, suddenly worried for him.

"That ship's like my woman. I'd know if somebody else had boarded her."

She blushed.

"He's warning us. He's getting closer, and he wants us to know he's here. Searching. Prying. Stalking. Waiting to pounce."

She shivered.

"You're shaking like a leaf. Let me get you a sweater before you blow away."

"No, let's both go in together. I don't want to be alone out here now."

"I'm sorry if I've frightened you. I didn't mean to. I'm here now. So you don't have to be afraid." He closed his hand protectively around hers and led her back into the house.

****

Patience thought the late-night phone calls had stopped, but they hadn't. She'd been asleep and he'd answered, and the caller had hung up, expecting to hear Patience's frightened voice.

"Who is this?" Nathaniel had shouted. "Answer me, now!" But the caller had broken the connection. There was no reason to tell Patience. It would just worry her. And that was the last thing he wanted to do.

****

Later, that afternoon, while Nathaniel was occupied on the *Fair Winds*, after he had called Cecilia and asked her to come over to keep Patience company, Patience looked up at her friend.

"He's pulling away," Patience said. "He's making leaving noises."

"Well, you know the rules. Visitors are only allowed to stay three weeks, unless they own real estate or unless he has means to support himself without seeking employment on the island. Or unless you're planning to marry him."

"Cecilia! It's not like that between us. His time's almost up. He's taken the *Fair Winds* out for provisioning, I think. He mentioned that he has reciprocal privileges at the Royal Bermuda Yacht Club. When he leaves, he won't be back. I can see it in his eyes. He just hasn't told me goodbye yet. Cecilia, I don't want him to go. How can I make him stay? How can I keep him here?"

"Darling, I've learned the hard way that you can't hold on to someone who wants to break free. Have you told him how you feel?"

"No," Patience admitted. "I haven't said the words. He could have an ocean of women, and has had, I'm sure. Why would he want me?"

"I think that's obvious. He doesn't want an ocean of women."

"It's not obvious to me. I'm plain, not spectacular, like my grandmother."

"You're every bit as beautiful as Diana," Cecilia argued. "You look exactly like her. Everybody always said so."

"But I don't have her fire, her spirit, her vivaciousness," Patience objected. "When she entered a room, she dominated it. She captivated everyone in sight. Absolutely everyone noticed her."

"You are capable of those same qualities. You may be quiet and unassuming, but you're just as brilliantly stunning in your own way."

"My grandfather adored my grandmother. She inspired the type of larger-than-life romance, the kind of love you only read about in fairytales. That's what I want."

"It will happen that way for you too," Cecilia promised. "You'll see. Maybe it already has."

"No, I think I'm going to have to practice being more like you, more fun-loving and adventurous," Patience said. "Maybe I should seduce him. You could help me."

Patience turned away until the laughter in her friend's voice stopped roaring in her ears.

"You, seduce a man? Patience, you don't have it in you. Leave that to the professionals like me. Just be yourself. You'll get your chance to shine. Has he kissed you yet?"

"Yes, and when he does, it feels like I'm floating...flying, like a longtail, soaring high above the island. And then I can tell he wants more and, Cecilia, so do I, but I—"

"Has he tried anything?" Cecilia accused, pacing the room like a mother tiger protecting her young.

"He tried, I mean we tried, that is, he tried and I... He wanted to make love with me, but I stopped him," Patience explained awkwardly, lamenting, "What's wrong with me?"

Cecilia hesitated, because she could see that her friend was seriously hurting, before adding, "Nothing is wrong with you. You have to move at your own pace. When the time is right and you feel safe with the right man...you'll know what to do. Are you sure you're ready for this?"

"For heaven's sake, Cecilia, you've been married three times. I'm twenty-seven and I've never been with a man. If I'm not ready now, when will I ever be?"

Chapter 26

Patience had fallen asleep on her bed and was still a little disoriented when Nathaniel gently nudged her shoulder.

"I was dreaming of a man, and I thought he was—I mean, he had the look of my grandfather," Patience said.

Nathaniel scratched his head. "Patience, your grandfather is dead," he said softly.

"Yes, I know." She remembered all the blood—on her hands, smeared on her dress, and on the carpet in the study.

"Your hands are stone cold." Nathaniel frowned as he took her small hands into his and rubbed them until the circulation returned. Then he put them to his lips and kissed them gently.

"All warm. Better?"

"Yes. Thank you."

"When did Cecilia leave? I told her to stay until I got back."

"I didn't need her here. I was reading, and I must have dozed off."

He sat on the bed, and they talked about who could possibly be shadowing them.

"It can't be anyone else but that man your grandfather referred to in his journal as Nighthawk. He knew about the gold. He helped your grandfather unload it. But I don't know his real name, and he's been impossible to track down all these years later. My guess is that now your grandfather is dead he's come back for what he considers his rightful share of the gold. Your grandfather knew he was dangerous. And it stands to reason he may be the one who was blackmailing William Whitestone and finally killed him."

Patience shivered. She suddenly felt cold again.

****

"We're going out," Nathaniel announced the next morning after breakfast.

"No, I can't go out," Patience wailed. "I'll have every well-meaning matron clucking over me. 'Poor Patience. She's all alone. So utterly alone. No man. No prospects. What will become of her?' They all feel sorry for me. They'll go to work on me and start trying to pair me off with their sons, the usual lineup of stuffy bankers, proper members of Parliament, and any number of other 'suitable,' available men. I won't be able to stand their pity."

Nathaniel folded his arms and stared at her.

"I told you before, you're not alone," Nathaniel said, putting his arm around her. "You've got me."

"For how long?" she whispered, looking up at him. He didn't answer.

Nathaniel had pretended not to hear her question. How could he reply when he didn't know the answer himself?

"Out where?" Patience wanted to know.

"Into town to shop."

"But I don't need anything."

"Well, then, I'll do the shopping. I just think you need to get out. You've been cooped up too long in this house. The only time you've gone out is for that business meeting. You need to have some fun." He worried that if she continued to remain cooped up, she'd have too much time to focus on the stranger who was stalking them.

"Okay, then we'll take my car," she agreed.

"No, we need some adventure. Let's take the scooter."

"Oh, no, not the scooter. Not with you driving."

"Get dressed. Your transportation leaves in ten minutes. I assume you have a helmet. Doesn't everyone in Bermuda have a scooter?"

"Of course, but you're not going to wear those shorts, are you?" she mocked. "Or I'll have to bring the first-aid kit."

"I'll be changed into my jeans before you even make it to your closet."

"Fine," she said.

"Okay, then. I'll start locking up the house."

Patience went into the bedroom to change into slacks and closed-toe shoes, grabbed a sweater, her helmet, and her handbag, and joined Nathaniel in the driveway.

"Hop on," he instructed.

She got on the bike and placed her hands around Nathaniel's waist. He turned around and stared into her eyes.

"What?" she asked.

"Nothing," he said and turned to the front. "It just feels good to have your arms around me."

"Don't take it too personally." Patience loosened her arms a little, thinking it felt good to be sassy.

Nathaniel started the scooter, and they sped out of

the driveway and out onto the winding roads into town. Patience tightened her grip against the real possibility of colliding with the rough-cut limestone walls that bordered the highway.

"Nathaniel, you drive like a maniac. You'd do better staying off the roads and sticking to the sea."

"I can't hear you," he shouted.

Or you don't want to. She had to admit it felt good to get out, to smell the fresh ocean air and the scent of the flowers, feel the wind against her face, and see other people. She loved to watch them as they went about their daily business, lived their quiet lives. And it felt so right to have her arms wrapped around Nathaniel.

When Nathaniel got to the first traffic circle, she closed her eyes, hung on tight, and screamed.

"Nathaniel, we almost got hit by that public bus."

"I had plenty of room."

By the time they arrived in town, parked on Front Street, and locked the scooter, her muscles were aching from gripping her hands so tightly around Nathaniel's waist.

"That was scarier than a roller coaster ride," Patience said.

"Have you ever been on a roller coaster?" he asked quizzically.

"Well, no," she admitted.

"I didn't think so. I'll bet there's a lot of things you haven't done." Nathaniel looked at her intently and she blushed. "But the ride was exciting, wasn't it?"

Patience frowned. "Yes, for a near-death experience. Well, where do you want to go first?"

"I'd like to talk about where you want to go and where you've been. Cecilia told me you'd never been off the island. Not even for school?"

"We have fine schools here," Patience remarked, thinking back to the only time she ever remembered her grandparents argue. Her grandfather had fought to keep her in school on the island. Her grandmother thought sending her to a school in England would be best for her. In the end, her grandfather's will was stronger. Anytime her grandmother had suggested a family trip off-island, her grandfather had voiced his objections.

"Why do we need to see the world, when we're living right here in paradise?" She recalled his words and his effort to make light of the situation. When her grandmother had started to cry, he had kissed her and taken her into his arms and said, "We don't need anybody else. We have each other. I need to keep her close, Diana." And something about the way his voice had pleaded and the fear his eyes had communicated had quieted her. Patience couldn't explain his reaction, but she loved him, respected his wishes, and knew he was doing what he thought best for his family. She had never felt stifled. She loved Bermuda and she didn't care if she never left.

"I attended locally."

Nathaniel shook his head. "Never even been to Europe?" he inquired.

"No. I told you. But I've always wanted to go to Virginia."

"Then you should."

****

Nathaniel had been all over the world several times now. Always running from something or toward something. He wasn't sure which. But whatever he was searching for, he hadn't found it yet. Until now. He was thinking he'd like to be the one to show Patience the places he'd been so they could experience them together.

Whitestone or von Hesselweiss or whatever his name was had kept his wife and granddaughter under lock and key. He'd probably convinced himself it was for their protection, but that hadn't been fair to Patience or her grandmother.

"Where do you want to go first?" Patience repeated.

"How about Gibbons Company? I've heard some good things about that store. Or A.S. Cooper & Son's, or maybe Davison's of Bermuda."

"Fine," she said. "They're all great department stores, and they're all on Front Street. Let's walk to the end of the block and start there, and work our way back."

Crowds poured into the street and flooded into the stores and boutiques to load up on designer clothing from Europe, jewelry, china and crystal, woolen fabrics, perfumes, local products and crafts, and tacky T-shirts. It seemed Patience had been in all the shops at one time or another, knew most of the shop owners, and was even related to some.

****

Patience looked forward to sharing everything about Bermuda with Nathaniel.

There were the touristy things that were a must on any visitor's shopping list—Outerbridge's Original Sherry Peppers sauce, Gosling's Black Seal rum, black rum cake, and Bermuda fish chowder.

"I want you to see all the galleries and studios, too," Patience said. "There's Carole Holding, Diana

Higginbottom, Birdsey prints are wonderful, and Michael Swan has the prettiest prints of pastel cottages and shutters. And then there's Pegasus. The shop is a bit of a walk from here, but it's got some great botanical prints and antique maps. It's a sailor's paradise."

"Now why should I buy from any other artist when I have my very own talented artist right at home, and I could have a PKW original?"

Patience, unused to compliments about her watercolors, blushed.

Nathaniel slid his hand down Patience's arm and latched his fingers around hers. It felt like the most natural thing in the world, and a little like a teenager on a first date.

She looked up at Nathaniel as their hands touched and she felt a tingle right down to her toes. She didn't cast off his hand. It felt too good in hers.

"We're here," she announced. He kept his hand in hers as they walked through the doors of Davison's.

The manager stepped up to greet them.

"Patience, it's so good to see you out, finally. I was so sorry to hear about your grandmother."

"Thank you," she said. "I appreciate the card and the flowers you sent."

"This must be the cousin," the man said, amused, causing Patience to guiltily let go of Nathaniel's hand.

"Uh, this is Nathaniel Morgan, from Virginia," Patience explained. "It's his first time in town."

"Fantastic. What can I help you find?"

"Well, right now, we're just browsing."

"Lovely. Just let me know if you need anything."

As Patience and Nathaniel walked through the

store, she was stopped by at least five more people who offered their condolences.

"Do you know everybody in Bermuda?" he asked.

"Almost. That's what happens when you live in one place all your life."

Two hours later, loaded down with shopping bags, Patience suggested they walk across the street to the harbor and rest on a bench while they looked at the waterfront.

"It's so serene, isn't it?" Patience asked. "I never get tired of watching all the boats."

"Yes," he answered. "Can you recommend a good jewelry store?"

Patience looked at him warily. He said he had no one to go home to, but he probably did have a girl back home. She had just assumed he was unattached. For all she knew, he might even be married. What an idiot she was, to think she even had a chance with him. He was leaving, and he wanted to bring his special girl a trinket, a sign of his affection. Why did the thought of another woman with Nathaniel make her feel so horrible?

"Of course. Astwood Dickinson," she replied without enthusiasm.

"Let me guess. It's on Front Street too."

"That's right." She laughed and gave him directions.

"I need to make a quick run, and I'll be right back here. You rest on the bench and guard the packages."

She watched him cross the street in hurried strides.

****

Patience hadn't asked him why he had a need for a jewelry store. Had she asked, she would have discovered how nervous he was around such places.

The last time he'd been in one, he was with his college sweetheart looking for an engagement ring. And that experience had ended badly, with his fiancée walking out on him the week before their wedding to run off with a golf pro. And not just any golf pro. *His* golf pro. It was humiliating.

If he had read the signs, he would have known from the beginning he had nothing in common with Jenna. When he spoke of history, he came alive with the magic of it, while her eyes glazed over. History bored her to tears, and she complained about his "obsession with something that was dead and gone."

In an attempt to bridge the gap, Nathaniel had arranged for Jenna to take private golf lessons at his club to get her interested in another one of his hobbies. He thought perhaps that would give them some common ground. As it turned out, the pro must have given her some extra lessons on the side. Her game never improved, but the pro had evidently scored a hole in one.

Nathaniel had wondered what Jenna could possibly find so stimulating to discuss over the dinner table with a golf pro. Then he discovered talk wasn't the only thing she found stimulating about the guy.

Jenna didn't see the connections of history like Patience did. Instead, she had been obsessed with picking out silver, crystal, and china patterns, and dealing with guest lists and invitations. Marriage had been her idea, and he had gone along with it, like a ship without an anchor, adrift in the ocean.

In a moment of honesty with himself, Nathaniel had been certain history would repeat itself in the form of another failed marriage like that of his parents. And if by some chance they did have a child together, Jenna would probably take off just like his mother did. And that would leave another devastated child to grow up without a mother.

As the wedding date approached, Nathaniel had been filled with a growing sense of dread instead of the happiness he knew he should have been feeling. It went deeper than a simple case of pre-wedding bridegroom jitters. Gran had called it. Gran, who had taught him everything he knew about people, the importance of family, and even about love.

"She's not the one," Gran had announced with simple conviction.

And with a sudden flash of clarity he had known it, too. But he would stand by his promise to Jenna. He was blindsided when she called him and told him things weren't going to work out between them. Adding to the indignity, she had broken off the engagement over the phone, afraid to face him—or not caring enough to bother. She danced around an explanation and never admitted there was someone else, never really apologized. So Nathaniel bailed on his life in Virginia and sailed away, leaving Gran to explain everything away to the relatives and guests. He never looked back or regretted his decision, except for the trouble it must have caused Gran.

By the time he returned to Virginia his grandmother was dying, and Jenna and the golf pro were married. So much for true love! It was no less than he expected. As a result, he had given up on golf and on marriage in general.

****

Patience looked at her watch. Nathaniel had been

gone a long time. She dozed off again and woke up when he nudged her shoulder. She didn't see a package. Maybe he didn't find what he was looking for at the jewelry shop. It wasn't her place to ask, anyway.

"Patience, I think you must have sleeping sickness," Nathaniel said. "Where were you just now?"

She had been dreaming of sailing to strange and interesting places, of doing unpredictable things, instead of the expected, every day for the rest of her life. She wanted to see the world. All the places she'd only read about. And she wanted to have the freedom and flexibility Nathaniel had to live his life how he chose. Instead of being suspended in a protective and suffocating cocoon spun by listening to all the tales her grandfather had spun for her and all the lies he had told.

"Nothing, really," she answered wistfully.

"Hey, I'm starving. You must be, too. Where can we eat?"

"The Lobster Pot. That's my favorite place for lunch. They have the best local lobster, and I'm craving an apple fritter with plenty of whipped cream."

"Lead the way." Nathaniel grabbed some of the packages, and when he put his arm around Patience's shoulder as they walked toward Bermudiana Road, she tried to push it off, with no success.

"What's up? You won't hold hands, and you won't let me put my arm around you. Can't you cut me a break?"

"Patience?" An older, fashionably dressed woman in front of them signaled.

"Judith," she acknowledged, guiltily.

"How are you doing, dear?" the woman asked kindly.

"I'm fine, thank you. We were just, Nathaniel suggested that—"

"I forced her out of the house to get some fresh air. I thought she needed a break."

"Of course she does. Nathaniel, it's so nice to see you again. It's comforting for Patience to have her family looking after her in her time of need. You do remember me from the committee meeting?"

"Of course. And it's a pleasure to see you again, Mrs. Overbrook. Thank you for your concern for Patience."

"Well, dear, we're so happy to see her back at the meetings. Patience, your ideas for the celebration are lovely."

"Thank you. I appreciate that."

"Well, if there's anything I can do, please call."

"I will," Patience assured her.

As Judith Overbrook walked away, Patience hissed, "You see? Everyone is talking about us. They think you're my cousin. How will that look if we're holding hands, or touching, or—"

"I couldn't care less how it looks," Nathaniel said boldly. "You sure do know a lot of people."

"They're friends, Nathaniel. Well-meaning friends. Let's duck into the restaurant before anyone else sees us."

"Don't I get any credit for being charming?" Nathaniel teased.

"A little."

After the restaurant owner expressed his condolences and Patience spoke with several other businessmen and acquaintances she knew in the lunch crowd, she and Nathaniel settled into a table at the back of the room.

"It's good and dark in here," Patience observed, looking around at the sleekly polished wood tones of the maritime decor. "Private."

"Why, what did you have in mind? Do you want to be alone with me?"

"Don't be ridiculous. I just want to be left alone. Don't you see?"

He reached across the table to stroke her hand.

"Trouble is, Patience, I can't leave you alone." Nathaniel got up from the booth and sat beside her on the upholstered bench seat, kissed her lightly on the lips, then more urgently, flustering and exciting her. "I can't stop touching you. I don't want to stop. Let's get out of here, Patience."

"I thought you were hungry," she whispered trying to catch her breath.

"I am," he said, looking straight at her until she blushed. *It was time, way past time.*

Marilyn Baron

PART FOUR

Destiny and Revenge

Bermuda 2013

Marilyn Baron

Chapter 27

It was time. Soon she would see. And he would finally get what he deserved. What he had been waiting for all these years. Revenge and reward. And wouldn't they both be sweet? "William Whitestone" got what was coming to him, and now Patience would pay for the sins of her grandfather. History was repeating itself. He didn't feel sorry for her. Not one bit. In fact, he hated her.

He had plotted and he had planned, and all his hard work was about to pay off. How would he do it? He'd thought long and hard about that, hidden away in his cramped quarters while she pranced around Marigold House without a care in the world. The pampered, spoiled grandchild. Well, things were about to change.

Would he shoot her? Too impersonal. Then it would be over too fast. Drowning would be easy, but too good for her. Accidental fall? No. Torture left a nice taste in his mouth. Slow and painful. Apparent suicide? She was so distraught over the brutal death of her grandfather and the tragic death of her grandmother so soon after. She had always been fragile. No wonder she couldn't go on living. Maybe he'd even force her to write her own suicide note.

He'd enjoy watching her beg and plead for her life, but there would be no one to hear her screams. He needed to make her suffer, the way he had suffered.

But first, of course, he would collect his due. After all, what would she need with money after she was dead?

He'd have to get her alone. But that sea captain barely let her out of his sight. He would have to lure the man away with a warning that Patience was in danger and demand that he meet him at a designated place in town. That would leave pretty Patience defenseless. Yes, it would be better to do it in the house where he had killed her grandfather. They'd start in the study. That would be fitting.

He needed a drink now. It would make the years of neglect and disillusion easier to swallow. Time to take the bus into town. No one knew him, so he could have a drink anywhere. He'd enjoy some fish chowder, washed down by a Dark 'n Stormy™. Prices were high in Bermuda, so he couldn't afford to splurge. Not yet. Killing William Whitestone had been satisfying, but in his rage he hadn't thought the plan through. He'd killed the man before he could arrange to squeeze more money out of him afterwards. Things would be different with Patience.

She and her sea captain were up to something. He knew they were. He had caught wind of it when he rifled through the papers on the boat, but the man had come back before he could make sense of what he was seeing. He'd had to leave before he was ready. Something about gold, a fortune to be had. He knew that Whitestone was an important man. And rich. And some of that money rightfully belonged to him.

He had tried to frighten Patience with phone calls, which had worked, up to a point, until the sea captain started answering the phone. And he didn't scare easily.

He was living with her in the house now, and that complicated things. So, no more threatening calls or notes to the girl. She was frightened enough.

He had set the stage brilliantly. She was primed. She would do anything he wanted now. He knew she would. It was time for action. He would make his move tonight. It would have to be tonight, before he lost his nerve. A little rum on the brain wouldn't dull his instincts or dampen his pleasure. She was a pretty little thing. Too bad she'd end up bloated and beaten, washed up on some beach. No, he couldn't afford to feel sorry for her. It must be the liquor that was going to his brain. No one had ever felt sorry for him. And when she was dead, he'd finally be at peace. With her demise, he could bury all the demons of his past.

Chapter 28

Nathaniel's brain was raging. He had to stomp down his anger before he saw Patience or she would suspect something was wrong. He remembered bringing her home from the restaurant with a mind to finally take her to bed. He'd had the overwhelming urge to be close to her, closer than the space across a restaurant table permitted.

It was all he could think about, but he'd made the mistake of stopping at the *Fair Winds,* telling her he'd be right up to the house. And that's when he had discovered the note.

The note that was now crumpled in his pocket. Someone had left it for him on the boat where he was sure to find it. It stated in no uncertain terms that Patience would pay if Nathaniel didn't meet him at Casey's, in town, tonight. He thought he had walked by Casey's earlier that afternoon. The bar was narrow and crowded. It was a good place to be if you wanted to blend into the background.

He knew he should call in the police. He didn't have the experience to handle something like this. The stalker was certainly dangerous, and he was getting closer. But this was nobody else's business. And the man had specifically threatened Patience with imminent death if he contacted the authorities. He didn't doubt the stalker would follow through on his threats. Who the hell was this man who was tracking them? He certainly wasn't discreet. He was sloppy, and he left signs everywhere. Maybe intentionally. Perhaps it was Nighthawk coming to collect his due? If it was Nighthawk, he'd have to be an old man by now, wouldn't he? He could take an old man. But evil transcended age.

Whoever he was, he had been in Marigold House, and on the *Fair Winds* several times. He was lurking, lying in wait for them, playing with them, biding his time. And now, apparently, their time was up. No doubt he was a contemporary of Patience's grandfather, one of a nest of agents Wilhelm von Hesselweiss had planted on the island. But Nathaniel was flying blind. He didn't know how many of them there were, or what had become of them since the war. Surely some of them had remained on the island. It had to be someone who knew about the gold. That could be any number of people. Island Eagle and Nighthawk could not have kept the gold a secret known only to themselves. The island was too small, too insular. They would have needed assistance to bring it ashore and to bury it.

If the stalker had gotten wind of the existence of a buried treasure, Nathaniel could find out what he was after and shut him down before word got out. And as long as he was talking to the man, he couldn't hurt Patience, Nathaniel reasoned. He wanted to get his hands on the bottom-feeder who thought he could breach his boat and threaten his girl.

So what if he was possessive of Patience? He had a lot invested in her. He may as well face it. He loved her. How had that happened? He had come for the gold, and now *she* was all he could think about. He would give anything, pay anything, relinquish every last ounce of the gold, just to keep her safe. He had never been as sure of anything in his life. If that was love, then yes, he supposed, he was in love. She would just have to deal with it.

He walked up the stone stairs slowly, trying to work out the best way to approach her. He used the key she had given him to get back inside the house.

"Patience," he called, trying to sound nonchalant as he walked in the side door.

"In here," she answered cheerfully, acknowledging his presence. When he entered the kitchen, she was busy at the counter, apron on, happily peeling and preparing. She'd been watching Nathaniel cook enough times that she thought she could accomplish a meal by herself. She hoped it wasn't too much to expect. With a large carving knife, she was trying to chop onions. Ingredients were scattered all over the granite surface of the island. A cookbook was propped up on the counter. Cabinets were flung open, the faucet was running and so were her eyes.

"Patience, what's the matter? Have you been crying?"

"Crying? Oh no, silly. It's the onions. I've been peeling onions."

"Hey, I thought maybe we should go into town for a drink or dinner or something, to finish off the day. It would do us good."

"Oh, but we just came from town, and I thought you said... I mean..." Patience was confused. She dropped the onion and the knife to crunch up her skirt in her fists. Her heart was beating fast, her brain going fuzzy. She must have misinterpreted his advances at

The Lobster Pot. She was nervous and excited at the same time. She'd thought he wanted her, and she was finally ready to give herself to him, and then he had disappeared to his boat. She'd considered waiting in the bedroom, but when he'd been gone so long she had dreamed up the idea of making dinner to keep herself occupied.

She must have misread his intentions. Why would someone so dashing and daring and handsome be interested in her when he could have anybody else in the world and probably did have someone else? A girl in every port. Wasn't that the expression? She turned away from the counter.

"Can't you see I'm making you dinner?" she chattered, spilling the words quickly to quell her nerves. "All on my own. I'm so excited. It's going to be fancy, Nathaniel. I found this great recipe, and I know I can do it. We simply can't go out to dinner tonight."

****

He smiled. "Hey, that's great." That was damn near perfect. He had counted on her not wanting to go with him. He didn't want her to go. Not for this meeting.

"Well, let me just whip into town for a while, then. I'll pick us up a nice bottle of wine to go with dinner. I'll be back before you even miss me." His heart was beating out of his chest. He was doing his best to calm her down, but he couldn't seem to gain control over his own ricocheting emotions.

"Not now, Nathaniel," Patience protested. "Please. What if the stalker comes back?" She didn't want to admit she was afraid. "Besides, I have a wonderful selection of wines here." She didn't want to let him go.

"Patience, I *need* to go into town for a while," he

said coolly.

"Well, okay," she relented. "But will you be back before dark? I don't think you've quite got the hang of the roads yet. I don't want them scraping my dinner companion off the street."

"What an appetizing thought. Umm, I hate to leave you alone, though. So, how about if I call Cecilia and invite her over to keep you company?"

"I can handle dinner without Cecilia. I have everything under control. Don't worry. Besides, I want this dinner to be just for the two of us." She blushed, and her eyelashes fluttered.

"Oh," he choked, his heart racing. He reached out and closed his hand over hers. Her eyes were still watery. He had to remind himself that it was only the onions. He didn't want to leave her, not now, not ever. He wanted to scoop her up for a never-ending kiss, drag her into the bedroom and toss her on the bed, but he couldn't afford to be late to Casey's. Too much was riding on it. On impulse, he leaned in and placed a quick, soft kiss on her lips. Patience kissed him back with a sweetness and a fire that took his breath away.

"That was nice," he said softly. "Hold that thought. I'll hurry back. But I want you to promise me you'll lock up while I'm gone."

"Nathaniel, I'll be fine. You won't be gone long. I'm not afraid anymore. Really."

"Sure, I know," he said, pretending a calm he didn't feel. He was only going to be gone as long as it took to wipe the floor with the bastard who was threatening Patience, and then he'd be back in time for the first course. He'd pay the man off, give whatever he wanted, and hopefully frighten him away.

He had money. If he needed to get his hands on some fast cash, he could always sell his boat.

"You have your key, don't you, in case I can't hear you from the kitchen?" she asked.

"Yes," he said, checking his pocket to make sure as he looked back at her one more time. That she had given him an extra key really did prove she trusted him. She was smiling now, trying to put on a brave face, for him. He could be brave for her, too. He was a pirate, after all. Fearless. That's how she saw him. And that's what he'd be, have to be, for her.

Tears gathered in her eyes.

He couldn't leave her hurt and mad, so he added, "Now, don't burn the dinner, dear."

Patience laughed in spite of herself. "I'll try not to."

****

Patience didn't even know if she could make dinner, but she was determined to finish what she started.

She locked the door behind Nathaniel, put on a CD, and listened to some Forties music. She liked the sounds of the Big Band era. It made her feel closer to her grandparents and helped to lift her mood and temper her disappointment about Nathaniel leaving so abruptly.

She would finish dinner preparations, set the table, and put on something fresh and sexy for Nathaniel. She had seen Cecilia operate. She could do that. Her heart was in freefall, and tonight she was determined to make Nathaniel fall in love with her, too.

The main dish was in the oven. The timer was set. An accompanying dish was simmering on the stove.

Patience went to her bedroom and turned on the shower, leaving the door open so she could hear the music while she showered. She sang along as she lathered up, washing her hair. Smiling, she daydreamed about what it would be like tonight. A candlelight dinner out on the veranda. Music pouring out into the moonlight. Stars everywhere. And then, after dinner, romance. She was finally ready, and tonight she would tell Nathaniel how she felt. She closed her eyes, let the warm soapy water wash over her while her imagination ran wild. She knew just how it was going to be between them. He would take her into his arms and press her close, and she would open her lips and—

Suddenly her naked body stiffened as a large, hairy hand reached in, snaked her from behind, and yanked her from the shower. She tried to scream, but another hand was covering her mouth. Her heart beat so fast she thought it would burst out of her chest. She shook from the shock, and the cold made her teeth chatter.

"Patience, don't make a sound, not if you want to live." The man spoke in broken English with a heavy, guttural German accent Patience found intimidating and frighteningly familiar. She gasped when she saw the flash of a sharp blade.

Fear shot through her, and she tried to struggle out of his hold, but the intruder was too strong.

"One wrong move and I'll gut you."

"W-what do you want?" She barely choked out the words. She didn't think he could understand her since the words were muffled against his hand.

Releasing her suddenly, he dangled her sheer, white robe in front of her so she could catch it, and when she did, he clamped his arms around her body again.

"Now, get dressed. Slowly. And don't turn around. He flicked the knife against her throat and drew a drop of blood.

She cried out.

"First blood." He laughed. "You're shaking. You're afraid. That's very good. You should be."

"Nathaniel," she whimpered, wanting to crawl into herself. She didn't know if she had said it aloud or thought it.

"Your sea captain is otherwise occupied. He won't be coming to your rescue. Not in time, anyway."

"What have you done to him?" she asked. She couldn't see the man's face. She did recognize his voice. It was the man who had threatened her on the phone. He sounded like an older man, but he had the thick, strong arms of someone much younger.

"Just threw him off course."

"But I locked the doors," she whispered.

"Yes, of course you did. Did you think that would stop me? I'm very resourceful. Did you like my little diversion, Patience?"

"Diversion?" Patience was puzzled.

"The fire," the man hissed.

"You set the fire on Nathaniel's boat?"

"Yes. It gave me a chance to get into the house, steal your keys, and make a set for myself. Did you and your sea captain have fun on Front Street today?"

How could he know?

"I've been here in your bedroom all afternoon, waiting for you. For us to have this time alone together. I think I've been very patient. You really should get the lock on your bedroom door fixed."

Tears began to slide down her cheeks. All she could think was that her dinner was going to burn and she'd never see Nathaniel again, never touch him, never kiss him, never get the chance to tell him or show him how much she loved him.

The intruder stroked her neck methodically and his fingertips skimmed the front of her robe. Disgusted, Patience tried to pull away. She couldn't stand his hands on her.

"You can struggle all you want. You can't get away from me." She was shivering uncontrollably now.

"Don't worry, I'm not interested in your body, not in the way you think, just your dead body. Yes, I'm going to kill you, Patience. Do you want me to tell you just how? First, let me tell you about how I killed your grandfather."

Still wet and slippery from the bath, and practically naked, she sprang on the balls of her feet, pivoting, to try to get a look at her attacker. But he grabbed her face and twisted it away.

"My grandfather?" she seethed. "You killed my grandfather? Why would you do that? How do you even know my grandfather?"

The man loosened his hold on her and whispered softly in her ear, "Because he was my father."

Patience sagged against him. She couldn't have heard correctly. She didn't understand.

"But how can that be? My grandfather had no other children."

He forced her face forward for one more moment, and then threw her roughly on the bed.

When Patience finally turned to face him, her mouth flew open in confusion and her eyes widened in shock.

"Grandfather?" she whispered, going pale. The intruder was younger than her grandfather, but as she stared at the man in the dimming light, he had the definite look of William Whitestone. "Is that you?"

"You think I'm your grandfather?" The man laughed wildly. "Or maybe your grandfather's ghost? I think you're going insane, Patience. Your grandfather is dead. There is a strong family resemblance, though, don't you think?"

"Who are you?" she demanded, her teeth still chattering from fear and the chill in the room. She pulled her filmy robe tighter around her.

"I suppose you deserve to know the whole story, since I'm going to kill you anyway. I think you'll be surprised. Would you like to hear it?"

She was too frightened to speak, but she nodded and huddled under the covers, scooting as far away from the apparition as possible.

Chapter 29

Nathaniel wrapped a shaky hand tightly around his beer, took a pull from the bottle, and then got up from his seat near the door to pace the length of the smoky bar again. The man was a half hour late for their meeting. It was getting dark. He had promised Patience he'd try to be home. She would be worried.

The jukebox was playing. The few tables that filled the narrow room were brimming with customers, but there was no sign of whoever had written the note. No one seemed to be looking for him. No one appeared to be nervous. He had looked every one of the patrons in the eye and received no acknowledgement, no response, no recognition.

He could have kicked himself. He had no idea what the man looked like. Why hadn't he given a description? Was he young or old? Heavyset or thin? Bearded or clean-shaven? Dark-skinned or light? Local or foreign? Had he ever been in the bar at all? If so, why hadn't he come forward? The man obviously knew what *he* looked like. He wasn't going to show. He was playing games.

Nathaniel got the sinking feeling that he had been tricked. Lured away from Marigold House and away from Patience. The man could be with her right now. She could be in danger. Nathaniel slapped some dollars on the bar to cover his tab and ran outside. A brief look around confirmed that no one was waiting for him here. His scooter was right where he had left it, untouched. He unlocked it, dragged on his helmet, and raced out of Hamilton like his life depended on it. Because he had a horrible feeling in his gut that Patience's life might depend on it.

Chapter 30

Patience held her hand to her galloping heart. The man looked so much like her grandfather it was uncanny. She wanted to cringe and flee from him in terror, and at the same time she stifled the urge to fling herself into his arms and cry out, "Grandfather!" But this man exhibited no tenderness like her grandfather. And the look he gave her jolted her system like a shock. It was a look of bitterness and pure evil, emotions she had no experience with. Yes, his thick German accent was the same as that of the man on the telephone. She was sure of that. But she couldn't put it together. It made no sense. He said he was going to kill her. What reason did he have to want to harm her? Why did he hate her so much? And what did he mean by saying William Whitestone was his father?

"If you want money, I have it," she offered, her body shaking. "You can take whatever you want that I have in the house. I can get more. Why have you come?"

"To tell you the story, Patience. I've waited a long time to tell you the story. Money is only part of it."

Patience bit her bottom lip until it bled, then took a deep breath. She scrunched the robe in her hand, bunching it up, letting it go, bunching it up again. She huddled further under the blankets.

"It's the story of a little boy in Dresden," the man

began. "Do you know Dresden, Patience? It's a city in eastern Germany. Have you ever been there? Of course, you haven't. Your grandfather would never have allowed that. Surely you've heard of it? Dresden was a beautiful city, one of the most beautiful in Europe, before the bombs destroyed it. But I'm jumping ahead of myself.

"I was about seven then. Too young to go to war. Too young to see and suffer the scars of war when it came to our city. After the military academy, where my father studied engineering and was first in his class, he served on a battleship and then became a *Kapitänleutnant* in the *Kriegsmarine*, a loyal Nazi. Next, he worked in intelligence in the *B-Dienst*. He was a shining star, so full of promise, my mother said, that they sent him off on a secret assignment, which explained why he couldn't visit us. But she promised me he would come back one day. She told me, 'He will love you. You'll see.'

"My mother said I should be proud of my father. I should be proud of *Kapitänleutnant* Wilhelm von Hesselweiss. But how could I be proud of a man I had never met? Oh, I'd seen pictures. She kept his picture in a place of honor, on a lace doily on a small table in our apartment. But he never did come home. He never wanted my mother or me. He never wrote to her, never even tried to contact us.

"I was a handsome boy, my mother said, just like my father. 'You're like an apple off the tree,' she liked to tell me. 'The image of your father.'

"So why did the other boys make fun of me and call me the son of a whore? Why? Because my mother never married the handsome *Kapitänleutnant*. He slept with her, had his fun with her, but then he left her, alone, to raise a son alone in the misery of war. She was a good woman. She didn't deserve to be treated the way he treated her.

"My father was an important man, my mother told me. He was doing an important job in the war. He didn't have time to worry about how we were faring. He was a wealthy man. I can see now how wealthy he was. So why were we starving? Because he didn't provide for us. When my mother became pregnant, her parents forced her out of their home. So the young boy went to sleep each night with a hunger in his belly so great that he didn't think he could survive until morning. And a craving for a father that was never satisfied.

"Never once did my mother speak ill of him. She loved him until her dying day. She waited for him and he never came. His name was the last word she breathed. He was not worthy of her love, and yet, for some reason, she worshipped him.

"My mother was just a statistic, one of the hundreds of thousands who lost their lives in the Allied bombing raids. The bombs that wouldn't stop raining down their death and destruction. We were running, but there was no escape from the fire. We were separated by the crowd. My mother tried to hold on to me, but she had to let go of my hand. One minute she was there, the next she was on fire. And I had to watch. I remember wishing I had died with her.

"Perhaps you've read about the firebombing of Dresden? It was worse, much worse, so much more painful than the newsreels and the history books paint it. You are a student of history, but nothing said about it is as bad as living through it.

"Who cared anything for a lost, motherless little boy, evacuated and orphaned after the war? A boy who had to fight for every scrap of food, every worthless mark. Every kind word. It was an empty life.

"You, on the other hand, were the pampered, spoiled little princess living in the big house on the beautiful island, with all the pretty colors. Not the drab life I was living. You were the little girl who wanted for nothing. Who worried about nothing. The little girl who had the love of both her grandparents. Yes, you see I know all about you.

"My mother was the most beautiful woman I've ever known," said the intruder, his eyes assuming a faraway look. "She sacrificed everything for me, for my *father*. And he never cared. I spent the rest of my young years in the orphanage where I was sent. Can you imagine what that was like? I could not get out of East Germany after the war because of the Soviet occupation. And, foolishly, I thought the Iron Curtain was the reason my father couldn't get to me. I was always waiting for him to come back. I thought he was struggling, all the time struggling, to find me. But even when it was possible to come, I waited, and still he didn't try to find me, his own son. Finally, I gave up hope.

"Eventually I did get out and began to track my father down. I followed the trail. It wasn't easy. Wilhelm von Hesselweiss had disappeared off the face of the earth. He thought he could hide from me. But he wasn't clever enough. He thought his new identity as William Whitestone was a secret. With the inadvertent help of an old friend of his, Karl Krauss, I discovered where he was. Karl was infatuated with my father too, couldn't stop going on about him. And he had also been in love with my mother. He said he had been looking for me all through the war years and afterward, and had lost track of me. He had wanted to take care of me. But of course, it was too late. He finally told me the story of my father, and I convinced him it was time for a family reunion. He thought he was doing my father a favor."

The man rambled on, lost in his story. Patience knew she should try to sneak away, but her heart went out to the little boy who had so tragically lost his mother.

"Are those tears I see in your eyes, Patience? Tears for your uncle?"

Patience stuck out her lip. "My uncle?"

"If William Whitestone was your grandfather, then yes, I'm your uncle."

Patience's head was spinning. There was something about the story that was familiar. Dresden, 1934, the photograph of the boy and girl intertwined in the garden. "Emilie. Was your mother Emilie?"

"You know of her?"

"I saw her picture."

"A picture of my mother?"

"Of Emilie. He didn't forget. He saved her picture."

"That's a lie. I don't believe you. I didn't believe him.

"He tried to embrace me," the man continued, adding sarcastically, "It was quite a touching father and son reunion. I thought he'd require proof. But when we finally came face to face, he couldn't deny I was his son. 'The resemblance is remarkable,' he told me. I think I even detected some pride and remorse in his voice."

"'You left her, left us, all those years,' I accused him. 'Not a word. She loved you. It killed her. She spoke of you often. Never a malicious word. She brought me up to love you. I wanted to love you. I tried to love you. But how could I love a father who left us behind, who abandoned us? In the end, I had nothing left but hatred for you.'

"'My son? Emilie's son? I didn't know.' That's what he told me.

"'You didn't know?' I said. 'Am I supposed to believe you? Is that supposed to provide comfort? How many years have I waited for you to acknowledge me? I thought you would surely come home after my mother's death to take care of things, to take care of me. You are so rich, so powerful. So important. My *father*. But you couldn't spare even a handful of marks for your son, your lover. You should have married her. We had nothing, not even your name. You brought shame on her and on me. Living through the war. In poverty. Only the garden. She had the garden and her memories. She died with your name on her lips. I thought you'd want to know that.

"'Do you want to know my name?' I asked him. 'The name of your own son? It's Friederich.'

"He looked at me as if he wanted to speak, to form the words, but he said nothing. My father cried," Friederich said. "He was bleeding, dying, from a knife wielded by his own son. A son he said he had never known about. If he had only known, he said, he would have gone back. Yes, he definitely would have gone back for his son. For Emilie. I didn't believe him, of course. He was such a smooth liar.

"He mumbled something about 'All this time,' about how he had been afraid for his family, looking over his shoulder, consumed by the fact that someone would be hunting him, and all this time he should have been taking care of his family in Germany.

"'Patience and Diana are safe,' he said to me. Then he crawled out through the garden, Diana's garden, he called it. He went on and on about how beautiful she looked when he first laid eyes on her. And how beautiful she was on her wedding day when they stood hand in hand under the moon gate. All the time he was losing blood and losing consciousness.

"At the end, he pleaded with me to save him so he could make it up to me, and finally, when he knew all hope was gone, he wanted me just to forgive him."

Patience did not believe her grandfather had begged for his life. Her grandfather was fearless.

"Then I heard your car in the driveway," Friederich continued. "I had to run, but first, he had to die. The knife wound was taking too long, so I shot him. I barely had time to escape when you came screaming down the steps. So, in the end, his thoughts were of you and of his wife, only of her. My mother meant nothing to him."

Patience tried to think back to the day her grandfather had died. "Sun, sun," she thought he had said, but now she knew he must have meant "Son, son." And she suddenly understood why her grandfather hadn't tried to defend himself. Once he got over the shock of discovering he had a son, he never would have raised a hand against his own flesh and blood. She knew it with all her heart. Because that's the kind of man her grandfather was.

And when he had asked for forgiveness, he wasn't seeking it from his wife or from his granddaughter but from Emilie and the son he never knew he had.

"*Auf wiedersehn, Liebchen.*" He had gone back to his native tongue, to German, to say goodbye to his darling, his sweetheart, his one true love, Emilie. His last thought had been for her. Patience staggered back from the thought.

"I can prove that he did think of her," Patience managed through her grief. "He saved her picture. I can get it. It's in the study."

"Do you think I'm a fool? You're only stalling. You hope to call someone. But you won't escape. You won't get away."

"Were you so consumed by hatred for my grandfather and me that you never fell in love, found a wife, or raised a family of your own?" Patience wondered. "Did you waste your life?"

She saw by his expression that he had.

"I was alone. I am still alone."

"Then I am sorry for you."

"Love is not important to me," Friederich insisted.

"Love is *everything*," Patience disagreed, challenging him in a voice that sounded more in control than she felt. "Your father loved your mother. Don't you want to see the picture?"

"Why not?" he said as if it meant nothing.

Patience got off the bed and stopped at the closet.

"I'm freezing," Patience said, teeth chattering, thoroughly chilled from the bath water, the cold air, and the taste of fear. "I need a heavier robe."

He rustled through the clothes in her closet and

pulled out a thick white terrycloth robe and tossed it to her. She slipped it over her sheer robe and tightened the belt, stuffing her hands in the pockets to seek additional warmth. She didn't dare risk asking him for panties, but she felt naked and vulnerable with nothing under the robe. He yanked her by the arm and pulled her down the hall, her wet hair spraying droplets in a trail along the highly polished wooden floor, and into the study.

"No, first, I want you to open the safe and empty the contents into this bag for me," he said.

"The safe is in the drawing room." She led him to her grandmother's portrait.

"You'll have to help me take the portrait down," Patience said, staring up at her grandmother, looking for guidance.

"You look just like her," Friederich commented. "Isn't that funny? And I look just like him. You have nothing of him in you."

She stuck out her chin defiantly. Despite what she had learned about him, she was still William Whitestone's granddaughter.

The man removed her grandmother's picture from the wall, and Patience entered the combination, fumbling with the dial. Finally, the safe clicked open.

"You can have it all, anything, if you'll just go," she pleaded, still shivering. "I won't report this to the authorities."

"No, you won't," he agreed. "Unless you can communicate from the grave."

He handed her the bag, and she began stuffing jewelry, loose diamonds, and cash into it. There was an envelope, but when she tried to put it into the bag, he grabbed it out of her hand and threw it to the ground.

He was only after valuables.

She picked up the letter. She had never seen it before. It was addressed to her in her grandfather's handwriting. It must have gotten stuck behind some of the jewelry boxes. She stuffed it into the pocket of her robe.

When he was satisfied that she had retrieved all the contents of the safe, she zipped up the heavy bag and handed it to him.

"That's all of it."

"That's a good start. But it's just a down payment for all the years I suffered. Imagine, if you will, Patience, what your fancy friends would think if they knew your grandfather's true identity. The true source of his wealth. Knew how, with his information and connections to the right people, I mean the wrong people, he was singlehandedly responsible for the deaths of—"

Patience's eyes blazed. "Stop. Don't. Don't take that away from him. My grandfather...your father...was a decent man."

"Decent? You know what he was, don't you? And you'll do anything, anything to keep the truth from getting out."

"What do you want?"

"Everything you have, but it's too dangerous. I can't let you out to go to the bank. I can't let you out of the house ever again. My father mentioned something about the gold before he died, and I saw the maps on your sea captain's ship."

"What gold?"

He backhanded her, and she winced from the pain of the slap. Blood leaked from her lip where he had broken the delicate skin.

"I've been watching the house. I've watched your sea captain digging in the garden. I don't think he was planting Easter lilies. It's not the season."

"All right. The gold is there, under the moon gate."

"How much?"

"We only just found it. I don't know for sure. A lot, I think."

Friederich's eyes sparkled. "All right, then, let's go. You need to start digging."

"Nathaniel will be back soon," Patience stalled.

"When he returns, I'll deal with him. In fact, you can both dig while I watch."

"If there's as much gold as I think there is, it will take a long time to dig it up. How long do you think you can keep me prisoner here without people getting suspicious?"

"As soon as you dig deep enough, I'll bury your bodies and no one will be the wiser. I'll be William's relative from Switzerland. No one will question me. I look just like him. I'll simply tell them that poor, bereaved little Patience was overcome with grief and she had to go away on a long trip to recover from the death of her grandparents. I'll enjoy living in this house. Ironic, don't you think? I'll take out the gold at my leisure, sell off your things one by one. I'm entitled."

Patience could see the way things were. But she tried to stall the inevitable.

"The picture. Didn't you want to see the picture of Emilie? It's in the study." He jerked her back down the hall and into the study.

"Where is it?" he asked impatiently as he dragged

her along.

Her hand paused on the doorknob, remembering the last time she had been in this room to put away the diary and slide the picture of her grandfather and Emilie inside the pages. She'd been avoiding this room as much as possible, and fear threatened to paralyze her as soon as she entered. She felt her grandfather's powerful presence everywhere. She thought she could see traces of the pool of blood on the carpet, and the pounding in her head returned. She clutched her grandfather's desk to hold herself upright. Friederich pushed her against the wood until she cried out.

Patience opened a drawer, shuffled through the diary, and found the picture. She could see her grandfather's gun sitting in the drawer, gleaming, loaded, waiting, like a viper about to strike. Her grandfather had taught her well. She could shoot that gun in her sleep. She was an expert with a target. But could she shoot this flesh-and-blood man? Her own flesh and blood? The man who had her grandfather's blood running through his veins? Even if she were successful, how would she explain it? Guns of any type were illegal in Bermuda. That didn't stop a man like her grandfather from owning one.

Her hand was shaking as she lifted the fragile picture and handed it to Friederich.

"She must have been a remarkable woman to have attracted the attentions of your father," Patience said graciously, and meant it.

He seemed mesmerized by the image of his mother and father together.

She'd only have a moment. A moment when he was stunned, focused only on the photo. *Conquer your fears, Patience.* She could almost hear her grandfather's voice calling out to her, trying to protect her, even from his grave.

"*So schön, nicht war?*" Friederich said to himself, tears sparkling in his eyes as he lapsed into German. "*Meine Mutter.* So beautiful." He stroked the face on the picture.

"Look how they loved each other," Patience urged. She felt dishonest for encouraging him and, at the same time, a sense of betrayal to her grandmother, because she knew it was true.

Then his countenance turned dark again. "That's not love. That's lust in his eyes. Can't you see it? He used her and threw her away when he was finished with her."

"No," Patience said, tears slipping down her face. "My grandfather was not like that. He would never have done that. He was a decent man. He would have come back for you, if he had known."

Angered, Friederich grabbed Patience by one arm while he turned to throw the picture on the desk. As she saw her last chance slipping away, she managed to snatch the gun and shove it into the deep pocket of her robe.

In the kitchen, the buzzer rang insistently, a jarring sound that clashed with the music still playing on the radio. The roast was done. Her first meal. Possibly her last.

Momentarily startled by the harsh noise, Friederich turned toward the kitchen, and Patience saw her opportunity. She lifted the firearm from the pocket of her robe and leveled it at him, stepping back a few inches to take aim. He sensed the movement and swerved.

Her hands shook, but she steadied them.

"I don't want to hurt you, but I will," she threatened. "Drop the knife and step back."

She heard Nathaniel's scooter in the driveway. Her heart beat faster, but she didn't turn away. The timer buzzer was ringing in her ears. Nathaniel has a key, she thought. He'll come in any moment. She didn't want him involved or hurt in any way. This was her mess to clean up.

"Patience," he was calling out frantically. He must have seen an extra scooter in the driveway and known she was in trouble. "Are you all right? Are you in there?" She heard the front door lock open, and suddenly he was bounding over furniture, knocking over tables to get to her.

"Where are you? Patience, don't you hear the buzzer? The dinner is burning. I..." He hesitated and froze when he came to the open study door and saw her weapon aimed at the intruder.

Friedrich took advantage of Nathaniel's hesitation to pull him in by his neck. He swung Nathaniel around and used him as a shield between himself and Patience. Friederich was much older, but his body was thicker than Nathaniel's lean one. Nathaniel tried to wrestle the intruder to the ground, but Friederich overpowered him.

As he lashed out, a flash of light on the corner of the end table caught Nathaniel's attention. The golden glow was enhanced by the lamplight. Nathaniel grabbed the heavy gold bar, raised it, and smashed it across the side of Friederich's head. Friederich went down like a stone. Nathaniel got up, rubbed his neck where Friederich had grabbed him, and started toward

Patience.

A hand grabbed his shin and pulled him down. He tried to escape Friederich's grasp, but the man's hand crushed his foot. Friederich rose and dragged Nathaniel up with him into a standing position, pressing his blade against Nathaniel's throat.

"Nathaniel!" Patience screamed. "Are you okay?"

"I'm fine, did he hurt you?" Nathaniel seethed, furious at being bested by an old man, but more frightened for Patience. "You're bleeding."

"No." The breath hissed out of Patience's body. "It's nothing." She tried to hold the gun steady, but her hand shook. How could she shoot the man with Nathaniel in the way? That changed everything. In that moment, she hesitated.

"Drop the gun unless you want a repeat performance of your grandfather," Friederich called out. "I will enjoy killing him slowly, right in front of you. You will have to watch another man you love die."

Patience swayed, remembering all the blood gushing out of her grandfather's body.

"Shoot, Patience," Nathaniel ordered, trying to get her to focus again. He didn't care a thing for himself. He had to make sure she was safe.

"Nathaniel, I can't. I might hit you. He killed my grandfather."

Nathaniel tried to struggle again, but Friederich gave him a shallow cut with the knife and drew blood. Patience focused on the blood and knew with certainty that the man would kill Nathaniel, would kill them both, if she didn't take action right now. The time had come to face her fears and wake up from her nightmare.

Patience turned toward the man, took a deep,

calming breath and placed both hands on the gun to steady the weapon and herself.

"Friederich," Patience warned deliberately above the jarring din of the kitchen buzzer and the frantic beat of the music. "Put down the knife and let Nathaniel go or I will be forced to shoot you."

Friederich laughed madly, doubting her resolve. Patience looked at Nathaniel and signaled, inclining her head to one side. "I think I will kill him now," Friederich said, with a wild look in his eye. "How much does he mean to you?"

Patience took another deep breath. *Everything,* she realized, and her eyes signaled that message to Nathaniel, but she said nothing and continued to focus on her grandfather's killer. There was a rapid movement in front of her as Friederich raised his knife to plunge it into Nathaniel's flesh. She was convinced he would follow through this time.

"Now, Nathaniel!" Patience screamed.

Nathaniel twisted away as she took careful aim for the center of her uncle's chest, found her mark, and pulled the trigger. Friederich's grip on Nathaniel slowly loosened. His face registered surprise, then pain, before he fell. His body lay lifeless on the Oriental rug, blood flowing everywhere, spoiling the airy yellow pattern.

Patience felt the blood rush to her own head and fought with everything she had to keep from collapsing.

Nathaniel ran to her and took her in his arms.

"Patience, are you okay?"

"I'm fine. What about you?" she demanded desperately. "Are you hurt?"

"Don't worry about me," he said, touching his shoulder. His hand came away with blood on it.

With one hand, Patience removed the belt from her terrycloth robe and pressed it to Nathaniel's wound. Within seconds, it was soaked with his blood.

"Sit down, and I'll call the police and straighten this whole thing out," Patience said, keeping pressure on Nathaniel's wound. Nathaniel managed to unlock the death grip she had on the weapon and pry the gun loose from her fingers, placing it on the desk. She dialed the emergency numbers.

Then she smelled the burning roast. "We'd better move into the kitchen. I need to shut off the oven and that incessant buzzer." Before they moved, she picked up the faded picture of Emilie and her grandfather.

"Who was he?" Nathaniel prodded, looking at the body, as Patience supported him while they walked together into the kitchen. "Did he say? Was he your grandfather's associate? Was he Nighthawk?"

"He was my uncle, my grandfather's son from Emilie."

Nathaniel's face mirrored his surprise. "Your grandfather had a son with the girl in the picture, the girl in the garden in Dresden?"

"Yes, that's right. A son he never knew about." Patience showed Nathaniel the picture. "You see?"

Nathaniel took the picture from her, stared at it again, tucked it back in the diary, and closed the desk drawer.

"He was going to kill us, both of us, after we dug up the gold, and then bury us in the garden," Patience said, holding up the bag her uncle had brought with him. "He came for this. The money and the gold. And he threatened to expose my grandfather. He was going to kill you, Nathaniel. I couldn't let him kill you."

"I know, sweetheart," he said, stroking her hair as they walked back into the study. "You're still trembling."

"Nathaniel, I shot my own uncle. His name was Friederich." Patience bent down, stepping in the pool of blood with her bare feet to feel for a pulse. Maybe, maybe he was still breathing. Maybe she could revive him somehow.

But he was already cold. The little boy from Dresden could not be saved.

"He's gone, Patience," Nathaniel said, gently. "You can see that he is."

Patience touched Friederich's forehead lovingly, brushed away a lock of hair that had fallen over his face. "He looks exactly like my grandfather, Nathaniel," she said absently. "I could have loved him. I would have. My grandfather would have welcomed him into our lives, into our family, opened up his heart for him, if he had been given the chance. I miss my grandfather. I miss him so much."

"I know you do," Nathaniel said. With his good arm he pulled her to her feet and into his arms. "I wonder what ever happened to Nighthawk?"

"You don't think my grandfather killed him, do you?" Patience asked quietly, afraid to hear the answer.

"It's possible. He would have done anything to protect you and your grandmother. You must know that by now. But maybe he just disappeared mysteriously from the island after the war.

"We know he spoke to your grandfather after the war about the missing documents. We know he exacted payments for them. But I got the sense that your grandfather thought this latest attempt at blackmail was

Nighthawk's doing. So he must have thought Nighthawk was still alive. From what you've told me, he never knew about his son.

"A man like Nighthawk collected enemies. I don't think we have to worry about him anymore. One way or another, he's probably dead by now. It's been too long. Surely someone has already dealt with him. He got what he deserved."

Patience shivered, thinking about how difficult the situation and the gun would be to explain to the authorities.

"You're just in shock now," Nathaniel said, wrapping his arm tighter around Patience. "He was a burglar, a drifter, Patience," Nathaniel prompted. "He came to rob the house, he threatened your life and you wrestled with him and shot him with his own gun. Isn't that how it happened?"

Patience shook her head. "You want me to lie to the police?"

"I want you to go lie down in the bedroom," Nathaniel instructed gently. "I will handle the police."

"No, Nathaniel. It's time I started facing life again. We'll handle this together."

But she let him comfort her, keep her body pressed close against his, and kiss her. She was cold, so cold. She had taken a man's life. Her uncle's life. How much different was she, really, from her grandfather?

Chapter 31

The police and the doctor were gone and Patience, after dressing, finally felt warm again. Nathaniel had built a roaring fire, and they huddled closely together under a quilt on the couch in front of the fireplace, staring into the flames.

They had eaten the dinner she cooked after all. Nathaniel couldn't stop talking about how good it was. Patience knew she had ruined the meal. The meat was burnt and tough, the vegetables overcooked, and the potatoes raw. But he didn't complain. In fact, he ate every bite on his plate. He hadn't stopped to get the wine, his pretense for going into town, so they drank some liquor from her grandfather's cabinet. It felt warm going down and loosened her inhibitions.

They talked about everything, ignoring only what had just gone on in the study. They spoke of his life, hers, nothing in particular, just enjoyed each other's company. Being together was enough.

"Tell me about your family, Nathaniel," Patience prompted.

"The Morgan men made their mark on Virginia," Nathaniel said proudly. "They were among the leaders of Colonial Virginia. My ancestors were former governors, statesmen, successful businessmen. They devoted themselves entirely to their work and to Virginia.

"As a consequence, loveless marriages are a long tradition in my family. The Morgans grew tobacco, but they were best at cultivating bad marriages. The Morgan men don't have any trouble getting women…just keeping them."

"Then maybe the Morgan men are marrying the wrong kind of women," Patience pointed out. "Tell me about your home, Nathaniel," she urged wistfully.

"Fair Winds is a large, historic plantation along the James River corridor, in the southeast part of Virginia, between the coast and Greater Richmond," Nathaniel explained. "We have access to the ocean, which is important. There were always sailors in our family. There's been a home on the site since the early seventeenth century."

"The James River," began Patience as she stared off into space, almost hypnotized by the fire. "It's 430 miles long and was originally known as Powhatan Flu by the English colonists who settled at Jamestown in 1607. They named it after the Indian Chief Powhatan. They renamed it for King James. The river begins near the western Virginia border, west of the Blue Ridge Mountains, and joins the Chesapeake Bay at Hampton Roads. I'm also familiar with all the major tributaries. You know, Thomas Jefferson lived on a tributary of the James River."

"That's impressive. How did you learn all that?"

"I know all about Virginia's James River Plantations," she said, as she conjured up a mental picture of an elegant Georgian-style brick mansion and stylish, laughing ladies in hoop skirts enjoying picnics by the water and romantic candlelight dinners. "I read about all the historic landmarks in a history book."

"You would like Fair Winds, Patience. Your parlor reminds me a lot of home."

"It sounds lovely. I would really like to see it one day."

"It's so peaceful along the river. It's beautiful country."

"Then why did you leave?"

"It's personal. I just couldn't stay. There was a girl I—"

"You don't have to tell me." There was a story there, she thought. Perhaps another woman had hurt him. But he would tell her when he was ready to talk about it.

"I want to tell you. I have to tell you. Her name was Jenna."

"Did you love her?" Patience asked, not really prepared to hear the answer.

"We were engaged to be married. I guess I thought I loved her."

"What happened? Did she hurt you very much, Nathaniel?"

"I think she injured my pride more than anything," he said, just realizing the truth of it. "She ran off with a...you promise not to laugh?"

"I would never laugh at your pain," she swore.

"She ran off with a golf pro. My golf pro."

Patience's lower lip quivered uncontrollably, and she had to bite it to hold back the urge to convulse with laughter. She forced her eyes to remain serious.

"That explains your irrationally hostile feelings about golf," she said evenly.

"Golf was *my* game. I introduced her to the sport."

"Apparently your pro introduced her to more than

the game," Patience said, finally breaking down. "Sorry, but you have to admit there is something humorous about it."

"It didn't seem funny at the time," he said. Looking back on those times and being here with Patience, his pain was only a distant memory. His feelings for Jenna didn't even come close to the feelings he had developed for Patience.

"I guess I never really loved her at all. I was more humiliated than anything else. I actually miss my golf game more than I miss her. Since she called off the wedding, I've been wandering around the world trying to figure out what I want to do with the rest of my life."

"And have you come to any conclusions?"

"Nothing definite." He was quiet for a long time, and then he asked, "Have you ever wanted to get married?"

"I never found a love like my grandparents had," Patience confided. "That's what I'm waiting for." She thought of how her grandfather had indulged and deferred to her grandmother. She was his true partner in life and his true love.

"Did you ever wonder why he married her, whether their meeting was truly accidental? Her father was a vice admiral. That would have proved useful to William during the war. Did you ever think that's the reason he chose her?"

She thought of Emilie. Of course he must have loved her. Enough to have created a child with her. But the love her grandfather had felt for her grandmother could not be denied. It was strong and true, and tangible. The kind of love you could feel whenever they entered a room. The kind of love that lasts a lifetime.

"Whatever crimes you think my grandfather is guilty of, not loving my grandmother is not one of them. I'm certain of that. What about your mother? Can you tell me about her?"

"My mother left when I was ten years old," Nathaniel admitted bitterly. "I barely remember her. I blamed myself for her leaving and wondered what I had done wrong to make her leave. I remember missing her desperately, hoping, always hoping, she'd come back. But she never did.

"My grandmother said she didn't leave me, she left my father. After that, my father left. But if she really loved me, why didn't she take me with her? My mother left, but my grandmother stuck. Gran raised me. She was a romantic. She said I'd be the one to break the Morgan chain of bad luck with women. But she was wrong. I'm never getting married. No woman is ever going to run from me again."

Patience stared at him, aching for the lonely boy who still missed his mother. The scars of that hurt were still there. She touched his cheek lovingly and he shivered.

"Not all women leave, Nathaniel."

"That's not a risk I'm willing to take."

She reached for his hand, and her heart swelled with love for this man. It made no sense. They had met such a short time ago. But she had known him forever. She had been waiting for him forever. They were, somehow, connected.

****

He held her hand in hers.

"I can't stay, Patience," he said, frowning. "I have to be honest with you. I owe you that much. Now that I know you're safe, I...I've gotten off course, somehow. It's not in my nature to stay anchored in any one place for too long. I don't need anyone but the sea."

Nathaniel knew that wasn't exactly true. He needed Patience. He'd never known just how much until he'd seen her in the study with that man. Until he thought he might lose her. But he wasn't going to stay. In fact, he had already packed his things. He planned to tell her tonight that he would be sailing in the morning.

She laughed. "Bermuda is the world's second most isolated island. No matter where you are in Bermuda, you're only minutes from the water. Surely you could find peace here, with the sea all around you." *And me.*

He caught her face in his hands.

"Patience," he sighed. How was he ever going to live without her? He took her in his arms and kissed her so gently, to try to ease the ache in his heart. But one kiss wasn't enough. It would never be enough. Her arms went around him and she raised her lips to his, seeking his warmth.

"Nathaniel, I love you," she said, as her tears started flowing. "I wanted to tell you, and I thought when Friederich had hold of me I'd never get a chance to tell you."

"Oh, God, Patience," he said, wiping away her tears. "You're still in shock. It's all the events of the evening. Please don't cry over me. You don't really love me. You can't love me. You don't even know me."

Love could make you crazy and content all at the same time. That was the ten-year-old boy talking, the boy whose mother had left him, who still held on to the belief that he somehow wasn't worthy of love.

"But I do. I know everything I need to know about

you. I know my own heart. And I feel as if we've known each other forever."

"You don't know everything about me," Nathaniel said, taking his grandmother's letter from his pocket and placing it, along with a pouch of diamonds, in her hands. "Here. Read all about Nathaniel Morgan's noble roots."

"What is this?"

"It's a letter my grandmother wrote to William Whitestone on her deathbed. She made me promise to bring it to him when I returned the diamonds he gave her. Now he's gone, it all belongs to you. So, go ahead, read her letter."

She took the letter and the pouch and read the words. "My God!" she said as she finished, "Your grandmother was Yvette, Nighthawk's mistress!"

"So now you see, it would be best if I left."

"But I don't want you to leave."

Nathaniel groaned and grabbed her to him roughly.

"I feel…so much for you…I don't want to feel," he managed. "My heart breaks with it."

"I know," she whispered.

"No, you can't possibly know. You can't know the depths of my feelings for you. I don't even understand them."

"Help me to understand, then," she said softly. "Don't go."

"I want to stay," he said, torn by some eternal, inner turmoil he could not explain.

"Stay and love me, Nathaniel. Love me now. Even if you must go. I need you to love me tonight." She was trembling, and suddenly he couldn't stop kissing her, touching her.

He carried her into the bedroom and laid her gently on the bed.

"Patience, I...we can't do this. You're not ready. And I'm leaving. It wouldn't be right."

She put her hand to his lips.

"No more talking. Touch me, Nathaniel. I need to feel you. Tell me you love me, even if it's not true. Even if it's just for tonight. I need to hear you say the words."

"Oh, God, Patience, but I do. I do love you."

Nathaniel let out a deep, shuddering breath as he broke down and let the tears come while he kissed her, his tongue lashing hers, his kisses pounding her lips, tears raging like rain in a violent storm. She grabbed onto him for dear life like a drowning woman, pressed herself into him, and refused to let go.

They were close. She wanted to be closer, pressing harder against him. Of course, he thought, she wanted to experience the passion she had only read about in paperbacks, the shimmering love she had witnessed between her grandparents. "Closer, please," she urged breathlessly.

Burning for her, he ripped away her blouse impatiently and clasped his hands to her breasts. Touched them, tasted them. She moaned. It was her first time, he knew, but he couldn't be gentle. His need was too great. And he knew she could feel the growing evidence of that need. He wanted to take it slow, for her sake. But he had to have her right now or he would die.

"Patience, I'm sorry. I don't mean to be so rough."

"Don't be sorry for wanting me as much as I want you, my love, my darling Nathaniel. Please, take me now. I want you to."

He tried to keep his need at bay, but her responsiveness was just fanning the flames of his desire.

"No, you deserve more. You deserve everything." He drank from her lips. They were bruised and swollen from his kisses. He touched them, savored them. Then he showed her how much he worshipped her. Touched her everywhere gently, sweetly until she trembled with need for him.

"Now, Nathaniel, now." She was asking, so innocently, for something she didn't really understand.

"Ssh, let's don't rush," he breathed softly.

He was shaking from his need for her, but he made his hands give her pleasure, more and more, until neither of them could stand it. She was writhing on the bed, moaning and bucking under him, her skin burning.

He touched her everywhere, tortured her with his hands and his mouth until he felt she was hot and wet and ready. He kissed her and drove into her, firmly but gently at first, and she struggled just a little under him before he lost control and she called out his name in surprise and ecstasy. His heart soared and his body made her his as they surrendered on the waves of passion together.

"Patience, you were made for me," he breathed, astonished.

"Oh, Nathaniel," she sighed.

He didn't know how he would ever leave her now that he had known her sweetness, her safe harbor.

"Did I hurt you, my sweet Patience?" he whispered, as they lay back, spent, on the sheets, tangled together.

"No, no, it was wonderful," she said. He kissed her

softly on the lips.

"For me, too, my love."

He held on tightly as if she might disappear into the mist.

They lay together like that, restful, coming together again during the night, until dawn broke through the open picture window. And, for the first time in his life, he knew true happiness. She had calmed his ancient restlessness and offered him his first sense of inner peace. He felt the anchor in his heart drop with a thud.

Patience was still sleeping when he left to load the boat. He'd had the entire night to think. It was wonderful. She was wonderful. He couldn't bear to leave her, but he knew he couldn't stay. It was in his nature to leave. It would break her heart and her spirit to leave the island. Hamilton Farnsworth had learned that the hard way. So he wouldn't ask her to.

She would be hurt at first. But she would only hurt more if he stayed longer and then left. He had battled storms before and survived. But he knew if he stayed, if he even saw her again or touched her again, he would lose the ability to fight his feelings.

He felt troubled about leaving the note and debated whether he shouldn't just leave without any goodbye. It would be better that way. That way she could hate him and then, in time, it would hurt less. He knew it was easier to hang on to anger than live with the pain of false hope.

****

When her eyes flicked open, Patience was sprawled face down on the satin sheets. The faintest early morning light had started to streak through the window when she felt Nathaniel bending over to press a soft, wet, final kiss to her neck. It tickled, and she tingled just from the touch of his lips against her body. Coming out of a deep sleep, her first instinct was to reach for him. But, for some reason, she held back.

"I love you, Patience," he whispered. "You're everything to me."

He caressed her shoulder and then her cheek. He was tender, he was gentle—and he was leaving. His hand lingered, and then he was gone, taking the warmth with him.

Patience choked back a sob until she was sure he had left her room, and then she let the hot tears flow. She would not beg him to stay if he wanted to go.

How had it happened? How had she let him in so close and so quickly to her heart? And why was he breaking it? He was her first love, and he had brought her such joy, propelled her to such heights of happiness. Now she was sinking into the depths of despair. She needed to talk to her grandmother and ask her if love was supposed to hurt this much. But her grandmother was gone. And now, so was Nathaniel.

He'd professed to love her, but he didn't trust her enough to let her love him back. He had no faith in what they were beginning to build together.

And then the doubts surfaced. How could he love somebody like her, so unworldly, so inexperienced, so naïve? She had been blindsided by the love she felt for him. Perhaps she had disappointed him in some way. Maybe she wasn't enough of a woman for him. She was a fool to have fallen so hard, so fast. She could hear Cecilia now. *Why did you give everything away to him? Why didn't you hold back? Why didn't you hold back your heart?* As if she'd had any choice about it. She had learned that to love another person was to hold nothing back.

But how could Nathaniel smoothly say all the right words and not mean them? How could he take her love and then leave? Perhaps she didn't really know him at all.

When they had made love, she had known then they were meant for each other. Could it be any clearer? He was running away from his destiny. He was the fool for throwing something so precious away so easily. Something she had freely offered, something she had given to no other man. Didn't he understand that? Didn't he understand her at all?

As the sunlight filtered through the curtains, she finally turned over and faced the ceiling. She could still feel the lump in her throat, but the tears had dried on her face. She wanted to run to the window, but she couldn't bear to see the *Fair Winds* sail away.

Suddenly remembering her grandfather's letter, she walked to the closet and pulled it from her robe. She needed the comfort of her grandfather's words.

My Dear Patience,

If you are reading this letter, I am probably dead. There are so many things I want to tell you, that I can't tell you. I know you have always thought of me as a strong and good man. But there are things, my dear granddaughter, about me that I never wanted you or your grandmother to know and that I hope you will never find out.

Did you know that at one time in my life, I never wanted a child, never hoped to have one, never allowed my wife to have her dream? But finally, when Diana stopped asking about a baby, when she had given up all hope, the miracle happened. Our daughter, your mother, Gwyneth, was born. And then the love I felt for her was beyond my control. From the moment I held her in my arms, I simply could not imagine a life without her in it.

I could never bring myself to talk to you about your mother. And that was wrong and selfish of me. But if you can understand how her death affected us, you can understand I believed it was better for Diana to erase all the pain by denying she ever existed.

One minute she was bright and laughing, the next she was gone, taken from us in a senseless automobile accident. By a miracle they saved her child, you. That is why I call you "my little miracle." And truly you are. Diana and I were determined to raise you as our own daughter, so you would never know the pain of growing up without a mother and a father. I grew up without my father, did I ever tell you? No, I don't believe I ever spoke to you about my past, a past that is better left buried.

By some incredible quirk of nature, you grew into the mirror image of your mother and your grandmother. You turned out to be the perfect imprint of my beloved Diana. Your blonde, curly hair is stamped in the same color of sunshine. Your dancing, bright green eyes could have been my wife's. The way you laugh, your shy, sweet personality, and the way you love and trust me, no matter how misplaced that trust, is so completely and purely Diana. In fact, I can't detect a trace of myself either in your visage, your spirit, or your personality. For that I am delighted and grateful, because I adore my wife and I don't want any evidence of my own flaws to infiltrate and contaminate you, my precious granddaughter. I have searched like a hawk for any signs, but if they are there, I simply can't find them. Biologically, it seems, I am irrelevant.

But, as for love, I could not have loved you better if you were my own dear daughter. And I did love your mother so much that even now, all these years later, it pains me to talk or even think about her.

I have enclosed a picture of your mother for you to have. It wasn't right to keep her memory from you. She and your father wanted you so much. They had such big plans for you. And it is a tragedy you never knew them, knew her. But just know that every time you look into a mirror you see her. Every time you laugh you hear her. Every time you experience beauty in the world, you feel her. You are good and fine, just like your mother. And she lives on in you.

All my love,
Your grandfather

Gwyneth. Patience touched her mother's name on the page and then touched her face in the picture, a picture that could have been a picture of herself. No one had ever spoken to her about her mother before. Never mentioned her name. Never displayed a picture. It was as if her whole life had been erased. Patience had known her mother's death in the auto accident must have been too painful for her grandparents. That she had replaced her mother in their eyes. She had become their daughter. When she was cut out of her mother's belly after the accident, in their eyes, their daughter had been reborn. And she couldn't take that illusion away from them.

Although she did look like her grandmother and her mother, that's where the similarity ended. Shy, deliberate, and sensible, she was not impulsive or prone to dramatics or fits of nerves, not governed by roller-coaster emotions like Diana. Her drive, determination, wit, reserve, and strength were all traits she had inherited from her grandfather. And she was proud of that. Like him, she had the capacity to go after what she wanted, to fulfill her destiny. Why hadn't he seen it?

Chapter 32

As the island receded on the horizon, no more than a shadow in the waves, Nathaniel stood on the moving deck, looked to the brightening sky, and fought back the certainty that he had made a horrible mistake. He felt it in the pit of his stomach. And in the empty place in his heart. He had only known Patience a few short weeks. Yet he was in love with her. It made absolutely no sense. But there was a connection. He had felt it the moment she first opened the door to him. When she was in his arms, it only became more powerful. But it was too late. That ship had sailed.

Nathaniel sat at the helm, almost catatonic, staring blindly at the horizon, unable to think or function, except to think of Patience. He remained that way for a long time. He had lost his bearings without her, his sense of direction. He couldn't make himself move forward.

"I have to go back for her, to her, to find her." He kept repeating that mantra. "I have to go back for her." And when his decision was made, he set to turning the boat about. Then he saw some movement on the deck and sensed another presence. Shielding his eyes from the rising sun, he saw a translucent figure, garbed in white. Was it a ghost or a spirit of some sort? A sea sprite or an angel? Perhaps his eyes were playing tricks on him in the growing glare of the sun.

"Mate, I'm getting hungry," the pale figure called out. "How about one of your famous Morgan omelets?"

All he could do was stare in amazement, and he didn't know where he found the presence of mind to stop the boat.

"Patience," he cried as he ran to her. "What are you doing here?" He thought he had dreamed her. "You're in your nightgown. You'll catch a cold. You're not even wearing shoes."

"No time," Patience said proudly. "When I saw you leave, I knew I had to go after you. So I stowed away."

"You came after me," Nathaniel whispered, humbled by her courage. "I left you, and you came after me."

"That's how much I love you, Nathaniel," she said quietly. "You should know that by now."

He took her in his arms and held her. Just held her. They swayed together on the deck.

"I was just turning her about," Nathaniel explained. "I was coming back for you. Come down below and let me make you warm, sweetheart."

"I got your note and your gift." Patience smiled. "I grabbed the package from the table on my way out."

He reached out to touch her neck as the beaming rays of the sun set her new necklace on fire.

"You're wearing my locket," he said, returning her smile. "I wanted you to have something to remember me by."

She lifted the bright gold heart-shaped locket from under her nightgown.

"I could never forget you, Nathaniel."

"I bought it when I went into town yesterday," he

explained. "A parting gift. I had it engraved with our initials—an intertwined P and N."

"Yes, it's lovely."

"It's just like that old silver locket you always wear around your neck, the one your mother gave you."

"That belonged to an ancestor, one of the first settlers in Bermuda, Elizabeth Sutton Smith, who is buried in St. Peter's Church near my parents."

****

What a thrill she'd felt when she opened the tiny, square box from Astwood Dickinson and realized the gift he had purchased in town was meant for her all along, not for another woman.

"And your note…" She'd read the note in his cabin while hiding, hoping he wouldn't discover her presence until they were too far out to sea for him to turn back.

"To a Girl with a Heart of Gold. Not much of a pirate, am I? I left the greatest treasure behind."

"Were you speaking of the gold, Nathaniel?" Patience asked. "You left it buried under the moon gate."

"Some things are better left buried," Nathaniel answered. "Precious memories are worth saving. And no, I wasn't speaking of the gold. And you know it."

"But you were willing to give up a fortune!"

"I've thought of a better use for the money. I was going to call you when I got back to Virginia. With the proceeds from the sale of the gold you could make a sizeable donation to the Bermuda National Trust to continue restoring and preserving the island and the environment. That would go a long way to nurture the intense and fragile beauty, the harmony of the precious island you love. It's the right thing to do."

"What a lovely idea. I could give it anonymously."

"No, you should give it in the name of your grandfather, as a legacy to the place he came to love, just as he loved your grandmother, and you, just as I love you. It would be a gift for the coming generations." *For our children.*

"But you know the truth about my grandfather," she said.

"Do I? Whether he came over here, was sent over here, whether he did or did not do the things we thought he did, we'll never know for sure, will we? And what does it really matter now?

"I've been doing a lot of thinking about it," Nathaniel continued. "Maybe fate had a hand in your grandfather's life. There was evidence that the Germans were going to seize Bermuda. They sent your grandfather to put their plan in motion. If another man had been put in charge, a man like my grandfather, the Germans might have succeeded and the story might have had a very different ending. The course of the entire war might have changed.

"What I do know is that if William hadn't come to Bermuda, he'd never have met your grandmother and you never would have been born. And I wouldn't have known you. So whoever your grandfather was, he was yours, and I'll always be eternally grateful to him.

"History has come full circle. Your grandfather could have destroyed the island, but his love for your grandmother saved it. And now you are heading the annual celebration to commemorate the discovery of the island."

Patience buried herself in his arms, crying tears of joy. "Do you understand how much this means to me?"

"Do you understand how much you mean to me? How long I've waited for you, my sweet, funny Patience? How much I love you? I thought I had to leave you before you left me, do you see? That's the way it always happens."

"I'm not going anywhere, Nathaniel."

"Promise me, promise me, my love," he said, crushing her to him.

"I won't ever leave you, Nathaniel," Patience vowed. "You're everything I want. Everything I've ever dreamed of."

"But you love your home," Nathaniel protested. "I didn't want to take you away from where your heart is. I struggled with that. In the end, I couldn't do that to you."

"Nathaniel, my heart is with you. It always will be. I do love my home and, for a moment, I didn't think I'd have the strength to follow you. But I am every inch William Whitestone's granddaughter. I don't want to live without you. I want to go wherever you go. That's how strong my love is for you, Nathaniel."

He whipped off his jacket and wrapped it snugly around her.

"No, my home is with you," Nathaniel said. "That's what I've sailed halfway around the world to discover."

He hesitated, and then smiled. "You know, I've been studying up on some facts about Bermuda. For instance, did you know that during the War of 1812, the British fleet departed Bermuda and successfully burned Washington, D.C., to the ground?"

"Oh, my," Patience said, her eyes fluttering. Any Bermuda school child knew that, but she played along for Nathaniel's benefit.

"And did you know that Princess Louise Caroline Alberta, Queen Victoria's daughter, put Bermuda on the tourist map by visiting in 1883?"

Patience smiled and struggled *not* to say, "She stayed in Paget for ten weeks. They renamed the Pembroke Hotel as the Princess Hotel in her honor."

"And did you know that the American painter Winslow Homer also visited Bermuda?"

Patience smiled and pretended ignorance, chuckling as she remembered the treasured Homer that hung on the wall in her grandparents' bedroom.

"Is that so?" Patience feigned surprise.

"Yes."

"Now you're playing dirty, sailor. Keep reciting those Bermuda facts. You're getting me hot. I'm afraid that omelet is going to have to wait until we've satisfied our other appetites."

"You're starting to sound just like Cecilia."

"No, it's the new Patience."

"I fell in love with the old Patience," Nathaniel mused, "but I think I'm going to like this new Patience, too." He kissed her lightly. "There are a lot of ties between our two countries—strong connections back to early colonial times. In fact, I think we need to explore those connections more intimately." He kissed her again, more slowly. "I've got an entire book about Bermuda down in my cabin, if you'd care to join me. It's got pictures and everything."

"I think I'm about to swoon. Tell me more."

"Those connections have been strengthened by trade, travel, and…" He paused for effect. "…intermarriage."

"Intermarriage?" Patience gulped, her heart galloping.

"Yes. I'd like to be back on the island before the business offices and banks close, so we can get the paperwork in motion."

"Paperwork?" she stuttered.

"For our marriage license."

Patience stared out to sea, clasping her new locket.

Nathaniel took her hand in his. "Are things moving too fast? Because if they are, we can slow it down, sweetheart. I know we've only just met, but I feel like I've waited so long for you, and I'd rather not wait another minute."

Wasn't this what Patience had secretly dreamed of, longed for? To be swept away by a dark, handsome pirate? She needed fast and adventurous. And she needed Nathaniel. She didn't want to be alone anymore. She had existed her whole life without him and thought she was content. But loving him changed everything. It opened up a world of possibilities. Was theirs as strong a love as the love her grandparents had felt for each other? She thought it must be.

"Marry me, Patience. I know we were meant to be together. For always."

"I thought you didn't believe in destiny."

"I didn't believe in a lot of things...before I met you."

"Meant to be. Oh, I like the sound of that. Yes, Nathaniel, I'll marry you."

"Then we'll be married under the moon gate, like your grandparents."

"How right, how perfect!"

"Picture it, with all your friends looking on."

"And Cecilia on the prowl for husband number four."

"Maybe we should introduce her to Hamilton Farnsworth," Nathaniel suggested. "Maybe husband number four, whoever he is, poor soul, will make her as happy as you make me."

"Oh, Nathaniel. Do I really make you happy?"

His arm tightened around her waist.

"Come down below and I'll show you just how much. And one day, soon I hope, we'll make a little miracle of our own."

After, when they lay together in his cabin, swaying with the gentle rhythm of the boat, still dazed and overwhelmed by their strong love for each other, Nathaniel said, "How does a honeymoon in Virginia sound?"

"Wonderful," she murmured.

"I want to take you to my home, to Fair Winds. And that's just the beginning, Patience. I want to show you the world, give you the world."

"I'd like to see it with you. But where will we live?"

"Right here in paradise," Nathaniel said.

"You mean on the *Fair Winds*?"

"No, in Bermuda."

Tears sprang into her eyes and Nathaniel kissed them away slowly.

Then Patience spoke of her grandfather. "Nathaniel, despite everything we've learned, I still love my grandfather. And I know he loved me."

"He was your grandfather," Nathaniel said simply, linking his fingers with hers. "Of course he loved you. How could he not? And so do I. I don't know how anyone, anywhere, could love another person the way I love you at this moment in time," Nathaniel pledged, answering all her questions.

Patience held the new gold locket in her hand, rubbed her thumb over the intertwined initials, P and N, overwhelmed by the immense love it represented. And she could hardly contain her joy when she looked down at the antique, square-cut emerald Nathaniel had put on her finger in the cabin. It had been his grandmother's. He had been carrying it on the boat since her funeral. When he put it on her finger he said he had finally found someone worthy to wear it. Someone he wanted to share the rest of his life with.

Nathaniel looked up at the heavens. The stars were aligned, their destinies realized, and their eternal searching souls were at last united.

"I wish you could have known Gran," Nathaniel said. "You would have liked her, and she would have loved you. She would have said her prediction had come true, that I'd finally found my destiny."

To find out where the centuries-old love story began, read *DESTINY: A BERMUDA LOVE STORY,* the prequel to *Under The Moon Gate*.

The relationship of star-crossed lovers Elizabeth Sutton and Edward Morgan founders off the coast of Bermuda with the shipwreck of the Sea Venture in the seventeenth century, when Edward is seduced by the captain's daughter and trapped into an unhappy marriage.

When Edward continues his voyage to Virginia to rescue the starving Jamestown Colony, Elizabeth, who finds herself pregnant with Edward's child, is forced to begin a new life without him despite following him as far as Bermuda. Will Edward return to discover the daughter he never knew existed? Can the lovers ever be reunited? Will their eternally searching souls finally fulfill their destiny?

Turn the page for a brief excerpt…

DESTINY: A BERMUDA LOVE STORY

Chapter One

Plymouth in Devon, England, Summer 1609

Edward Morgan placed the chain of the heart-shaped locket around Elizabeth's neck and lowered his mouth to hers for a searing farewell kiss. He wanted to brand this moment in his memory. She was so young, so impossibly beautiful. She tasted sweet, so sweet. And she was his.

"Now we are officially promised to each other," he vowed.

Elizabeth lifted the gleaming silver locket and smiled at the intertwined E's newly engraved in script on the back of the pendant.

"Oh, Edward! You had our initials engraved. It's so fancy. But the only promise I need from you is that you'll come back for me."

"I promise that wherever I am, no matter what happens, I will find you, Elizabeth Sutton."

"I will be waiting," Elizabeth answered with a certainty that signaled nothing could ever come between them. "Forever, if I have to."

A word about the author...

Marilyn Baron is a public relations consultant in Atlanta. She's a PRO member of Romance Writers of America (RWA) and Georgia Romance Writers (GRW) and winner of the GRW 2009 Chapter Service Award. She writes humorous women's fiction, romantic suspense, and paranormal. She graduated from The University of Florida in Gainesville, Florida, with a Bachelor of Science degree in Journalism and a minor in Creative Writing.

Born in Miami, Florida, Marilyn lives in Roswell, Georgia, with her husband, and they have two daughters. She loves to travel. Her favorite place to visit is Italy, where she studied for six months in her junior year of college.

She loves Bermuda and hopes her readers will love "visiting" this romantic and exotic destination getaway in her new novel *Under the Moon Gate,* and its prequel *Destiny: A Bermuda Love Story*, and find it as charming and inviting as she does.

Author e-mail:

mbaroncom@aol.com

Petit Fours and Hot Tamales blog:

www.petitfoursandhottamales.com

To find out more about Marilyn and her books, visit her Web site at:

www.marilynbaron.com